# INCINERATOR

**Also by Niall Leonard**

Crusher

NIALL LEONARD

# INCINERATOR

delacorte press

Text copyright © 2014 by Niall Leonard
Jacket art by blacksheep-uk.com

All rights reserved. Published in the United States by Delacorte Press,
an imprint of Random House Children's Books, a division of Random House LLC,
a Penguin Random House Company, New York.

Originally published in paperback by Definitions,
an imprint of Random House Children's Publishers UK,
a Random House Group Company, London, in 2014.

Delacorte Press is a registered trademark and the colophon
is a trademark of Random House LLC.

Visit us on the Web! randomhouse.com/teens

Educators and librarians, for a variety of teaching tools,
visit us at RHTeachersLibrarians.com

*Library of Congress Cataloging-in-Publication Data*
Leonard, Niall.
Incinerator / Niall Leonard.
pages cm
Sequel to: Crusher.
Summary: "Following the bloody deaths of his mother and father, Finn Maguire is
determined to make a fresh start, running a boxing gym in the bruised and bitter heart of
the city. But when loan sharks target his business partner and his lawyer vanishes with all
his money, Finn is dragged down into London's underworld once more, with only his fists
and his wits to keep him alive."
Provided by publisher.
ISBN 978-0-385-74363-1 (hardback) — ISBN 978-0-449-81845-9 (ebook)
— ISBN 978-0-385-74364-8 (trade paperback)
[1. Gymnasiums—Fiction. 2. Boxing—Fiction. 3. Criminals—Fiction. 4. Adventure and
adventurers—Fiction. 5. London (England)—Fiction.] I. Title.
PZ7.L55116Inc 2014
[Fic]—dc23
2013044093

The text of this book is set in 10.5-point Palatino.

Printed in the United States of America
10 9 8 7 6 5 4 3 2 1
First American Edition

To Chris, Chris, Anne, Terry and Julie.

*Thank you for listening.*

# one

I'd have to buy a new mop. No matter how much bleach I used on this one I could see a faint pink tinge to the trail it left, and I suspected it had cleaned up a lot of blood and teeth in its time. I'd found it in a musty cupboard when we'd first moved into this place, and I kept putting off buying a new one because after spending thousands on the lease and the equipment I couldn't bring myself to cough up for a new mop when there was nothing wrong with the old one, apart from the bloodstains . . .

Out for a run a few months earlier, I'd passed the old gym where Delroy had taught me to box, on the first floor of a tall narrow red-brick warehouse above a second-hand furniture shop crammed with plastic sofas and sad chintzy armchairs cleared from old folks' houses when they'd been carted off to care homes.

Between the front windows of the gym an estate agent's sign had been nailed up. I could just about read FOR SALE without stopping to decode it. Somebody ought to buy that place, I thought. Open it up again, hire Delroy to teach boxing. Fill it with workout equipment. There were plenty of fitness freaks around here, judging by the number of runners in the parks, and no decent gym for miles. It would take someone with energy and imagination and a ton of money, of course . . .

I'd been running for another twenty minutes before I'd realized that somebody could be *me*. The money I'd inherited after my dad died was sitting in a Spanish bank account doing nothing. Why the hell not?

I decided to bounce the idea off Delroy.

Years before, when he'd taught me how to box, Delroy had been a huge black bear of a man, for all his bulk unbelievably fast. The gym back then was full of vicious half-wild kids who would have a go at anybody—I was one of them—but Delroy had never needed to throw his weight around or even raise his voice. None of us had ever wanted to see him angry.

Now he spent most of his time slumped in his front room watching boxing on a big cheap TV with a lousy picture. He was still a big black bear, but he wasn't as fast as he used to be—he couldn't even get out of his chair without a stick. The stroke had paralysed the entire left side of his body, and he'd spent something like eighteen months in rehab and recovery.

I'd been to visit him a few times and always left feeling bored and frustrated that I hadn't been able to help him. But the day I'd told him my idea about re-opening the gym, and how he could run the coaching again, Delroy's face lit up. His grin was still crooked, but he seemed to grow ten years younger before my eyes. He wasn't available for hire, he said, but he'd go halves with me on the lease. Winnie, his loud, huge wife, clapped her hands and started praising Jesus, saying I'd been sent from God to heal her man. I'd always loved Winnie, so I didn't ask her who'd sent Delroy the stroke in the first place.

Here came Delroy now, stumping up the

stairs, grunting and panting. I knew better than to go and offer help. Early on I had suggested he didn't have to turn up at six just because that was when I opened the doors, but he had insisted. "You and me is partners, Finn. I need to be there. You'll probably sleep in anyway."

I went to empty the mop bucket. A few coats of paint had brightened the place up, and I'd fixed all the broken windows. We still needed new lockers—only half of the old ones opened, and half of those wouldn't lock—and as for the plumbing . . . when I tipped the grey-pink water into the old-fashioned earthenware sink the whiff from the plughole suggested something fat and hairy had crawled down the drain and died.

But surveying the place, with its rows of running machines and elliptical trainers, and the refurbished boxing ring and the floor-to-ceiling mirrors, I still felt an electric buzz of excitement. *Maguire's Gym.* I actually owned and was running a business, at seventeen, even if I did have Delroy as a partner.

He'd reached the top of the narrow stairs by now and stopped to catch his breath. I smiled as I heard his voice boom, "You mopped the floors already? God's sake, Crusher, you is the boss of this place. You shouldn't be doing the skivvying."

I didn't want to hire a cleaner for the same reason I didn't want to buy a mop—we didn't need any more staff. Sam and Daisy, who looked after the front desk, were in their twenties, and from the day we opened I had to insist they stopped calling me "Boss," because it made me cringe.

"I don't mind mopping the floor, Delroy, honest."

"I know you don't mind," said Delroy. "It's just you do such a shit job. You should stick to boxing. And making the tea."

"You want some tea?"

"Boy can take a hint."

"You know where the kitchen is."

Twenty minutes later the joint was jumping. Delroy had hooted with laughter when I'd told him I wanted to open at six every day, but I thought plenty of people would prefer to work out first thing in the morning, while they still had the energy, before schlepping off to the office. Maguire's would never be the sort of setup you'd see in a style magazine, with flawlessly beautifully models on treadmills grinning like idiots and never breaking a sweat, but I reckoned if we kept the prices low enough and the place clean enough we'd attract customers who wanted a basic gym with no frills.

So far it seemed to be working. The house my dad and I had lived in I'd rented out to a young Polish family, and now I lived over the shop, in the tiny apartment on the top floor. It was dark and dingy, and damp enough to grow mushrooms, but I didn't do much up there anyway except sleep.

While I acted as manager-cum-janitor Delroy looked after the fighting. His body might have been crippled but his mind was as fast as ever and his eyes missed nothing. He could spot bad habits before you'd even properly acquired them and double the force of your punches just by telling you how to place your feet. He could analyse a fighter's strengths and flaws by listening to them spar, or maybe smelling them; how his instincts worked was a mystery to me, but they worked, and fighters who listened to him could see and feel the difference his input made.

When I had started training with Delroy there hadn't been many female boxers, but that had all changed since the last Olympics. The first time I signed up two women for boxing lessons I saw him raise an eyebrow—the one that still worked—but if the prospect of encouraging girls to thump each other bothered him, he said nothing.

Fifteen minutes later he'd been driving them as hard as he'd ever driven me: "To hell with glowing, ladies, I want to see some sweat!"

There were two women in the ring this morning, circling each other, throwing jabs, dodging and feinting while Delroy observed, calling out advice. I was pounding away on one of the treadmills, seeing how long I could hold my top speed, and I found myself staring at the door before I even realized why. *She's usually here by this time on a Sunday.* I felt Delroy's eyes on me and glanced over. He was frowning like I'd screwed up, but before I could figure out what was bothering him he'd turned his attention back to the sparring.

"Finn, hi."

"Nicky, hey." She must have slipped in while I wasn't looking.

It was five kilometres from Nicky's house to the gym, and it looked like she'd run all the way, but she didn't stop for a breather; she slung her bag on its usual hook, checked the band that held back her honey-blonde hair, climbed up onto an elliptical trainer in front of me and went straight into her workout. I kept running, trying not to stare at the muscles flexing in her ass. It was unprofessional. I stared anyway; I just couldn't help it.

I'd seen a lot of Nicky in the last few months, but then she was my lawyer, and I needed to. She'd sorted the money I'd inherited from my dad, and got hold of the title deeds to that house in Spain I still hadn't seen. When I'd come to her for advice about the gym she'd helped me buy the lease and set up the partnership. She'd handled all the negotiations, arranged the transfer of the funds from Spain and even found me an accountant to keep the books. Our meetings consisted mostly of her handing me forms and telling me what they said and where I should sign, and me signing them. Reading had never been my strong point, but I didn't feel embarrassed about that when I was with Nicky; she managed to make me feel as if severe dyslexia was kind of cute.

The day we opened she had turned up with a bottle of champagne, which I helped Delroy to drink even though I hated the stuff. She even signed up as our first member, though Maguire's Gym was kind of downmarket for a girl as classy as her. But it was all strictly business . . . or that's what I kept telling myself.

Nicky clambered down from the elliptical trainer, returned to her bag and pulled out a towel. As she wiped her face I admired the play of muscles across her back and the way her skin glowed, even under these cold neons. She turned and caught my eye before I looked away. I could feel my face burning, and hoped she'd missed it. I focused on keeping my speed up, but she wandered over in my direction.

"Finn, has Judy been in yet?"

"Judy?" My mind had gone blank.

"We were meant to be sparring together. Kind of early in the day for it, but . . ."

Judy! I remembered her now—a wiry short woman with frizzy hair tied back in a bun, and a hell of a right hand.

"Haven't seen her, sorry." I reached forward, switched off the treadmill, and hopped backwards from the running bed as it slowed. "I'll spar with you if you want," I said.

She grinned. "Finn, you've got twice my reach. I'd end up smeared all over your glove."

I turned to the two women in the ring, who had finished their session and were clambering down through the ropes. "Tracey? You or Marcia up for a round with Nicky here?"

Tracey glanced at the clock. "Sorry, Finn, I've got a Sunday lunch."

"I'll do it."

I turned to find Bruno behind us. He'd only been coming to the gym for a week or two, but he was in good shape. Slim, gangly and dark, he looked Arabic, even if Bruno didn't exactly sound like an Arabic name. But our members could call themselves anything they liked as long as they paid their subs. He struck me as slightly clueless and I wondered if he knew what he was letting himself in for, but he only outweighed Nicky by a kilo or two, and he was pretty much her height.

"OK . . . but both of you take it easy, yeah?"

Across the ring I saw Delroy watching. He

seemed dubious. I remembered he'd quickly taken a dislike to Bruno, for some reason I'd never been able to fathom. But I thought if I kept an eye on proceedings there shouldn't be a problem.

"I'll go glove up," said Nicky.

"I'll help," I said. I'd shown her plenty of times the right way to wrap her hands before putting gloves on, and she was perfectly capable, but she let me do it anyway. She seemed a little distracted as I fastened the bindings off and slipped on her gel sparring gloves.

"Hey. Focus," I said.

"Sorry." She grinned, blew her fringe up out of her face. "Stuff at work."

"This will sort all that out."

"I hope so." I glanced across to where Delroy was checking Bruno's gloves. He'd switched from bag gloves to heavily padded sparring ones, heavier than Nicky's, but she was too slight to wear the exact equivalents. "Remember what I told you. Keep moving. He'll hit harder than you're used to, so try not to let him."

"Thanks," she said.

"And Nicky . . . go easy on him, yeah?"

*  *  *

For the first minute or so she did. They circled each other, weighing each other up, throwing the odd jab, but then Nicky stepped in with a right hook that connected clean with the point of Bruno's jaw, snapping his head back. She had plenty of strength, I knew, but it surprised me how much force she put into the shot—almost as if she had lost control. Bruno closed up his guard and increased the distance between them, forcing her to come closer if she wanted to make contact.

She was up for it. She smacked at his raised arms with left and right, then dodged back, all the time moving, side to side, switching direction. I was reminded of a tiger I'd seen once in a run-down zoo near Brighton, endlessly pacing up and down, staring through the plate glass at the slack-jawed punters staring back. Even as a kid I'd understood that that tiger was slowly going crazy. It wasn't a good image to come to mind.

It occurred to me that I really didn't know that much about Nicky. She'd always struck me as calm, level-headed, unflappable, but now I realized that as a lawyer she must deal with stress and conflict every day, and all that pent-up frustration and aggression had to go somewhere. I was starting to think I was seeing it now.

Bruno was cooler and more patient than I'd expected, but you could tell he was getting fed up with getting whacked by Nicky, padding or no padding. I suddenly realized how little I knew about Bruno, too. He'd been to the gym less than half a dozen times and would always work away quietly for the best part of an hour before slipping out again. Occasionally he'd linger nearby when Delroy and I were having a conversation, and if we addressed him, he'd just grin and carry on with what he'd been doing as if he didn't really speak the language. When he did speak his accent was pure London, with only the faintest hint of Arabic, so I guessed that was just shyness on his part. But Delroy always said that you only saw a man's true character when you put him under pressure in the ring.

Now Bruno's eyes were gleaming under the rim of his sparring helmet and his cheeks were glistening with sweat. He threw a few counterpunches but Nicky was always too fast, dodging to the left or right or leaning back just enough to let his shots go wild, and then coming in under his open arm with a hard sharp jab to the ribs. Around me I could hear the half-dozen customers easing off on their exercise machines as they sensed the aggression in the air and stopped to watch what was unfolding in the ring.

Delroy too seemed to smell the hostility and the adrenaline, and normally he got off on it, but now it was starting to rattle him. "Ease up, now! Back off!" he shouted, and somehow it got through to Nicky, and she stepped back.

Bruno dropped his guard. He planted his feet, lowered his gloved fists almost to waist level, and stood there with his head tilted to one side, as if Nicky was a problem he had to work out. Unable to resist an open shot she came piling back in, threw a right, and it was Bruno's turn to lean out of range. His left came up in a blur, connected with her ear and sent her staggering.

"Enough!" yelled Delroy, but nobody was listening. As he threw his crutch aside, fumbled for the ringside bell and clattered it, I grabbed onto the ring ropes and hauled myself up and through, but I was too late.

The bell was clanging continuously but Bruno paid it no attention. Nicky had bent over, and her knees were going, but Bruno wouldn't let her fall—he pounded her again and again with short, vicious uppercuts to her chest that almost lifted her off her feet. Stepping back he cocked his right arm for a haymaker, but I grabbed his elbow before he could deliver and heaved him away, driving him back to his corner with my forearm hard against his chest. I expected him to lash out at me, and I was ready for it, but he relaxed right away and lowered his fists. He hadn't lost his temper or lost control—he'd known exactly what he was doing. Now he dropped his arms and danced on his toes like he'd been having some harmless fun and was ready for another round.

"Bruno!" I snapped.

His face registered no emotion whatsoever. "Bitch was out of control," he shrugged.

"You're done here. Get changed and go." He stared at me and I stared back. "Leave, now, Bruno."

He glanced over at Nicky, who by now had collapsed, coughing, onto the canvas, then he sighed, ducked through the ropes, jumped down and sauntered towards the changing rooms, undoing his gloves with his teeth and not once looking back.

"You sure you're OK?"

Nicky was sitting on the bench in the ladies' changing room, bent forwards, flexing her jaw from side to side while I stooped beside her.

"I'm fine. It just really bloody hurts, getting punched in the tits."

"Yeah, I know," I said.

"I don't think you do." Somehow she managed to giggle. She straightened up and arched her back, touched her breasts and winced.

"I'm really sorry. I should never have let that happen. We're banning Bruno from ever training here again."

"It wasn't your fault, or his. It was me who lost it. I knew we were meant to be sparring, but I just . . . really wanted to lay into someone, and he happened to be there."

"Why did you?"

She looked at me, and shook her head, and

turned to grab her towel. "I'd better make a move . . ."

"Is everything all right? With you and Harry, I mean?"

As soon as the words were out of my mouth I wanted the cracked lino floor to open up and swallow me. She'd talked about her husband a few times, and from what I could make out they always seemed to be arguing. But it was none of my business if her marriage had problems. What was I going to do about it anyway?

When she looked at me now, though, she didn't laugh, or politely suggest I should scram; it was almost like she was flattered that I cared. I guessed she was about to tell me something, but thought better of it, and held a hand to her jaw again.

"I need a shower," she said.

She stood, and I did too, and held up a finger up in front of her face.

"Put that away, Finn. I don't have a concussion."

"What day is it?"

"It's Sunday, and tomorrow's Monday, and you're coming to my office at three to sign the completion."

"The what?"

"For the purchase of the freehold. Have you forgotten?"

When Nicky had helped me buy the lease she'd mentioned the whole building was for sale. That had worried me—I thought we might get chucked out by the new owner— until it occurred to me that if I bought the building, that wouldn't happen.

"No," I said. "Well, sort of. I'd forgotten what day of the week it was."

"Then how the hell were you going to test me for a concussion?" Now she sounded like her regular self again. When she started to pull off her T-shirt I suddenly realized where I was, and made a run for it.

"Don't use all the hot water, all right?" I called over my shoulder.

"Tell you, Finn, we are damn lucky she didn't sue. That's what puts gyms out of business."

"How would she sue us? She's our lawyer. It would count as conflict of interest or something."

"I'm serious, boy! Next time it happen, maybe it won't be a friend of yours, who gets up and walks away and laughs about it. Maybe some girl end up in hospital."

"Delroy, there won't be a next time."

Delroy shook his great grey head and sighed. We were sitting around the table of his poky kitchen drinking rum from shot glasses— heavily diluted, at Winnie's insistence. Delroy's wife didn't approve of strong drink, and Delroy had a hard enough time walking when he was sober. Watering it down was fine by me; I didn't really like the taste anyway, and I only sipped at it to keep Delroy company.

I ate at their house most nights, and loved it there, and they seemed happy to have me. It was warm and bright, and even the po-faced Jesus pictures Winnie had pinned up everywhere didn't stop the place feeling cheerful. It was certainly cosier than the mouldy-smelling apartment over the gym, but then a bus shelter in the rain would have been cosier than that place.

"You business tycoons too busy talking shop to stir the chicken?" Winnie complained as she bustled in. The smell of her cooking filled the house and my mouth was watering. The first time I tasted her jerk chicken and sweet potato

I wolfed down three helpings and nearly died of indigestion. Now I made sure I took my time.

"I'm not falling for that one," Delroy grunted. "I know what you like when someone mess with your cooking."

"I hope you are hungry, Finn, there's an awful lot of food here." She tutted as her glasses steamed up, then took them off and wiped them on her flowery apron.

"Course the boy is hungry. He work all day, seven days a week. Up at five and he never stop, painting, fixing windows, cleaning. Boy's a one-man army."

"It doesn't count as work if you enjoy it," I said.

"It's because you work for yourself," said Delroy. "Take orders from no one, that's what make the difference."

"All the same, boy your age ought not to be working every hour the good Lord sent," said Winnie. "You need to get out more, make some friends your own age. Not hang around with grumpy old farts like Delroy here."

"I am younger than you, woman!"

"Maybe I find you a nice girl from my church you can take to the pictures."

"Finn don't want none of them God-botherers," snorted Delroy. "He take a girl to the movies, he want one who'll sit in the back row. He's looking for heaven in this life, not the next."

"You is disgusting, Delroy Llewellyn!"

"I'm fine, Winnie, thanks," I said.

"You got a girl already?" Winnie beamed.

"I wish," I said.

"Look at him!" Winnie grinned. "Boy blushing like a Caribbean sunset. You tell us everything now. What's she like?"

"She's married, that's what she's like," grunted Delroy.

I stared. If this was a wind-up it was kind of close to the bone.

"Hush, you!" scolded Winnie. "Finn wouldn't go with no married woman."

"She's a lawyer, and she's married to a rich man who works in the City, and she's ten years older than Finn, and she spend more time with him than she do with her husband." Delroy poured himself another shot of rum, and this time took a swig without watering it down. Was that why he'd been scowling at me this morning as I waited for Nicky to turn up? Because he thought I had a crush on her?

"Well, how is it Finn's fault if she like him?" protested Winnie. "What woman wouldn't take a shine to a big handsome fella like him?"

I felt my face redden. Delroy had seen right through me. Of course I fancied Nicky—how could I not? She was beautiful, clever, funny, and a day I didn't see her at the gym felt . . . wasted somehow. I knew that, even if I'd never acknowledged it, and never would. To Nicky we were simply lawyer and client, I'd been sure. We were friendly, yeah, but . . . Delroy seemed to be suggesting Nicky felt the same way about me as I did about her, and that was bull—it had to be.

"You're hallucinating, Delroy," I said. "I thought it was her who got punched in the head today, not you."

Delroy was staring into his empty shot glass. "I seen the way she look at you. Believe me, boy, that woman going to break your heart."

"That's what women do, isn't it?" I said.

"Hark at him," Winnie tutted sadly. "Man of the world."

And then the doorbell rang.

Winnie went to answer it, grumbling about local kids playing knock and run, while Delroy and I sat there in awkward silence. I was kind of flattered that he was taking an interest in my love life, or the lack of it, but all the same I wished he'd mind his own business and let me make my own mistakes. Another part of me was wondering if it was true what he'd said about Nicky, that she wasn't just there to prop up the business and offer professional advice.

True, she'd been there when my mother was attacked, and come with me to the hospital where they tried in vain to rescue her, and stuck by my side through the purgatory of questions that had followed. Nicky had held my hand at the inquest when the details made me want to weep or throw my chair through a window or both. OK, she was more than just my lawyer, but Delroy must have been imagining the rest. Nicky was way older than me, way smarter, way classier.

So what if she worked out at our gym, and

23

came running with me? It had come up in conversation that her house was just not far from the Thameside path where I ran most mornings. And early one morning she'd overtaken me, and since that day we ran together a few times a week, and talked about nothing in particular, but that didn't mean she had the hots for me . . . did it?

Lost in thought, I took a while to catch on that whoever was at the door wasn't coming in and wasn't going away either. Winnie's voice was growing louder and shriller and more insistent, and I was just thinking I should go and find out what was happening when I heard someone push their way into the house, ignoring Winnie's protests, which by now had risen to a shriek. While Delroy groped behind him for his crutch, I kicked the chair back and pushed through the bead curtain into the hall.

A shaven-headed bloke the size of a wardrobe was standing in the hallway blocking the entire front door, his arms folded and his fat mouth a tight grim line. Winnie was in the doorway to the front room, scolding someone loudly in such a thick Caribbean accent I couldn't understand a word she was saying, but I got the gist: someone had barged in to rob them. Delroy and Winnie had nothing worth stealing, I knew, but details like that never bothered the twitchy lowlifes that roamed this area looking to fund their next fix any way they could. Not that the gorilla in the doorway looked like your typical smack addict, but I figured I'd help Winnie out first and analyse the intruders' motives later.

A bloke in his mid-twenties, shorter and slighter than the first, emerged from the front room lugging Delroy's cheap flatscreen TV under one arm and ignoring Winnie's protests. There was a sour tang of stale tobacco from his clothes, his fingers were stained yellow with nicotine, and he wore his greasy hair. in a daft old-fashioned quiff with sideburns that almost reached to his broad, square chin. All he needed was the glittery jumpsuit and the tacky gold sunglasses.

"Would you mind putting that back, please?" I said. It sounded absurdly polite but I knew that was the approach Winnie would prefer.

Elvis weighed me up and dismissed me with a glance. "Look, just mind your own business, kid, all right? And there won't be any trouble."

"There's already trouble," I said. "Winnie, get in the kitchen."

"No, Finn, this is not your problem," said Winnie, but there was a catch in her voice, and when I looked at her face I saw she was crying, and a surge of indignation sent adrenaline coursing through my body. Through everything that had happened to Delroy she had never lost heart or given up hope, and to see her humiliated now filled me with a rage I could barely contain. All thanks to those two leather-coated creeps carting Delroy's worthless crappy supermarket TV out the front door.

I strode out after them. They were headed for a big shiny Merc parked at the curb with its boot open. By now I knew these two were definitely not typical burglars, but I didn't care any more.

"Yo, jerk," I said. "I asked you nicely."

Elvis turned, the TV still under one arm, and sighed as if I was a parking ticket he'd have to tear up. He glanced at his glamorous assistant. "Sean?" he said wearily.

Sean the Wardrobe turned back and lumbered towards me, smirking. He was big and packing plenty of muscle but he moved like a hippo with piles, and that crappy cheap leather coat he was wearing would restrict his movements. He wore leather gloves too—either he thought they made him look hard, or he bit his fingernails—and when I saw him open his big meaty right hand I thought, He's planning to punch me?

I was almost insulted, but I let him take a swing, dodged and came up and threw all my weight into a straight right to his jaw. His big fleshy face rippled under the impact like a half-set jelly and he stumbled backwards.

By now Elvis was loading Delroy's TV into the boot of the Merc, but I figured he wouldn't drive off without his boyfriend. I let Sean find his balance and watched him come to the boil, shaking his head and screwing up his piggy little eyes. He came back at me twice as fast as before, his great fists flying, but so wild they might have been passing asteroids. I slipped up close and sank a left into his solar plexus, feeling the wind gush out of his body and watching him sag like a punctured blimp. He fumbled for my collar, plainly hoping to hold me still long enough to clobber me with his other fist or maybe a head-butt, but I grasped his wrist and locked his gloved hand back and twisted his arm round and he fell heavily to his knees, wailing a high-pitched protest that sounded weirdly like Winnie. Delroy was in the doorway now, watching, Winnie behind him sobbing and pleading with him to intervene.

"Bring the TV back," I called to Elvis, "or I break his arm."

"Dammit!" said Elvis, and he slammed down the lid of the boot.

"Fine," I said. "Have it your way."

"Finn, don't," said Delroy.

I looked at him. I wasn't really planning to break Sean's arm, but I was pretty sure I knew how to dislocate it. Dislocation was painful, but it could easily be fixed, although fixing it was even more painful.

"Let him up," said Delroy.

I released Sean's arm and stepped back. He knelt there, clutching it and cursing under his breath, until his boss came back, stood over him, sighed in frustration and kicked him in the ribs.

"Get up, you useless prick," he said.

"If I have to bring that TV back myself," I said, "I'll be using your ass for a wheelbarrow."

But Elvis ignored me and instead pointed a stubby little finger at Delroy. "You were warned," he said. "Next time you're late, we'll take all your bloody furniture, not just that cheap piece of crap." He glared at me. "And thanks to this Boy Scout, your rate's just doubled. You don't like it, talk to Mr. Sherwood." He turned and shoved Sean the Wardrobe back up the path towards the Merc.

I let them leave and turned to Delroy, who was leaning on his crutch, his knuckles white and his black face paler than I'd ever seen it.

"Delroy?" I said. "What the hell's going on?"

"You borrowed your stake in the gym off Sherwood?"

"What else was I going to do? We didn't have six thousand pounds lying around." Delroy was slumped in his armchair in the front room, opposite the empty stand where his TV had once stood. Now there were just a few balls of dust and some loose cables with the connectors half wrenched off.

"You could have borrowed it from me," I said. "I can afford it. I told you, my dad's friend in Spain left me a shedload of cash—what the hell else am I going to use it for?"

"That's your money," said Delroy. "I wanted us to be partners. If I took the money off you, where would that leave me?"

Winnie bustled in again, her eyes still red and swollen, clutching a can of furniture polish and a faded yellow cloth. She sprayed the stand and wiped it down, as if she could clean up this horrible bloody mess with a duster.

I'd heard a few things about Sherwood, none of them good. Cars had been burned out, windows broken, knees smashed with baseball bats in alleys behind dodgy pubs. You had to be stupid or utterly desperate to borrow money from him. And Delroy and Winnie weren't stupid.

"I been paying it back out of my disability allowance," said Delroy. "Fifty pound a week." He was staring at the floor, as if he was afraid to look up and see the gap where the TV had been. "But this week the bank messed up, and the money came in a day late. I called Mr. Sherwood and all, tried to explain, but they kept saying he was busy."

Fifty pounds a week? How could Delroy ever afford that sort of money? I knew Winnie was still working as a cleaner, although she was nearly seventy. The way she'd talked it about it made it sound like something she did for the company of the other cleaning women, and to keep herself busy. Now I cursed myself for ever letting myself believe that. She couldn't afford to stop working, because I had come to them with a stupid scheme about opening a gym, and she had gone along with it to make Delroy happy. I'd thought I was being clever and helpful when all I had done was landed them in debt to a loan shark.

"I'll get your TV back," I said. "In fact, to hell with that, I'll buy you a new one. A big one."

"It's not your problem," muttered Delroy.

"It doesn't matter. I want to," I said.

"Forget it, Finn," he sighed. "I watch too much TV anyway."

I had to fix my screw-up somehow. And it was going to take more than a new television set.

# two

Nicky didn't show up the next morning, either for our run along the river or at the gym, and for once I was glad. She would have sensed something was bothering me and nagged me to tell her and insisted on helping to sort it out, but I had the feeling this wasn't the sort of problem that a lawyer could help with. Sure, I'd be seeing her that afternoon, but maybe I'd have come up with a solution by then. This was my screw-up, and I wanted to see what I could do without getting any more of the people I cared about sucked in. Back at the gym I heaved away at the weights harder than ever, clanging the metal bricks till my muscles burned, punishing myself for my blindness, my stupidity, my selfishness. Delroy watched me from the corner of his eye as he prowled around the gym, grunting terse words of encouragement to the punters working out and training, but didn't come over to talk about the night before. There was nothing to be said anyway. When I'd changed and showered I simply told him I'd be back in an hour or two and he didn't ask where I was going.

The loansharking business was getting squeezed nowadays by those Internet lenders with adverts everywhere and interest rates in four figures, but even so there was always room for bottom-feeders like John Sherwood, taking on borrowers no big firm would touch. He ran small ads in free newspapers and put postcards in newsagents' windows describing himself as a "local friend in need" who would even bring cash to your house. That sounded like good service, but then his operating methods relied on knowing where you lived. As soon as something went wrong—and something always went wrong—he wasn't so easy to reach. His adverts featured a mobile phone number, but if you called it, all you got was a voicemail message telling you to leave a number for someone to call you back.

When I was thirteen or so, running wild

around West London, one of the places me and my fellow brats had hung out was a snooker hall that had seen better days. A sign outside the door barred entry to anyone under sixteen, in theory, but no one could be bothered to enforce it. If you could cough up the hefty deposit for balls and cues and had enough pound coins to keep the table light on you could play all day. There were usually older blokes hanging around, some offering a range of drugs to anyone who asked. For the most part we ignored the pushers, but one thing I did learn was that a loan shark called Sherwood had an office nearby. Once or twice I'd glimpsed a slim bloke in a sharp suit, usually with a couple of heavies in tow, slipping in through an unmarked doorway in the alley outside.

The snooker hall was a few minutes' walk from the bus stop on the main drag, lined with pubs and clubs that only came to life at weekends. The entrance was off a narrow side street, and its doorway was barred now by a steel grille filled with rotting litter and leaves; behind the dusty filth-spattered windows slabs of chipboard had been screwed up to stop looters ripping the place apart for its pipes and wiring. Either it had run out of money or the cops had finally got their act together and put it out of business. As I glanced at the doors, their handles wrapped in rusted chain, I couldn't work out whether I felt nostalgic for the fun I'd thought I'd been having here or angry at myself for wasting so much of my youth in this dump playing bad pool and losing all the money I'd made from shoplifting cigarettes and booze.

But all that was past, I thought, and there was no point in beating myself up—especially in this neighbourhood, where you could usually find a crack addict to do that for you. I went round the side to the grimy alley with its unmarked door, noticing a sleek new convertible Merc parked in a private off-street bay opposite—a motor way too classy for this part of town.

It looked like my luck was in.

I banged on the blank double doors and after a few moments heard footsteps clomping down the stairs and a rattling of the lock. When the door was shoved open Sean's head emerged, and when he clocked who it was standing there his face went bright scarlet, adding a lovely pink tinge to the purple bruise my fist had left on his face the day before. Even though he was indoors he was still wearing his leather gloves, I noticed. Maybe he had a skin condition.

"I'd like to talk to Mr. Sherwood," I said.

I could see uncertainty and indecision jostling under Sean's beefy features. He seemed unsure whether he should tell me to piss off and slam the door again, or step out into the alley and see if the previous day's encounter had been an unlucky fluke. I stared at him and waited, ready for either but hoping for neither. If he did slam the door again I'd have to stand there knocking on it till Sherwood came out for lunch or something, and it was starting to rain, and I'd look like a berk.

"You got an appointment?" said Sean finally. I nearly laughed at his effort to sound efficient and professional—he came across like one of those self-important grannies who work as doctors' receptionists so they can have a nose through patients' medical records.

"I'm here to repay a loan," I said.

Sean squinted, and his little eyes nearly disappeared into the fleshy folds of his face. "Wait here," he said, and slammed the door shut.

It re-opened a few minutes later and Sean urged me in with a sharp jerk of his head. The stairs were covered in cheap vinyl, but at the top the floor was so thickly carpeted I couldn't hear my own footsteps. The long hallway was moodily lit, painted in muted beige colours and lined with bland abstract prints in metal frames. The effect was meant to be classy and upmarket, but it reminded me of one of those budget business hotels where travelling sales-men watch porn. Sean led the way up the corridor to a pair of wooden doors, rapped gently with one leather-gloved knuckle and waited, while I examined a nearby oil painting showing a hay cart fording a stream. It looked old, and it didn't really go with the modern abstracts, but maybe Sherwood thought it gave the place class.

"Yeah," said a voice from inside.

Sean opened the door and stood back rever-ently.

Behind the desk, flicking his finger across a

tablet PC, was the same slim, sharp-suited guy I used to glimpse in the alley. Sherwood was in his late thirties now, I guessed, with an overdone tan, neatly cut hair and rimless glasses. He looked quite respectable, more like an accountant or a high-street estate agent than a loan shark. But then he had goons like Sean and Elvis to handle the business that involved smashed teeth and turds through letter boxes. Elvis was here right now, I noticed, perched against a side table eating peanuts from a bowl, relaxed in stone-coloured chinos and a sweater. His outfit didn't go with the greasy quiff, but then only a glittery glam-rock jumpsuit would have gone with that quiff.

Either Sherwood was genuinely checking something on his screen or he was merely feigning a lack of interest in my arrival. I approached his broad, bare, bleached-wood desk and stood there waiting. At last he put the tablet aside and looked up at me over his glasses with eyes of washed-out blue.

"Mr. Maguire, hello," said Sherwood. His accent was Scottish, Glasgow at a guess, with a hint of head-butts and razor blades. There was a solid modern chair facing his desk, but he didn't look at it or invite me to sit. It didn't surprise me that he knew my name; by now he knew what had happened at Delroy's house the day before, and he would have found out I was responsible. Addressing me by name was meant to rattle me—to make me think he knew everything about me there was to know. But of course he didn't.

"Mr. Sherwood, I came to apologize to you and your staff about what happened yesterday," I said. That took Sherwood by surprise, as I'd intended; he was expecting me to act defiant or macho. But he'd struck me as vain and egotistical, and I guessed that flattery might be the best way to get his guard down. "I'd no idea your people were there to collect on a legitimate debt," I went on. "I thought they were stealing Mr. Llewellyn's TV, and I sort of waded in. I'm very sorry."

Sherwood did a good imitation of being amused. "These misunderstandings do happen," he said. "Just as well no one called the police." Yeah, right, I thought, like they'd back you up. Then I thought of all the coppers I'd encountered, and how they would have looked at me, a scruffy overgrown teenager, and then at prosperous, plausible Sherwood. They'd have done whatever he wanted them to.

"Fortunately I made my own enquiries first," went on Sherwood. "From what I heard, I thought you would come looking for me. And here you are." He smiled, not warmly, and let the silence hang a minute in the air. He liked playing games, I could tell. Getting customers to sweat was one of the perks of his business.

"Take a seat," he said finally. I sat, and tried to shift the leather-and-wood armchair closer to his desk, but it was too heavy to move easily. I could sense Elvis lurking behind me, where I couldn't keep an eye on him.

"I understand you're here to repay a loan," said Sherwood. "But I don't think you're one of my clients."

"Delroy told me he borrowed six grand from you," I said. "I can get hold of that much in a day or two."

Sherwood sighed and smiled and fiddled with a fat black fountain pen. "Sorry, Mr. Maguire," he said. "I wish it was that simple."

"I understand there's interest on top," I said. I didn't name a figure; I suspected whatever figure I suggested, Sherwood would double it.

"My arrangement was with Mr. Llewellyn, not with you," said Sherwood. "In fact, strictly speaking I can't even discuss Mr. Llewellyn's business with anyone but him. We take the Data Protection Act very seriously in this firm."

Data protection? Now he really was taking the piss. I bristled, but tried to hide it.

"The thing is, you're a successful business-man, Mr. Sherwood," I said calmly. "I can't understand why you lent Delroy that money in the first place. He'll never be able to pay it back. You've taken his TV, and he doesn't have anything else worth seizing."

"Yes, that TV is pretty much worthless, but that's not the point," said Sherwood. "He promised to make his payments on time, and he broke that promise. It was by way of a re-minder."

"Look, like I said, I can repay that loan my-self, with interest. You won't need to send any more—reminders." I glanced at big Sean to show I could think of a better name for him. "And realistically it's the only way you'll ever get your money back."

"That's not quite true," said Sherwood. "Mr.

Llewellyn offered his family home as collateral, and I accepted."

I felt my mouth opening and closing gormlessly. When I finally managed to stammer, "His home?" it came out as a pathetic squeak.

Watching me flounder, Sherwood's chilly grin finally reached his eyes.

"You can't take his home," I said. "Where are he and Winnie going to live?"

"The local authorities have a wide range of bed-and-breakfast accommodation," said Sherwood. "They cater for all sorts—asylum seekers, gypsies, benefit scroungers . . ." Behind me I heard Elvis snickering.

"Delroy's had a stroke. He still uses a crutch. That house has been specially adapted for him. He can't live in a B and B."

"Then maybe he should race back to Jamaica," shrugged Sherwood. "Those people have huge families, so somebody over there will look after him. He'll probably be happier back where he came from anyway."

You smug, slimy racist, I thought. But I didn't say it. I had done enough futile bleating, and it was time to bring the discussion back to the only thing Sherwood cared about.

"How much do you want?" I asked. Let him name the figure.

"Even in that area, that house of theirs is worth . . . a hundred and fifty thousand pounds?" He grinned as he said it, as well he might. Delroy had borrowed six, and Sherwood wanted one hundred and fifty to cancel the debt? That must have been how he paid for his fancy oil paintings.

"That's presuming you can get hold of Delroy's house," I said.

"The paperwork is watertight, believe me," said Sherwood. "I do this for a living."

"There might still be complications," I said. I knew Sherwood would have a brief on his payroll—but then I had Nicky. She decorated her office with the shrunken heads of shyster lawyers.

"Ah," said Sherwood. "I wondered when we'd come to the threats."

"I'm not the one making threats," I said.

"I know you're acquainted with McGovern," said Sherwood. "But so am I. And believe me, I've been dealing with him a lot longer than you have. I wouldn't count on him backing you up."

McGovern? Who the hell had told him I knew McGovern? Last time I'd seen London's most notorious gangster he'd held a gun to my head and told me to forget I'd just seen him shoot a man in the face. I still hadn't figured out why the Guvnor had let me live that time. Why on earth would he lift a finger to help me now?

But if Sherwood thought he might . . . ? I could see now why he'd told Sean to let me in, why we were having this conversation, why we were negotiating. I was still only seventeen years old. I couldn't spend any of my inheritance without my lawyer's signature. Whoever Sherwood had spoken to, they'd told him that I was pals with the Guvnor. And it was true McGovern liked me—otherwise my corpse would have been piled up with the others in that blood-spattered Pimlico restaurant. All the same, I'd have to tread carefully. I'd seen what happened to the last bloke who invoked the Guvnor's name without permission—he was the one with his brains all over the wall.

"Mr. Sherwood, let's call it twelve grand, cash. No strings, no lawyers, and I can get the cash to you by Wednesday. Nobody else will ever get involved, that's a promise." It was funny how trying to sound calm and reasonable, when really I was ready to smack someone, made me feel calm and reasonable. I'd have to remember that.

"Fifteen," said Sherwood. I chewed my lip while I pretended to think about it. Then I shrugged and smiled, and stood up, offering him my hand. He stood too and grasped my hand in both of his. His touch was cold and slimy, like a handful of old dead fish.

"We have a deal," he said. But he didn't let go of my hand. "That means you and I have a deal, Mr. Maguire. Fifteen grand by this time on Wednesday, and Mr. Llewellyn's debt will be cancelled. Otherwise . . ." He sighed, like a ham actor in a TV soap.

"I'll be here," I said.

As I rode the Tube into the City for my appointment with Nicky, I wondered how I was going to explain why I needed fifteen thousand pounds in cash at such short notice. It was my money, of course, and she always insisted it was up to me what I did with it, but the way things had been set up I still needed her signature to get hold of it. She was bound to be curious about what it was for, and I wasn't sure if I should tell her. I'd back her any day to take on Sherwood in court and string him up with his own rancid guts, but once we left the courthouse all bets would be off. He'd find a way to make Delroy and Winnie, and me, pay. I decided I'd just tell Nicky I needed cash for some second-hand gym equipment. She'd probably guess I was up to something, but with any luck she'd just think I was buying bent gear that had been pushed off the back of a lorry, and wouldn't ask too many questions.

All the same it was going to place a barrier between us, for the first time, and I wasn't sure how I felt about that. Nicky was like the big sister I'd never had, except what I felt about her wasn't at all brotherly, I knew now. I thought I'd been doing a good job of hiding my feelings from myself and everyone else, but I hadn't fooled Delroy for a minute—and if I hadn't fooled him, I probably hadn't fooled Nicky either. I didn't know if I would even be able to look her in the eye at this meeting.

As usual Lincoln's Inn Fields was a mêlée of lawyers in gowns and smart suits scurrying back and forward between their offices and the Royal Courts of Justice on the eastern side of the square. Nicky's building didn't look quite as intimidating as the first few times I'd been there; I knew now that she and her partner Kamlesh Vora were just tenants on one half of one floor, sharing a receptionist and secretarial staff with other small firms in the same building. The woman at the front desk gave me a professional smile, like she recognized me, but with an odd hint of tension and weariness.

"I'm afraid Ms. Hale isn't in today," she said. That explained the weariness—she must have been telling people the same thing all morning. It didn't explain much else, though.

"I had an appointment at three," I said.

"I'm sorry. Would you like to reschedule?"

"Did she say what the problem was?"

"She hasn't been in touch at all, I'm afraid. She just didn't come in this morning."

"Have you tried her mobile?"

"We've left messages, but no one's heard back from her yet. We do have access to her diary, if you'd like to make another appointment."

For the moment I was stumped. It wasn't

like Nicky to drop off the radar. I'd always been able to contact her, even way out of office hours. Once when I'd got through to her in the evening I gave her a hard time for answering her phone when she should have been having a life. She'd laughed. "I do have caller ID, Finn," she'd said. "I didn't think you'd be ringing me up to waste my time."

"What about Mr. Vora?" I asked the receptionist. "Is he in?"

"I'll try him for you."

When Vora opened the door to let me into his and Nicky's office it took me a moment to recognize him. He was normally neat, dapper and expensively dressed, but today his tie was crooked, his neat white fringe of hair stuck out at odd angles and it looked like he hadn't even shaved. When I told him I was supposed to be signing completion documents with Nicky that day—I didn't mention the fifteen grand—he actually wrung his hands. I'd never seen anyone do that before.

"I am sure this will all be sorted out when Nicky returns," he insisted, but he didn't sound convinced.

"But where is she? It's not like her to just disappear and not let anyone know where she's going, is it?"

"We are all human, Mr. Maguire." Vora pulled at his hair in agitation. "She maybe has problems at home, or a personal crisis of some sort . . ."

"Have you tried her home number?"

"Her husband says she went out late last night and did not return. That is all he knows."

"Did they argue?"

"Look, Nicky has always been one hundred per cent reliable. I am sure when she returns she will have a perfectly reasonable explanation."

He sounded like he was trying to persuade himself as much as me. In fact, Vora's appearance was rattling me more than the mysterious missed appointment. It was far too early to be panicking like this, unless . . .

"Jesus, Mr. Vora . . . Look—never mind the documents for now. I need to get hold of fifteen grand. By Wednesday. What about you— can you authorize it?"

Vora blinked some more. His lips worked as if they were trying to form words but had forgotten how.

"I am not strictly speaking a partner in the firm," he stammered finally. "I retired recently. I am merely acting as a consultant while Nicky looks for a new partner."

"Yeah, whatever, but you have access to my money, the client account, don't you?"

"I do, yes, but—there appears to be a problem—"

Damn, I thought. "What sort of a problem? You mean you can't get access to the money?"

"I can get access to the account, yes, but . . ." Vora's voice trailed off.

"But what? Mr. Vora—tell me the money's there."

"I've asked the bank to double-check," stammered Vora. "But—"

Shit. *SHIT!* "Do you know if she took her passport?"

Vora blinked. "Her husband says her passport is missing. It seems likely she did take it, yes."

"You're telling me Nicky Hale has taken her passport, cleaned out the client account, and disappeared?" Whatever that trick was for sounding calm and reasonable, I couldn't remember it now.

Vora stroked his sweaty bald head, trying to pat down the wild white hair that rimmed it. "I'm truly very sorry . . . this has never . . . I am so sorry, Finn . . ."

The female constable on the front desk of the Holborn cop-shop looked like she was more used to dealing with mugged tourists and lost iPhones than lawyers absconding with their clients' money. It took some explaining but finally I was shown to an interview room and offered the traditional grey plastic chair and grey plastic tea while I waited for a detective to arrive, my thoughts tumbling and tangling in my head like shirts in an overheated tumble dryer. I'd needed that money to complete the purchase of the building—what would happen to that? And what about Delroy and Winnie, and their loan? What the hell was I going to tell Sherwood? I'd never bothered with the police before—even when I'd tried to help them they'd always treated me as a suspect rather than a witness—but now I didn't have a choice. I couldn't fight or blag my way out of this hole.

A few months back I had fallen for Zoe

Prendergast, and she'd distracted me with her assets while her boss arranged for me to be turned into Spam. Now Nicky had taken me for half a million quid, and I'd never even got to sleep with her.

As I sat there, sipping the insipid milky lukewarm liquid from a dribbly plastic cup, I thought about all the trouble Nicky must have gone to—winning my trust, egging me into buying that gym so I'd authorize transfer of my inheritance from Spain straight into her client account . . . Had buying the freehold of the building been my idea or hers? It was hard to believe it had all been a scam.

In fact, the more I thought about it the less I believed it. I'd liked Nicky, and I thought she'd liked me, and—apart from Zoe—my instincts usually weren't that far wrong. Delroy had said Nicky would break my heart, but I was pretty sure he hadn't meant she was going to rip me off. I'd sat with her after that pummelling she had taken from Bruno and looked into her eyes and she'd told me she'd see me today. She'd made several appointments for today, in fact, from what her receptionist had said, and why would she bother if she had been planning all along not to be here? The more clients she pissed off, the sooner her theft would be spotted. If it was a theft.

If she *hadn't* run off with my money, then what had happened to her?

The door opened and a sharp-faced woman entered. She was thirty-something with dark hair, high cheekbones and the expression of a copper who hated dealing with the public but had drawn the short straw in the station canteen. Her short cropped hair and smart suit suggested she wanted her colleagues to assume she was a lesbian so they'd stop hitting on her and let her get some work done.

"Finn Maguire?" Her accent was Brum and I noticed she didn't bother calling me "Mr." Two words in and she was already patronizing me. "I'm Detective Sergeant McCoy, this is Detective Constable Whelan." I honestly hadn't noticed she had a DC with her, a guy in a rumpled suit who didn't look much older than me, so nondescript he faded into the background like a stain.

By the time I'd explained my problem the

look on McCoy's face suggested my story was a wind-up that someone was going to regret, starting with me.

"You're how old—seventeen?—and you had half a million pounds in the bank?"

"I inherited it from my dad. He was left it by a family friend." I'd told her all this already. I hadn't told her Dad had been murdered over it, because that was none of her business. It didn't matter anyhow; like most cops she'd jumped to a conclusion early on and was ignoring anything afterwards that didn't fit. "My lawyer had control of it, not me," I explained again.

"Only she's absconded with it."

"I don't think she has."

"Well, has she or hasn't she?"

"She's not the sort of person who would."

"Believe me, for that sort of money a lot of people would." I noticed that she'd shifted from sceptical to sardonic, which was progress of a sort.

"I think it's more likely something happened to her."

"Let's hold off on the conspiracy theories for now. Give us the facts, and let us do the investigating, OK? Your lawyer Nicky Hale has disappeared, and so has your money, is that right?"

I could see where this was heading. Nicky had gone, her passport had gone, and the money had gone. As far as McCoy was concerned she could skip straight from recording a crime to marking it "case solved" and heading to the pub to celebrate.

"Yeah. That's right."

"I might as well tell you now, you're unlikely to see that money again."

"Then what the hell are we all doing here?"

"Oh, she'll be caught eventually, don't worry. But chances are she'll have blown all the cash by then. If she hasn't already." McCoy actually found this funny, I realized—a lippy kid with more money than he knew what to do with had been taken to the cleaners by his bent brief. McCoy realized she shouldn't have let her amusement show in her voice. She cleared her throat, looked down at her paperwork and clicked her pen pointlessly.

"Right—is there a number where we can contact you, Mr. Maguire?"

\* \* \*

My first thought as I emerged from the station into the cool evening was that there was little point heading straight back to the gym. Delroy could manage without me till closing time, and anyway I didn't want him to read on my face how deep in shit I was—how deep in it we both were. Things were bad enough, but my deal with Sherwood had made everything worse. Detective Sergeant McCoy had made it very clear that as far as she was concerned, this was a case of fraud, not robbery, and the suspect had made a clean getaway, so what was the point of hurrying? She'd glanced at the institutional clock on the wall of the interview room. It was after six. In the morning she'd make a few calls to confirm what I'd told her was true, and then the police investigation would clank and grind into motion like some clapped-out British car built in the seventies. As soon as it did, anyone who'd ever been involved with Nicky would hire lawyers and clam up. I had at best a few hours to find out what had really happened to her, starting with her husband.

I'd never met the guy, though I'd seen his car in the drive of Nicky's house—a sleek, sculpted BMW with one of those metal roofs that fold away into the boot. The house itself was a double-fronted Victorian number behind wrought-iron railings, all red brick and white-painted woodwork, immaculately maintained, like the cover shot on one of those glossy property mags for the stinking rich. Beyond the house you could just about glimpse the tops of silver birch trees running the length of their enormous rear garden. When I'd mentioned to Nicky that it looked like a great house for kids to grow up in, her smile was faked and sad. I'd known instantly that she'd wanted children but couldn't have them, and I'd wondered why, and knew I couldn't ask. All I could do was mentally kick myself.

The thick cream-coloured gravel crunched beneath my trainers as I approached the massive and gleaming front door, its stained-glass panes glowing from a light deep within the house. The noisy gravel was there to deter burglars, I knew; it almost deterred me, as I realized how scruffy I looked. Even with half a million quid in the bank I'd never have fitted into this universe. Certainly not now.

The doorbell rang like a distant cathedral

bell, and I saw movement flicker through the rippled stained glass. A tall, heavyset figure resolved itself as it approached and reached for the latch of the door.

Nicky's husband Harry was roughly the same height as me, but instead of my mousy spikes his jet-black hair was neatly trimmed. His blue eyes were cool in his tanned face, and that cleft chin made him look like an old-fashioned Hollywood heartthrob. He was wearing a spotless white cotton shirt and blue jeans, and his feet were bare. He was muscular and fit, and he moved with a sort of twitchy nervous energy; he was frowning at me with irritation, as if he knew my face but couldn't place me.

"Mr. Hale?" I said.

"No one here by that name," he said. He watched me flounder but didn't elaborate.

"Sorry, I thought Nicky Hale lived here—"

"Nicky is my wife," he said. "Her name's Hale."

"Sorry—right." She'd told me all this. "Mr.—Anderson, isn't it?"

"Oh, yeah, you're her trainer. Finn, yeah? Nicky's not in."

"I know. I'm looking for her."

He thought about that for a second. Maybe he was wondering what sort of trainer doorstepped customers who hadn't turned up, while I was wondering how he knew who I was when we'd never met before.

"Like I said, she's not in. And I don't know when she'll be back." He sniffed and rubbed his nose. I shuffled on the doormat as if making to leave, hoping he wouldn't notice me placing my foot where I could slip it forward to block the door if he tried to shut it.

"When was the last time you heard from her?" I said.

"Sorry," he said. "This isn't a good time. Try her mobile." He moved back, ready to close the door. I didn't put my foot in the gap—I didn't want to get in his face just yet.

"Mr. Anderson, could I come in? It really won't take very long."

"Actually I was just about to go out," he said. This must be how double-glazing salesmen feel, I thought.

"It's just that Nicky's my lawyer, and it looks like she's run off with all my money. I was hoping to speak to you before the cops turn up."

Anderson blinked. "What do you mean, run off?"

"The cops think she's absconded," I said.

Now he seemed to be paying attention.

"Holy crap," he said eventually.

"Can I come in?"

He looked at me as if calculating which would cause him more grief—keeping me out or letting me in—before he finally stepped back and held the door open.

Anderson led me along a long hallway with a red and cream chequerboard floor and into a massive library lined with bookshelves. With its deep button-backed sofas and its mottled leather-bound books the room struck me as cheesy and old-fashioned, not the sort of decor I would have expected Nicky to like. Between the bookshelves were hung ornately framed classical paintings, all depicting ancient countryside scenes with milkmaids in suspiciously clean smocks, apart from an odd one depicting a heap of dead partridges . . . or pheasants, or possibly grouse—my local supermarket stocked more frozen burgers than fresh game, so I was no expert. The place might have been cosy in the evenings with the fire going, but right now it was as bleak and chilly and cheerless as a funeral parlour. I noticed a tall mahogany cupboard to one side with ostentatiously locked doors. Was he that paranoid about people stealing his brandy?

Anderson looked as if he would have preferred to sit back in an armchair like the lord of the manor, but right now was too rattled by my news to relax, so he paced the room, rubbing his forehead. "I'm sorry, I had no idea you were a client of Nicky's," he said. "I thought you were just her personal trainer."

"I'm not her trainer," I said. "She works out at my gym, that's all."

"Oh yeah, your gym." Something about the way he said that suggested he'd driven by once to have a look, and not been impressed. Nicky must have told him about me, and whatever she'd said had made him curious.

"Sorry, but how could you not notice your wife had gone missing?" I said.

"We had a row last night. She left the house. I thought she'd gone to stay over with— friends."

"How often did that happen?"

"Have you ever been married? Sorry, silly question. How old are you, twenty?"

"Can I ask what you two were arguing about?"

He held his hands open in a hopeless gesture. "Nothing. Everything. Are your parents still together?"

My parents hardly ever fought, I wanted to tell him—they were happy together . . . right up to the day my mum walked out. But that was none of his business.

"My parents are dead," I said.

"Sorry. Look, Finn, if you're right, and she really has run off . . . I've got to start making some calls. And you need to find yourself another lawyer." He ran a hand down his face, pinching his nose, as the implications sank in. "The police are going to turn this place inside out. They're going to think I knew what she was planning. What a bloody mess." He looked back at me. "Can I ask—how much did she take you for?"

"I don't think that's what happened," I said.

"I don't want to believe it either," said Harry. "But here we are."

"You think she's capable of something like that?"

"Honestly? Yes, I do." He hesitated, as if reluctant to bad-mouth his own wife, then seemed to decide it didn't matter any more. "She's a selfish, spoiled . . . bitch. I'm just sorry you had to find out this way. Anyway, like I said, I've got to start making calls so . . ." He walked to the door to show me out.

"Can I use your loo? Sorry," I said.

He eyed me up and sniffed, as if wondering if I was going to run off with his toilet roll. But the good manners that were probably beaten into him as a boy eventually prevailed, and he nodded towards the hallway. "Of course," he said. "There's one in the hall, under the stairs."

Crap . . . I'd been hoping there wasn't. I checked to make sure he wasn't watching, found the loo and opened the door noisily, switched on the light—the walls were hung with cartoons of hunting scenes—and shut the door again, but from the outside. Slipping off my trainers I sprinted upstairs in my socks on tiptoe, trying not to make the treads creak.

The upstairs landing was long and dimly

lit and stretched on for half a mile, with about a hundred doors leading off. I didn't know what I was looking for but reckoned whatever I found would tell me more than Anderson was going to. The door immediately ahead of me was the master bedroom, I discovered, and the bed was neatly made and scattered with plump shiny cushions. A book lay open on a bedside table—I didn't have time to decipher the title—and the wardrobes were all firmly closed. If any clothes had been strewn about in a frenzy of packing, they'd all been tidied away now.

I hurried up the landing and tried the furthest door. The air in there was slightly staler, as if the windows and the door were rarely opened. A guest room? The bed was made up like the first one, except instead of a pile of cushions a small holdall sat half sunk into the soft quilt. It was full, but not zipped up. Peeking inside I found several neatly folded blouses of the cut Nicky liked. There was a leather address label hanging off one handle. I lifted it and squinted at the name written on it . . . *Susan Horsfall.*

"Are you lost?" Anderson had come up the stairs even more silently than I had, and caught me red-handed. No point making feeble excuses, I thought.

"Sorry, is this Nicky's?"

"I really think you should leave now." Harry's air of sympathy and commiseration had evaporated, and he had planted his feet wide apart as if he thought this might get physical. He was big and fit, but that didn't worry me unduly—he didn't look like he was used to getting smacked in the face, at least not by a bloke his own size.

"If Nicky did do a runner, why would she have left this behind?"

"If I ever see her again, I'll ask her." He stood to one side, pointedly. I raised my hands in surrender and left the room. As I walked back down the landing I could hear a mobile phone ringing from below in the hall, distant and muffled, as if it was in a coat pocket. The ringing stopped as I reached the foot of the stairs, Anderson a few steps behind me. As we headed in silence towards the front door the ringing started again. It was a ringtone I'd heard before, on Nicky's phone, and it was coming from a drawer in a little side table near the front door.

"Aren't you going to answer that?" I said.

"They can leave a message," he said.

"What if it's Nicky?" I said. I didn't know why Nicky would ring her own mobile number rather than the house landline, but I could tell I'd pricked Anderson's curiosity. He pulled open the drawer, lifted out a smartphone in a distinctive silver sleeve—it *was* Nicky's smartphone—and glanced at the screen.

"It isn't," he said. He cancelled the call, threw the phone back in the drawer and slammed it shut.

"Funny she didn't take her phone," I said.

"Not really," said Anderson. "She'd hardly want to keep in touch, given the circumstances."

"Shall I leave my number in case she does?"

"I'm sure she already has it," said Anderson, tugging open the door.

"I'm terribly sorry, I can't leave just yet," I said, mimicking his public-schoolboy veneer of politeness. I could see him tense again, ready for an ungentlemanly scuffle. "I left my shoes."

Anderson looked back and saw my tatty grey trainers lying at the bottom of the stairs where I'd slipped them off. He strode over, picked them up gingerly, returned and slung them at me.

"Thank you so much," I said. I exited meekly, and when the door slammed shut I quickly pulled my trainers on and raced away into the gathering dusk without doing them up. The laces whipped at my shins, the gravel grated accusingly under my feet, and my heart was pounding. I didn't want to hang around long enough for Anderson to discover I'd lifted Nicky's phone when he went to fetch my shoes.

A few streets away I slowed down; there were still no angry shouts of pursuit or police choppers with night-sun searchlights circling. I stopped at a pub on the Thames towpath, sat down at a table and took out Nicky's phone. Thirty-two missed calls, twenty-two voice-mail messages. She'd always used a security code to lock it, but I'd seen the combination a million times, and when I tapped in the numbers the phone blazed into life. Lots of missed calls from me, Vora, and someone called . . .

Joan Bisham? Anderson had had a point . . . if Nicky had absconded, she would have had to abandon her phone—but why would she have packed a bag and then left it?

Anderson hadn't seemed deeply distraught that his wife had left him. Or even that surprised. If anything he came across as excited and a bit hyper, but maybe that had been the cocaine talking. I'd met enough coke users to recognize the twitching and the constant sniffing and the dilated pupils. I wondered how Nicky had felt about her husband's drug use and the implications for her if their house had been raided.

I couldn't sit outside this pub all night. It was going to take me hours to go through this phone, reading all the messages to see if they offered any answers about what had happened to Nicky. I hated reading at the best of times—it felt like flossing my brain with barbed wire—and until she vanished Nicky had been doing most of the hard work for me. I felt a pang of self-pity that was immediately washed away in a surge of anger. Why the hell was I feeling sorry for myself when Nicky might be in danger?

If she was in danger, and not halfway to some sun-kissed island on the Indian Ocean.

Maybe I was refusing to believe the obvious explanation—that I'd been hung out to dry yet again by a good-looking woman. But something had been bothering Nicky that morning in the gym. Something had upset her or frightened her. Something had made her so furious she had lost all control in the ring, and her phone might hold the key to that something.

Before heading home I quickly checked her email app. Most of it was densely packed text that gave me a headache looking at it, but halfway down one short subject line caught my eye. It read DEAD MEAT and the sender field was blank. Somehow I didn't think it was a message from her butcher. I touched the header and the message opened. It too was short and to the point, and it didn't take me long to figure out.

UR GONNA DIE IN AGONNY NOSY BITCH

# three

The gym was dark and locked when I returned. When I stayed out after closing time Delroy usually left me a note—only a few words: he was as good at writing as I was at reading—saying he'd see me tomorrow, or something equally obvious, but it was always reassuring. Tonight there was nothing, although he'd tidied the place up and emptied the bins and wiped down the stark little kitchen. I should have called him, I realized with a pang of guilt. I knew he felt that he'd let me down and embarrassed himself, but it was nothing compared to how I'd made things worse that morning at Sherwood's office. I wanted to tell him that, but first I had to make it right somehow, and not just dump more worries in his lap.

I stomped on up the dim stairs, cursing the bulb overhead. It was about forty years old and gave off less light than a luminous watch, but it was too high up to reach without an extra-long stepladder, and we didn't have one, and I was the only person it was a problem for anyhow. My little place, tucked under the sloping eaves of the building, was as cold and dark and empty as when I'd left it early that morning, which felt like months ago. A little more of the wallpaper had peeled off on the section above my bed; one night the whole lot would no doubt slop down onto me and give me nightmares about being a mouldy filling in a stale sandwich. For the first time I missed the ramshackle little house where I'd lived all those years with my dad, and I wondered if the tenants in there would mind if I crashed on the floor. But when I thought about it, it wasn't the house I missed. I couldn't feel nostalgic about the place where I'd found my father slumped over a table with his head beaten in. It was Dad I missed, and his lovable, idiotic conviction that somehow everything would turn out all right in the end.

I heard a wooden banging down below, and

realized someone was thumping on our bolted doors with the heel of their fist. I thought maybe another drunk had taken the place for a nightclub, and tried to ignore it, but the banging went on, faint and angry and persistent. I sighed, skipped back down both flights of stairs again, drew back the heavy bolts, swung the door open, and stared.

"Where is she?" said Nicky.

Except it wasn't Nicky. She certainly looked like her—she had the same neat athletic build, and wore her hair about the same length, pulled back from the same delicate, intelligent features. But this woman was five years younger, and her hair was fairer.

"If you mean Nicky Hale, that's what I'd like to know," I said.

"You're sisters?"

She'd marched into the flat as if she'd expected Nicky to be hiding under my bed. Now the way she was looking around the place suggested she couldn't believe a human being could live here.

"Half-sisters. My name's Susan Horsfall."

"Right," I replied vaguely. "I saw your

name . . . on a holdall at her house." I was still trying to get my head around this. Half-sisters? This woman didn't just *look* like Nicky—she walked like her, spoke like her. I'd seen twins who looked less alike. "Nicky told you about me?"

The look of amused disbelief she shot me blew away any lingering hopeful illusions.

"No," she said. "Harry told me you'd been round, when I went looking for her. Nicky was supposed to be coming to stay at my place, only she never turned up."

"Why was she coming to stay with you? Because they'd argued?"

"They never stopped arguing," Susan said. "She'd had enough. She said she was going to leave him. I never thought she really would . . . and certainly not this way. Harry says she cleaned you out."

"Just about," I said. "Look, now you're here, can I offer you something? A drink, or . . . ?"

She glanced towards the greasy stove and battered kettle on the corner unit. "I'm good, thanks," she said. When I followed her look I could see why she'd wrinkled her nose. God, this place was a dump, I realized. But she seemed to unwind a little, at least, and took a seat on my creaky old settee.

"For what it's worth, I'm really sorry. It's hard to believe she'd do something like this, but she was desperate. She'd been so unhappy the past few months . . ."

"So Harry really didn't know what she was planning?"

"Are you kidding? This is going to cause him an unbelievable amount of grief, especially at work. I suppose that was one of the upsides, for her."

"What does Harry actually do?" I said.

"He's an account manager for a private bank in the city. Makes loads; more than Nicky ever did. She always claimed she didn't care about money."

"You didn't believe her?"

"She obviously cared about yours," said Susan. I must have looked pathetic, because she smiled at me with pity. "I'm sorry, Finn," she said. "I'm sure she liked you. You're definitely her type. She's always gone for big strapping men like you and Harry."

"Did she ever tell you about these?" I picked up Nicky's phone from my rickety dining table and unlocked it. It opened where I'd left it, on the nameless poison email, and I passed it to Susan. Her eyes widened as she scanned it.

"There's another half-dozen like that," I said. "And twenty more in the Deleted folder. She was getting about three or four of them a day."

"Lawyers make enemies," said Susan.

"They're mostly the same," I said. "I think this was just one enemy."

"It certainly wasn't Harry," she said. "He'd never spell 'agonny' with two n's."

"Unless he was covering his tracks," I suggested feebly. I hadn't noticed the two n's but I didn't want her to know that.

"Harry's a shit, yeah," said Susan, "but he'd never have hurt her."

"OK," I said. "Then it was someone else. I can't believe she ran away."

"But if she was getting threats," said Susan, "wouldn't that have been one more reason to run?"

I suddenly felt deflated, confused and despairing. I'd imagined myself riding to Nicky's rescue, wherever she was, and winning her breathless admiration. I could see now I'd been fooling myself. Everything I'd done in the last few months had been part of a colossal con and I might as well have gone out and blown my inheritance on lottery scratch-cards and cider. Nicky had led me around on a string like a lovesick puppy, and thanks to her I'd made promises I couldn't keep to people who would take it out on me and my friends in blood and brain damage.

"Have you shown these messages to the police?" Susan said.

"Not yet." I held my hand out. She passed the phone back to me, and stood up to leave. "It doesn't make any difference," I said. "I have to know. I have to find her, or find out what happened to her. And I'm not leaving it to the cops, because they're useless."

"Finn . . ." She swept her blonde fringe out of her eyes in a gesture so familiar my heart twisted in my chest. "Has it occurred to you . . . Nicky might not want to be found? If you liked her, maybe you should let it go. Contact the Law Society, put in a claim, find another lawyer. There's plenty more where Nicky came from."

"What's the Law Society?"

"They run an insurance fund. All practising solicitors have to pay into it. If one of them runs off with a client's money, the fund repays it. That's probably what Nicky expected you to do. They have an office in the City some-where—Google them."

After Nicky's sister left I paced the tiny flat trying to figure out what to do next, but my mind kept sliding back to something she'd said, words that had snagged under my skin like a splinter. About how Nicky had been deeply unhappy for months. She'd felt that way all the time I knew her? Had I been just a distraction, some comic relief? I could see what Susan had meant about Nicky's type: there was a distinct resemblance between me and her husband Harry, if you disregarded the dimple in his chin and the expensive haircut and the posh accent and the private education and the BMW coupé in his drive. But maybe that's why Nicky had liked me—I was a younger, dumber, more pliable version of her husband without all the trappings of success that she resented so much.

The bed squealed and groaned as I planted

my big ass onto it, and the noise sounded a lot like the dispirited voice in my head. I was swinging between feeling sorry for Nicky and feeling sorry for myself, and neither was getting me anywhere. I would do what I always did when the thoughts running round and round in my head started to wear a rut in my brain: I pulled off my clothes, pulled on my sweats, and hit the street.

A brief summer shower had left the pavements gleaming, and my trainers splished through shallow puddles as I weaved through the drunks staggering out of the pubs after last orders. In twenty minutes I reached the park by the canal, where the trees were rustling ghosts of green and the paths were pale grey shadows; in the bushes around me rats fought over stale crusts and foxes screwed, screeching. Disregarding the darkness I ran faster and faster until I was running full tilt, my pulse thumping in my head and sweat gushing from my pores, deeper into the night.

When my bedside alarm spewed out its horrible cheesy fanfare it felt like I'd only just closed my eyes. The morning sunlight was bursting through my flimsy orange curtains, but although I hit snooze and tried to grab another few minutes of shuteye, it was no good. I lay there staring at the slope of the peeling ceiling instead. I had hoped the run and a good night's sleep would straighten out my thoughts, but they seemed to have curved back on themselves and melted together in a mess like overheated plastic. Had Nicky really been planning all along to rip me off, or was it just a spur-of-the-moment thing? I didn't want to listen to her sister, but then Susan wasn't the one who'd cleaned out my account.

Lost in a dark maze of contradictions I showered, shaved and ate breakfast in something like a trance before mopping the gym floor, wiping down the equipment and stomping downstairs to open the doors. Delroy showed up at his usual time, grunting and panting as he reached the top of the stairs, and I brought him a cup of tea without him having to ask.

"If this is your apology for disappearing last night," he said, "I accept."

"I did call the office," I said. "But no one answered the phone."

"Then why didn't you try my mobile?"

protested Delroy. "Or text me?" Dammit. My dad had been so crap with his mobile phone I'd expected Delroy to be too, but he always kept his charged up and ready, though nobody ever called him except me.

"Sorry," I said.

"So what was you up to anyway?"

"I had some business in town."

"With that Nicky?"

"No, I didn't see Nicky."

He seemed relieved. If only he knew.

Half an hour later the gym was throbbing with activity, and I was busy extracting a bent pin from the bottom of a massive pile of weights some macho twerp had dropped while showing off. I caught the acrid smell of cheap tobacco and looked round.

Sherwood's greasy gopher Elvis was swaggering down the aisle between the running machines like he owned the place, or soon would, a lit roll-up glued to the corner of his mouth. I looked over at the front desk. Daisy was staring at me, her face pale with fear. I didn't like to think what Elvis had said to her when she'd tried to stop him entering.

Elvis paused in front of a treadmill where

Pam, one of our regulars, was running. He smirked as he watched her breasts bounce, tapping ash from his roll-up onto the floor.

I walked up behind him and plucked the stub from his fingers, and when he turned I screwed it out on the lapel of his leather jacket. "No smoking," I said, and offered him the crumpled stub. He ignored it.

"Nice place you have here," he said, glancing back at Pam, whose face was now bright red, and not from exertion. "Is it insured?" Subtle he wasn't.

"Members only," I said, "and I don't think you'd pass the physical."

Delroy emerged from the changing room, and when he saw me talking to Elvis he stopped and braced himself, as if I was going to send Elvis over to him.

"Mr. Sherwood says hello." Elvis smiled at me, as if I might have forgotten who he worked for. His teeth were the same sickly shade of yellow as his fingers.

"Tell him he can send a postcard next time," I said. "I'll see him tomorrow, like we arranged."

"Today," he said. I might have blinked.

Surely Sherwood hadn't heard already about Nicky stealing my money? "Like, now," said Elvis.

"I'm busy," I said. I needed time to go to the Law Society offices and sort out my compensation claim. I didn't want to turn up in Sherwood's joint clutching an IOU. Also I didn't want him to think I would jump whenever he clicked his fingers. Then again, I didn't want it to look like I was avoiding him, either. "I'll see him at four," I said.

Elvis shrugged like he didn't give a damn, coughed, cleared his throat and spat on the floor. Then he turned on his heel and walked out. As he passed Delroy he gave a cheery nod like they were old mates, but kept walking. I went to fetch the bloodstained mop.

"Finn?" asked Delroy. "What the hell you up to now?"

"Don't worry about it," I said. Worrying wasn't going to help. Talking to Delroy might have helped, but it was too late for that.

"I've printed out the form for you," said the helpful bloke at the Solicitors' Regulation Authority. He looked younger than me, in a pinstriped suit that was too big for him, and his big head wobbled on his skinny neck like those nodding dogs you sometimes see on the back shelves of cars driven by old ladies in strange hats.

I picked up the form. I really hated forms, though this one at least wasn't as densely packed with gibberish as the ones Nicky used to wave at me. My reluctance must have been obvious from the way I held it, because the clerk piped up, "It's only six pages long. And three of those are a diversity survey. You know, race, sexual orientation—they're not strictly necessary."

"And how long will it take to get compensation?"

I was trying to avoid looking directly at his face because of its magnificent crop of pimples, but I saw him grin proudly. "We aim to deal with your case within thirty days as a rule. Unless it's complicated. But from what you've said, this doesn't sound complicated."

"Thirty days?" He didn't seem to notice the desperation in my voice.

"If you fill it in now, I'll submit it straight away. Do you need a pen?"

Ignoring his acne I stared at him. Was there any point explaining that in thirty days' time I might well be in plaster from the neck down, eating my meals through a straw?

"You can take the form home with you if you prefer."

Back at Nicky's building, a few streets away, the receptionist tried to tell me the offices of Hale and Vora were closed, but I wasn't having any of it. From where I stood I could see Vora in a cubicle at the back, photocopying a heap of papers, and I insisted on talking to him. Perhaps the receptionist was too mad to care, because Nicky had done a bunk without paying her bills, but she let me through.

Maybe Nicky didn't want me to find her, and maybe she did think I'd get my money back. Or maybe somebody had got to her. Either way I had to know, and that meant following every lead I could find.

Vora stared at me with trepidation when I entered. He seemed less panic-stricken than the last time I'd seen him, and had recovered some of his style, but his skin was grey with stress and he looked tired and old. I felt sorry for him, till I remembered that he had got out of the firm when it was still solvent. Probably with a generous pension.

"I've just been to the Law Society and the SRA," I said.

He nodded in resignation. "You should get compensation, Finn," he said. "It's an open-and-shut case."

"You think so?"

"I—don't know what you mean."

"Do you really believe Nicky would do a runner?"

"Last week, I would never have believed it, no."

"Did you know she was getting death threats? Via email?"

"Yes, I knew. She used to be on Twitter, and Facebook, but the abuse got so bad she gave them up. It happens, especially to women."

"Why didn't she report it?"

"She did, for all the difference it made."

"And she never found out who was behind it?"

"Some creep. You can't respond to these idiots—she never took it seriously."

"Maybe she should have."

Vora thought about what that meant and frowned.

"What cases was she working on?" I asked.

"She mostly dealt in corporate affairs, nothing high-profile or controversial. But she did have a few personal clients, like you . . ."

"Any chance you could put me in touch with these other clients?"

"That would be unethical. Unprofessional— I could get struck off."

"So what? I thought you'd retired." Vora rubbed his forehead, looking older by the minute. "Look," I said, "I'm not convinced Nicky ran off with my money, and I don't think you are either. If she didn't, something must have happened to her, possibly connected to a case she was working on. I just need to get into her office, take a look at her correspondence . . ." Though at my reading speed, looking at it would be all I could do, I thought.

Vora chewed his lip, torn between doing the legal thing and doing the right thing. "You don't need to get into her office," he said at last. He glanced through the glass walls towards the reception area, but no one was watching. "I've been copying her case files, so I could pass her clients over to another firm. The police will expect to see the originals, but these . . ." He gathered up the copies he had stacked on the table and dropped them into the two box files. "I'll just copy them again," he said. "But don't mention my name. I don't know how you got hold of these, OK?"

There were a few empty cartons lying about that had originally held photocopy paper. Vora clipped the box files shut and handed them to me, and I wedged them into the cardboard box.

"Good luck," he said.

"I'll find her," I said. "Or I'll find out what happened to her."

"If something did happen . . ." Vora hesitated. "Watch out it doesn't happen to you too."

They were only legal papers, but the weight of the files nearly pulled my arms out of their sockets before I made it as far as the Tube and finally got to rest the box on my lap. The carriage rumbled and rocked and swayed westwards, the other passengers playing on their smartphones or staring into space, while I peeked into the box.

At school I'd eventually been diagnosed as dyslexic, but by the time they'd organized remedial classes I'd been expelled for fighting . . . and dealing drugs, and criminal damage. There were adult remedial classes I could take now, but I'd never got around to it because I couldn't be bothered and I was too embarrassed. Now I wished I'd swallowed my pride; it was going to take me months to read all these. I didn't have Sherwood's money, and I would barely have time to dump this lot at the gym before my appointment at his plush brothel of an office over the pool hall. I counted my options: I could tell Sherwood I needed more time, I could tell him to go ride a donkey, or I could follow Nicky's example and disappear . . . any or all of which would leave Delroy and Winnie in the firing line.

I didn't have any options at all.

Sean the Wardrobe smirked when he saw me standing on the doorstep outside Sherwood's offices, like he knew something I didn't. I studied the bruise on his face. "It hardly shows now," I said. "Did you dab a bit of Estée Lauder on it?" The smirk wilted into a sulky glower and he stood back to let me go first up the stairs. At Sherwood's office he reached past me to open the door, without knocking this time, and I wondered why until I realized Sherwood was not behind his big desk. Elvis was there, though, perched on the same unit in the corner, like a pet lizard. He said nothing, just watched me, and I guessed this was another of Sherwood's games.

My mum had taken me to the dentist once, when I was about eight, to get a tooth extracted. I knew it was going to be painful and I wanted to get it over with, but this particular jerk of a dentist seemed to go out of his way to prolong the anticipation to screaming point. I had sat waiting in the padded chair for what seemed like a day and a half, staring at a rack full of gas cylinders and some dubious-looking chemical flask with a long clear tube leading to a mask, while Mum tried to distract me with daft questions about my favourite video games. I was reminded of that experience now.

Already I was getting less respect than on my last visit. Sherwood knew something was up.

"Flynn, hey," said Sherwood as he appeared from a door in a recess beyond his desk, shrugging on his jacket. He was wearing a different suit, as sharply cut as the first. In his line of work I didn't imagine he took a lot of board meetings or did many media interviews, so presumably the designer labels were all about image, and pretending to be a legitimate businessman when he was anything but. "Dean, get me a coffee, would you?" Elvis sniffed and left the room. So his name was Dean? Maybe he modelled himself on that old movie star James Dean—though they had nothing in common beyond the pout and the quiff and the mumble.

Sherwood had got my name wrong and pointedly not offered me a drink—silly slights intended to needle me. When I was eight I had tried to snatch the forceps from the dentist and do it myself, and now I felt the same impulse.

"I don't have the money, Mr. Sherwood. And I won't be able to get hold of it by tomorrow."

"Ah," said Sherwood. He sounded disappointed that I'd cut short the foreplay.

"My lawyer's disappeared, and she had access to my accounts."

"That's one I hadn't heard before," said Sherwood. "But how exactly is it my problem?"

I took my wallet out of my pocket, tugged my credit card from its pocket and offered it to Sherwood. He looked at it as if his new kitten had brought him half a rotten rat from the garden.

"There's nearly nine thousand pounds in that account," I said.

"*Nearly* nine thousand?"

"Eight and a half," I admitted. Nicky had set it up for me so I would always have access to some cash, and I'd rarely taken out more than forty quid a week—I hated having more than that in my wallet. I did wonder why Nicky hadn't cleaned out that account too, but then she had been in a hurry. "The PIN is six-seven-four-three."

"And you expect me to go to some machine outside a supermarket and stand in line to collect the money you owe me. Is that it?"

"I'd give you all of it now, but my lawyer has to countersign the cheques."

"And what's to stop you phoning your bank and getting that card stopped?"

"I'm not going to do that. I'm not stupid," I said.

"Really? Because that's not the impression I'm getting." Elvis—Dean, rather—giggled. He had reentered silently behind me, and now he placed a china cup of coffee of Sherwood's desk, slopping some into the saucer. He wasn't good waiter material. I stuffed the card back in my wallet. So much for that idea.

"You came to my office, Flynn," said Sherwood. "You made me a business proposition, which I accepted, and now—just one day later—you're offering me a fraction of what I'm entitled to?"

"It's the best I can do."

"I don't think so. Try harder."

I was about to tell him about the compensation fund and how I could pay him back in a few weeks, when I realized it would be futile to make excuses and start bleating for terms, and when you were weak it was never good to let it show.

"Why don't you tell me what you want?" I said.

"I want the money you owe me."

"Then you'll have to wait."

"Maybe I'm getting old and crabby," said Sherwood, "but I don't like lippy bloody teenagers telling me what I have to do." He was genuinely angry, I realized, and on one level I felt glad to have finally got under his skin. "You must take me for a right moron, coming in here and boasting about your pal the Guvnor and how he was looking out for you."

"I never mentioned McGovern," I said. "You did."

That might have been true, but Sherwood didn't like me pointing it out.

"Who gives a crap?" he shouted. He expected me to flinch, but I'd been shouted at before, by guys a lot scarier than Sherwood. He realized losing his cool wasn't having the desired effect, and he pulled himself together, and smirked instead. "Your pal McGovern's over," he said. "He's history. His bent cops got caught, and the Feds were so far up his ass they could read his mind."

He had his facts wrong. The Guvnor's bent

cop had turned on him and got shot. I knew, because I'd been there, but this wasn't the time to be picky.

"McGovern's run off to Siberia or somewhere and he's not coming back," sneered Sherwood. "It's a whole new set of faces now. Ever heard of the Turk?"

"The who?" I said.

"Didn't think so," said Sherwood. He smiled because he knew something I didn't, and sat back in his kid-leather executive chair. "OK, you want to negotiate new terms for your loan." I noticed he wasn't talking about Delroy's loan any more, and I had a feeling any negotiations were going to be a bit one-sided. "Dean tells me you're running a gym. Does it make any money?"

"We get by," I said.

"You lease the place or own it?"

I knew what Sherwood wanted to hear. "I own it," I lied. Maybe he had heard that Nicky had disappeared, but he didn't know she'd disappeared before I'd managed to buy the freehold of the building, or he wouldn't have asked.

"Who's got the title deeds?"

"I have," I lied some more.

"Well then, let's say three grand a month, for two years, using this business of yours as collateral," he said. "Bring the title deeds round here Monday and we'll draw up the papers."

"I don't have a lawyer any more," I said.

"Not a problem." He smiled. "Mine will look after the paperwork. All part of the service."

I'd never afford those payments, I knew, but that's how Sherwood wanted it. He had no interest in owning a gym—he wasn't the sort of guy who'd get up at five to mop a floor, and I doubted he would ask Dean to do it. He was planning to shut it down, gut the building, flog it for flats and walk away with the profit. Except that was never going to happen, because I didn't own the building. But he didn't need to know that yet.

Lying had given give me time to think of something. Right now it was important to look reluctant.

"I own the business with Delroy. I need to discuss it with him."

"What's to discuss? Tell him. He got you into this."

"It's not just my business—that's my home,"
I protested. "If you take it over, where do I
live?"

"Make your payments and it won't be an
issue," said Sherwood. "And if you come up
short, drag yourself to Russia and borrow it
from McGovern." He flicked his head at Dean,
who heaved himself upright and slouched
over to open the door.

"Did you ever meet Nicky Hale?" I said.

Sherwood blinked, as if annoyed at me for
changing the subject. "Never heard of him,"
he said.

The doors to Sherwood's office slammed shut
behind me, and I tugged my collar up against
the rain. It had been a shot in the dark anyway.
Sherwood was going to benefit from Nicky's
disappearance, sure, but he was small-time,
a punk and a bully—I couldn't believe he'd
have had a solicitor abducted just to get his
hands on my tatty little gym.

So who was this new guy, the Turk? Sherwood hadn't just heard of him, he'd talked to
him, judging by the smug way he dropped
his nickname. It seemed to me that boasting

about the big sharks you knew wasn't a sensible thing for small fish like Sherwood to do. But that was his business, I decided, and it was high time I minded mine.

I had to come clean to Delroy. When things got sticky in the boxing ring I had always liked having Delroy in my corner, wiping me down, taping my cuts shut and telling me where I was going wrong. If he couldn't offer advice he'd slag me off, wind me up and make me angry, and that used to work too. I just hoped that this time he wouldn't get dragged into the ring with me.

# four

"What are you going to do?" asked Delroy, as we wiped down the gym's sparring kit in a quiet interval before the evening rush.

"I think as long as we keep making the payments," I said, "I should be able to string him along."

"How? We don't turn over anything like that much."

"I'll cover it for now," I said. The money Nicky hadn't taken might keep Sherwood satisfied for a month or two. I could see Delroy wanted to protest, but he just nodded. He was out of his depth, I realized, and weak and ill and weary, and again I felt ashamed that I had ever got him involved in this business.

Delroy hung the last helmet up on a hook to dry off. "Oh yeah," he remembered. "You have a visitor." I looked around. "She's up-stairs." I would normally have expected him to announce news like that with a dirty grin, but he just looked grim, and abruptly I knew who it was.

Susan Horsfall was sitting on my ripped vinyl sofa, reading. She had draped my discarded shirts over the back and, I noted with some embarrassment, picked up my discarded underwear from the floor and put it in the bin liner I was using for dirty laundry.

"Make yourself at home," I said.

She jumped, and looked up and laughed, a little nervously. "Finn. Hey. Sorry—your friend Delroy sent me up, and I thought you'd be here, or at least be back soon. And there wasn't much in the way of reading material except these . . ." She held up one of the case files I had carried away from Nicky's office. I decided this wasn't the moment to explain why my place wasn't strewn with novels and magazines. "How did you get hold of them?" she asked.

"They're the files on Nicky's other clients," I said, ducking the question for Vora's sake.

"You really think she hasn't absconded? That something happened to her?"

"Presumably you do too," I said, "or you wouldn't have come here."

She wasn't as cocky as the last time we'd met; she looked worried, and slightly ashamed. "I couldn't sleep last night," she said. "I kept thinking, what if you were right? It's easier to believe she did do a runner, that she's safe somewhere spending someone else's money, than . . ."

"Whatever the alternative is," I said.

"Nicky and I didn't always get on," said Susan. "I mean, there was a lot of crap in our childhood, and some of it was my fault. But the thought of her being taken, maybe being held prisoner, and nobody even knowing . . . it's horrible. I wouldn't wish that on anyone . . . even my cow of a sister." I could see she was trying to lighten the darkness with a feeble gag, and it wasn't working. I heard a catch in her throat, and the papers trembled in her hands.

"If you want to do something about it, you could help me," I said.

"How?"

"You could tell me what's in those files. I'm not the fastest reader in the world."

"You think one of her clients might have had something to do with her disappearing?"

"I've no idea," I said. "I'm just shaking all the trees to see what falls out."

She turned back to the two box files. "There are only two personal clients here, as far as I can see," she said. "Joan Bisham, and Jeremy Zeto."

"Who's Joan Bisham?"

"Property developer being charged with insurance fraud. A building her company bought—some old pub—mysteriously burned down, with two squatters inside. One of them died in the fire. This guy Leslie survived." She passed me a photocopy of an article from what looked like a local free newspaper. The main picture was of a man in his thirties with half of his face swathed in bandages.

"Fraud? Why isn't she being done for attempted murder?"

"Her husband got done for the fire. The insurers think she was in on it. The case comes to trial in a week or so."

"What about the other file?"

"Zeto? There's not much to that one. He's a vicar being done for drink-driving."

"All that paperwork for one drunk driver?"

"Nicky really went to town on the defence, by the look of it. Witness statements . . . psychiatric report . . ."

"Let me have a look." I held out my hand and she passed the report to me. It was unreadable jargon, as I expected, but at least there wasn't much of it—it was only two pages long. Maybe Zeto was paying for his own defence, and that was all he could afford. I dug through the rest of the papers in the box file. About a dozen witness statements, so dense and closely typed my eyes ached just glancing at them. What had Nicky been trying to do—drown the prosecution case under loads of bumpf?

Under that bundle was a single printout of a photo that seemed to have been blown up from a website mugshot, of a heavily built bloke in a cheap suit with jowls that bulged over his collar. A copper, I knew almost immediately, probably from the way his narrowed suspicious eyes seemed ready to follow me around the room. He wore a shallow grin that suggested that while the picture was being taken the Met's PR department was holding a gun to his kidneys.

"Who's the filth?" I said.

"Officer in charge of the case, I think."

I flipped the photo over. On the reverse was Nicky's handwriting: *DS Ian* something.

"Can you read Nicky's handwriting?" I asked, as casually as I could.

Susan glanced at it. "DS Ian Lovegrove," she read out. "North Met Traffic division. There's a phone number too, but no email . . . What do you suppose this is?" She held up a black square of plastic—a memory card. It must have been lying loose in the box file when Vora stuffed the copies into it.

"Let's stick it in the PC and have a look," I said.

My old Dell laptop wheezed and clanked into action, and after an age of waiting presented us with a desktop. I clicked on the icon for the SD slot, and we waited another hour or two for the window to open. I wished I'd bought a machine that wasn't powered by elastic bands while I'd still been able to afford it.

The memory card held only one file, a digital

video. I double-clicked on it, aware of Susan hovering at my shoulder. She used the same scented soap as Nicky, I noticed, and deep down I felt a stab of desire.

The video was grainy black and white. The camera was mounted behind a windscreen, recording a journey along an anonymous stretch of night-time motorway. White numbers flickered in the corner—the time and date, I supposed. The viewpoint seemed quite high, which suggested the vehicle was either a coach or a truck, travelling in the middle lane, overtaking vans and caravans on one side and being overtaken on the other by speeding saloons and big four-by-fours. These days a lot of trucks had cameras in the cab, I knew, to act like black-box flight recorders, providing footage that could be used in the case of an accident. The figure in the corner of the picture flickered between 64 and 65—presumably the speed of the truck the camera was mounted in. I kept my eye on the overtaking lane to the right, waiting to see this demon vicar come tearing past, when in the middle of the screen a shifting constellation of brake lights dead ahead burst into life, flashing, weaving, and swerving from side to side.

Zeto's tinny little hatchback wasn't overtaking the truck—it was coming straight towards it at top speed down the wrong side of the motorway, in the middle lane. I'd heard God moved in mysterious ways, but how he'd managed to keep Zeto from killing himself and twenty other drivers was sure as hell a mystery to me. The truck with the camera mounted in its cab jammed on its brakes while cars ahead of it lurched and rear-ended and side-swiped each other to get out of Zeto's way. Finally one white box-van with nowhere to go slammed into Zeto's car, not quite head-on, piling it into the central barrier and leaving it perched there with one wheel hanging off, while the box-van rocked and wobbled to a halt behind a crowd of dented, crumpled vehicles. The camera truck too had slewed to a halt, and the video showed dazed drivers climbing groggily out their cars before the image froze, crumpled and cut to white noise.

"Jesus," I said. "This could make us a fortune on YouTube."

"Finn, this is evidence in a court case," said Susan. "We shouldn't even be watching it."

"Relax," I said. "I'll send it back. Once I've copied it." I clicked on the file and dragged it to my desktop. The laptop grunted and wheezed as it started copying the file. It would only take it most of the night, I reckoned. "How much communion wine do you have to neck to pull a stunt like that?" I asked Susan. She was flicking through another printed report.

"About a crateful, I'd imagine," she said. "But this says his blood-test results are awaiting confirmation." She stood up and promptly banged her head on the low ceiling.

"Mind the low ceiling," I said.

"How the hell do you put up with it?" She rubbed her scalp. "You must be what, six foot three?"

"I generally move about on my hands and knees," I said.

Susan chucked the folder back into its crate. "I can't see how this stupid vicar can have anything to do with Nicky disappearing."

"Neither can I, right now," I said, "but I'd like to find him and ask him."

"And what about Nicky's phone?"

"What about it?"

"Do you still have it?"

"Why?" I said.

"Shouldn't we show it to the police?"

"When I've finished with it," I said.

"But don't they need to know about these threatening messages?"

"They already do," I said.

And that was true, because according to Vora, Nicky had told them. Knowing the cops, of course, they'd never make that connection now. They'd have stuffed Nicky's original complaint down the back of a filing cabinet and forgotten about it. If I wanted to know the truth, that meant finding it out for myself— not passing the buck to a bunch of uniformed jobsworths whose most urgent priority was a cup of tea and a biscuit.

"You liked Nicky, didn't you?" asked Susan.

"She was a friend," I said. "Is."

"I got the impression she was more than that."

I didn't want to lie, but I didn't know what the truth was, so I said nothing.

"Because you're taking a hell of a risk for her. Interfering with evidence. We could be charged with perverting the course of justice, even."

"Maybe, if the cops ever find out." I looked at her. She laughed. She resembled Nicky so much I felt as if I'd known her for months, instead of days; and for a moment I wondered if she was doing it on purpose.

"I'm not going to tell them," she said. "You need me to help, I'll help."

"Could you dig out an address for this arsonist property developer?"

Joan Bisham's place was in a quiet, prosperous suburb a twenty-minute bus ride away. I had thought a property developer would live in something flash and sleek, maybe designed by an architect, but I was wrong. Hers was a huge rambling, crumbling red-brick house that had been divided into a dozen dingy flats not long ago—one stretch of wall still bore a crudely painted 14A and a wobbly arrow pointing to the basement. There were two front doors to choose from, but I went for the one that looked the cleanest, and heard a bell ring somewhere in the distance. A few minutes later the door was jerked open by a smartly dressed woman in her forties with big brown eyes and shoulder-length chestnut hair that didn't quite conceal intricate earrings of blue stones on gold wire. We hesitated a moment, surprised to recognize each other, and I realized where I'd seen her before—on one of my visits to Nicky's office she'd been leaving as I arrived.

I could tell Joan Bisham couldn't place me, and not knowing seemed to make her anxious and irritable. Or maybe she was like that anyway; last time I'd seen her face it had worn an expression of bitterness and disappointment. It did again now, and I realized bitterness was becoming permanently etched on her features, which was a shame because she was still quite a looker.

"Hello again," I said, with what I hoped was a charming smile.

She eyed me with distrust, wondering if I was going to produce a religious magazine and start hectoring her about the Apocalypse.

"Do I know you?" Her voice was hard flinty South London.

"Finn Maguire. We met at Nicky Hale's office. I'm a client of hers. Trying to track her down."

"She's not hiding out here, if that's what you're thinking."

"I'm trying to get in touch with all her former clients."

I could see that she took me for an idiot, and would have shut the door except she was enjoying mocking me.

"What, you trying to start some sort of protest group or something, to demand compensation?"

"Not exactly."

"What, then?"

"It's a long story."

"Don't have time for long stories, sorry." She stood back to close the door without even the perfunctory smile the middle class give to doorsteppers they wish would drop dead.

"I thought it might have something to do with that squatter," I said.

She held the door back an inch at the last second, looking alarmed and angry.

"The one who died in that fire at your development," I went on, though I guessed she'd known what I'd meant. "Or maybe the one who had his face burned off. I thought maybe someone was out for revenge."

Maybe she thought I was talking bull, but I could see her wondering if it was a good idea to turn me away without finding out what I knew.

"What do you mean, revenge?"

"Like I said, it's a long story."

Bisham led me through a dim warren of hardboard partitions and peeling paint to a kitchen decorated with patches of damp and equipped with units so warped they no longer fitted. In her sharp slim business-like trouser suit she looked out of place, and I wondered how she kept up appearances while living in a house no self-respecting crack dealer would cook up his shit in.

"Nice house. Lots of character," I said, trying not to sound sarcastic, and failing.

"It's a dump," said Bisham. "But once it's been refurbished I should get more than I paid for it." She lit a cigarette and leaned against the counter with her arms crossed over her bony chest. I was glad she didn't offer me a drink, because I could see pellets of mouse shit on the corners of the worktop and I guessed there was plenty more in the cupboards, and on the crockery, and in the kettle too by the looks of things. Maybe my place wasn't so bad after all.

"Yes, I'm sure it has a lot of potential." I was trying to be polite but I thought I sounded like an estate agent, and Bisham seemed to think so too, and to hate estate agents as much as I did. "What were you saying about this dead squatter?" she demanded.

I didn't actually know where I was going with that so I didn't answer it, although I could tell her patience was wearing thin. I nodded instead at a small camera perched on top of a cupboard, a single blue light glowing beside its lens. "I see you have a CCTV camera," I said. "Is that in case of burglars?"

"You see anything worth burgling?" She took a deep drag of her cigarette.

"The camera?" I joked feebly.

Bisham tapped her ash into the sink, stared coldly at me, and finally deigned to answer. "It's my son's. He put it up there so he can see when I'm in, and when his dinner's ready. His room's right at the top—saves me climbing five flights of stairs."

She had a son? "How old is he?" I was hoping small talk might warm Bisham up a bit—I always thought parents loved boasting about their children, or complaining about them, or both at the same time. But this one didn't seem to.

"I'm still waiting to hear this long story," she said.

"Did you know Nicky Hale was getting threatening messages?" I said. "Via email and Twitter?"

Bisham's dangly golden earrings jangled faintly when she shrugged. "She never said nothing to me. Was it something to do with my case?"

"Hard to tell. They were mostly just threats." Luridly descriptive and obscene threats, but I wasn't going to go into detail. I had managed to read about fifty messages on Nicky's phone, and by the time I'd given up I'd felt ready to puke, and not from the effort of squinting at the screen. In youth custody I had met a few inadequate sickos who hated women, but not many with the sheer stamina and command of obscenity this guy had—I was pretty sure it was a guy, judging by his obsession with female anatomy. But he was always careful to omit any details that might identify him, or suggest exactly why he was picking on Nicky.

Bisham just snorted. "Now she knows how it feels."

"What?"

"I've been getting them for years. Threats. Obscenities."

"How many years?"

"Two or three. Changed my phone number, changed my email address, changed my on-line name, but whoever it is always finds me again in a few weeks. I thought it was pathetic and kind of funny at first, like those sad old flashers in the park. Now . . ." She sucked her breath in through her teeth, and I thought I saw her shudder. "It just . . . it gets to you, you know? Wears you down."

"Have you reported them?"

She snorted smoke and rolled her eyes at my naivety.

"But Nicky knew about it?"

"Yeah. She tried to track the senders down, got nowhere. Told me I should keep a note of every one I got so we could use them in evidence. Keep a note! I didn't need to keep notes, I couldn't get rid of the bloody things."

"And she never mentioned that she was getting them too?"

"No, and I'm not surprised. They make you feel like a victim, angry and scared and— helpless. Nicky wouldn't have liked that. And maybe she thought I'd blame myself for getting her involved."

"You trusted her?" I said. Suddenly I needed to know that I hadn't been a mug to put my faith in Nicky. I wanted someone to back me up, even if it was an embittered woman I barely knew living in a derelict toilet.

Bisham seemed surprised by the question. "Nicky? Yeah. I trusted her."

"And you have no idea who was sending the threatening emails?"

"Oh yeah." She laughed bitterly. "I know damn well who's sending them. He's in Dalston, doing six to ten for arson."

"Who?"

"My ex-husband. Used to be my business partner, when we had a business. It's his way of keeping in touch." She screwed her cigarette out in the sink. "And those stupid insurers still claim we're working together."

"How the hell is he sending threatening emails from prison?"

"Christ, it's easier from the inside than it is out here. They can get anything, that lot. Drugs, women, guns. And get anything done for them."

What could Nicky have done to infuriate Bisham's husband? I thought. Would he really have nobbled her just to get at his wife?

Bisham seemed annoyed that I was staring into space. "So what's all this about a squatter looking for revenge?" she said.

I wondered what she was talking about, until I realized that was the story I'd given her on the doorstep.

"Er—it's just a theory," I said. "I thought maybe a mate of the guy who got killed in that fire wanted to get back at you, and went for Nicky instead."

"You've spoken to him?" asked Bisham.

"Not yet," I said. I must have looked as sheepish as I felt.

Bisham tossed her soggy cigarette stub towards the bin and missed. "So everything you told me earlier was bull, is that it?" she said.

I tried to placate her. "I'm just trying to find out what happened to Nicky." It didn't seem to be working.

"How the hell did you get hold of my address?"

I realized too late I should have thought of an answer for that question before I arrived. I could hardly tell her I'd stolen Nicky's files and Nicky's phone. "Nicky sent me a letter that was meant to go to you," I improvised. "I never got round to sending it back. That's how I got your address."

"That's all lies," she snapped. She straightened up and jabbed her forefinger towards my face, its long fake nail like a razor blade painted crimson. "What are you after?" She must have been two-thirds my height but she was tensed like a rattlesnake and the anger was coming off her in waves. "And who are you anyway?"

"I told you, the name's Maguire. I can leave you my details if it helps."

"You can shove your details, and get out of my house."

"No problem," I said, raising my hands and

circling round her to get to the door. There was a potato peeler on the counter near her right hand and I half expected her to grab it and lunge at me. I made it to the hall, and as I headed for the door with her on my heels I saw a round, pale face behind greasy spectacles peering down the stairs.

"Mum?"

He was a podgy kid of fourteen or so, pale as an albino, with bulging blue eyes under a shapeless black hoodie that was too big for him and oversized headphones draped around his chubby neck.

"Everything all right?" he quavered. It was hard to tell if his voice had broken yet. He seemed frightened to come down the stairs,

"Everything's fine, Gabe. I've got this."

I admired the kid coming to his mum's aid, but if things had got rough I doubt he would have been much use, apart from sprinkling dandruff on me. I grabbed the latch and let myself out. "Thanks for everything," I said, and heard Bisham's final curse cut off as the door banged shut behind me.

I tried to make sense of what I'd learned, but soon ended up more confused than I'd been when I arrived. I wasn't a shrink, but I didn't need to be to know that Joan Bisham was a borderline nutter with a fearsome temper on a hair trigger. I didn't envy Nicky having had to deal with her. But Nicky was a good lawyer, one who never gave up—why would Joan Bisham have wanted her to vanish only a week or two before the case came to trial? That could result in the trial being delayed for weeks, months even. Is that what Bisham had wanted?

This was all guesswork, I realized with irritation. I didn't know how much to believe of what Bisham had told me, or whether she really had been another victim of those toxic emails. Then again, if anything would drive you to the brink of insanity, it would be a relentless stream of obscene and threatening messages for months and years on end. I knew from hard experience there were at least two sides to every failed marriage; I might never get to know the whole truth, but maybe I could get another angle on what had happened . . . if I spoke to Bisham's husband James.

The bus slowed as it approached my stop, just across the road from the gym, but the doors didn't open. I heard the bus driver leaning on the horn, and looked forward through the bus windscreen. Someone had parked a big Mercedes saloon right at the bus stop, and three stocky men were climbing out of it, wearing ski masks. Not a good sign—this wasn't the season for skiing in West London. Two of the men carried lump hammers, and the third, the one with the crowbar, flicked the bus driver the V sign as he and his pals sauntered across the road—towards my gym. I could guess what they were planning to do, and I reached for the button that rang the driver's bell and stabbed it again and again.

"I can't open the doors until we're at the stop!" the driver called back.

I cursed and scanned the panel above the door, spotted the emergency lever and wrenched it down. The doors sighed open, painfully slowly, and ignoring the driver's shouted health and safety lecture I rammed my body into the gap, squeezed through and burst out, nearly falling onto the tarmac before regaining my balance and belting round to the back of the bus. I had to leap back almost immediately as a skip truck thundered past, followed by an endless stream of speeding traffic. There was nothing I could do but stand and wait and watch, as on the other side of the road two of the winter-sports fans walked around the gym's car park smashing head-lights and windows on my customers' cars, while the third, a hulk wearing leather gloves, tipped brake fluid over roofs and bonnets, gig-gling as it trickled down, bubbling and scorch-ing the paintwork and gathering in puddles of chemical goo on the concrete.

By the time I got across the road at least two car alarms were blaring, echoing off the front of the gym and the grafittied walls of the car park in an ear-splitting cacophony. The guy with the brake fluid had just unscrewed the lid of a second bottle when I caught up with him, grabbed his arm and wrenched it back so that the blue liquid splashed across the front of his jacket and spattered his masked face. He shrieked and cursed and I pulled the mask off his head, and of course it was Sean the Wardrobe—I'd recognized him from his walk and those stupid leather gloves he always wore. Still holding his arm, I used that mo-ment of hesitation to tip him off balance and send him staggering across to crack his shins on the low brick wall that surrounded the car park.

I turned to see Dean's other helper running straight at me, leaving me no time to dodge. The impact knocked the wind out of me and we both staggered backwards, colliding with big Sean, who was still cursing and limping. I felt Sean's hamlike hands grabbing at my jacket, trying to hold me steady so his pal could take a swing, but the other guy decided to nut me instead. He pulled his masked head back like he was cocking the hammer of a gun, and I froze, until the very last instant. Then I drove my foot down on Sean's instep, hard, and twisted my body to the left. I felt the other guy's wool-clad skull brush my ear and even smelled his cheap aftershave as his forehead missed my face and collided with Sean's cheek. That close up I could hear the bones crunch in Sean's face. Sean's pal recoiled groggily, offering me the chance to sink the toe of my trainer into his nuts. While he doubled up in agony I tried to wrench myself free of Sean's grip, but even blinded with rage and pain he still managed to grab a handful of my hair in his left hand and nearly rip it out of my scalp. I grabbed his bunched fist, ducked and twisted round until I had him in another armlock, and this time I was really going to break his arm, and dislocate it too, if I had the chance. But his mate with the crushed nuts had recovered quicker than I expected and now he came after me.

I used Sean as a barricade to keep him off by wrenching on his arm some more, and most of his mate's flailing punches hit Sean, who was squealing curses at both of us. I was kind of enjoying myself at this stage, which is never a good sign, and was trying to think of some smartass remark to get them even angrier when a shattering pain on the crown of my head made my eyes water and my knees weaken.

I was forced to let go of Sean so I could turn to face Dean, who had come up behind me. He'd pulled off his own mask to reveal a grin like a terrier that had cornered a rabbit. He had clubbed me with the blunt end of the crowbar and now he coolly flipped it in his hand so the sharp end was pointing at me. He feinted with it while I dodged and backed off, hoping my vision would clear before he came at me, and hoping too that I could make the three of them get in each other's way. But with the wall of the gym behind me I had little room to retreat or manoeuvre.

The bonnet of the Ford to my right was long and low and I was just about to jump up on it and run over the roof when Sean came rolling over it towards me like a walrus on a water-slide, pushing the car down on its springs and leaving an enormous dent in the bodywork. From the corner of my eye I saw Dean lunge with the crowbar, and I stepped forward, gritting my teeth as his knuckles cracked on the top of my head, taking most of the force. I threw a right but the crowbar's point still came down hard, biting into my right shoulder, and it skewed the punch so it barely connected with Dean's face. By that time Sean was on top of me, blood running down his mouth and chin, and his massive paw clutched at my throat.

I was still running the odds in my head and wondering what had happened to the friend they had brought along, and when he was going to join in the fun, when I felt Sean's attention wander for an instant. In that instant I grabbed the hand that was gripping my windpipe, found the little finger and wrenched it back until I felt it pop out of its socket. My fists followed the now-familiar sound of Sean's squeals to his face, where I landed a good right to top up the bruise I had given him the other day. His legs folded and he went down weeping. I was bracing myself for Dean to come back with that bloody crowbar again when I saw what had distracted Sean.

Delroy had come out of the gym. He had propped his back up against a car, and was standing solid as Dean and Sean's pal hammered at him with his fists, trying in vain to penetrate his guard. As I watched I thought Delroy had been too long out of the ring, because his arms were too high, and sure enough the heavy noticed that and swung a punch in low. That was when Delroy unleashed a right that nearly took the heavy's head off his shoulders, sending him reeling. He was about to topple when I finished the job, barrelling into him, bringing us both down in a heap with me on top, ready to finish Delroy's good work. But something was obscuring my vision—blood was running into my eyes, and now I was being grabbed and hauled roughly to my feet. By Dean? Or Delroy?

When I was thrown face down across the bonnet of the Ford—narrowly avoiding a long livid trail of brake fluid mixed with auto paint—and felt the familiar bite of handcuffs on my wrists, I realized this was neither Dean nor Delroy. Mashed in with the shriek of the car alarms were sirens and the squawking crackle of police radios. The poky car park was a heaving mass of uniformed coppers. Two of them dragged me upright and frogmarched me towards a police van waiting with rear doors wide open. I saw Sean and his mate being manhandled into another, Sean yelling in agony every time his hand was jogged. Of Dean I could see no sign. Delroy, I noticed, was being closely questioned by a female cop, and presumably telling her that I had been trying to protect my business from being vandalized, but then the door slammed shut and my skull started to throb and I realized that every time I turned my head I was spattering blood around the place like an avant-garde art project.

*   *   *

I'd been a guest in several West London cop shops since I turned twelve, but this one I hadn't seen before. Thanks to budget cuts my local nick had been mothballed a few months earlier and the coppers that hadn't been laid off were relocated to this place—a tatty 1970s office block painted in loony-bin beige with dodgy neon lights that pinged faintly as they flickered off and on again. The cut the crowbar had left in my scalp was patched up by a pale, tired, monosyllabic medic who had never heard of any of the officers I had got to know a few months ago, after my dad's death. One of them, Detective Sergeant Amobi, I had almost got to tolerate. For a copper he seemed relatively intelligent and open-minded, which was probably why he wasn't around any more.

But by the time I was brought from the holding cells to an interview room the atmosphere seemed to have lightened a bit. I was no longer being shoved around like a thug hauled in for fighting in the street. I presumed Delroy and witnesses from the gym would soon set the record straight and I could go home. But one pallid cup of tea went cold, and a PC brought me another, and told me someone would take my statement "soon." But that cup of tea went cold too, because the police's concept of "soon" isn't the same as yours or mine. We're not being paid by the hour.

"Mr. Maguire. We've been looking for you."

Detective Sergeant McCoy was wearing a different suit, but she had the same frightened assistant in tow, hiding behind a manila folder and clearly itching to leave the scruffy suburbs.

"Well done, you found me. Can I go home now?"

"Not just yet. Somebody still has to take your statement."

"Why don't you do it?"

"Sorry, this is way off my patch. I'm here about that solicitor of yours that went AWOL. Nicky Hale?"

There was something extra-smug about the way she asked, as if she already had all the answers and wanted me to beg her to share them.

"Have you found her?"

McCoy settled into the chair opposite me and her sidekick sat at her elbow like her shadow, only less useful. "I've been looking into your background, Mr. Maguire. Quite the dark horse, aren't you?"

"I'm not any shade of horse," I said.

"Friend of the famous. Infamous, rather." I stared at her, refusing to toss that ball back. "This brief of yours, Nicky Hale, did she know you were a big pal of the Guvnor?"

"I'm not. But don't let that stop you making up theories."

She smiled as if I was being coy. "Don't you think you should have mentioned your connection to him when you first reported Ms. Hale's disappearance?"

"There is no connection, as far as I know. I'm not a pal of the Guvnor. If I was, do you think scumbags like Sherwood would try to nobble my business?"

"When the cat's away," said McCoy. "We've been getting a lot of this recently. Small-time criminals scrapping over territory."

"I'm not a criminal. I run a gym, and Sherwood's trying to strong-arm money out of me. I think it's called extortion, which is the sort of thing the police are supposed to prevent."

"Have you made an official report of this . . . extortion?"

"I'll make one now," I said. "Have you got a pen?"

"So you're saying there's no connection between today's incident and Nicky Hale's disappearance?"

"No, I'm not saying that, because I have no idea what happened to Nicky Hale."

"Is that why you've been calling on her family and clients, asking questions?"

I wondered who had complained about me. Joan Bisham? Or Nicky's husband?

"Somebody had to," I said. I was pleased to see McCoy bristle a little.

"We've made very thorough enquiries into Ms. Hale's disappearance, if that's what you're getting at."

"And what have you found out?"

"We're still missing a few pieces of evidence."

"So nothing, basically, is that it?"

"At the moment we're trying to track down her phone."

Ah . . . Nicky's phone. McCoy pinned me with a stare. Her eyes were two different shades of brown, I noticed, but I didn't mention it. She probably knew that already, and it might have sounded like I was chatting her up.

I went for sarcasm instead. "Have you tried ringing it?" But I'd already hesitated too long.

"Ms. Hale's husband says the last time he saw his wife's phone was when you visited him in his house. Shortly after you left he discovered it had disappeared."

"Well, has *he* tried ringing it?"

"So you have no idea where Ms. Hale's phone might be?"

I shrugged, as if mystified, but I had the feeling McCoy wasn't fooled for an instant.

"Well," she said, "if you happen to come across it, do let us know." Why was she backing off? I nearly protested that it was her bloody job to find the phone, not mine. I didn't particularly want her to look harder, but all the same . . .

"Why do I get the impression," I said, "that you're not bothered if this phone never turns up?"

She smiled again—she had a gap in her top front teeth too, and I found myself wondering if she could wolf-whistle—and held a hand out to her assistant. He wordlessly opened the folder and handed her a sheaf of photographs, and she turned them the right way up and slid them across the table to me.

Stage by stage, in blurry colour stop-motion, a woman in a baseball cap and sunglasses approached a glass cubicle and handed something over to the uniformed bloke inside. It was an immigration checkpoint somewhere in the EU, judging by the blue sticker on the glass of the cubicle showing a circle of yellow stars. The border guard made some gesture, and the woman pulled off her hat and shades. She was Nicky Hale, with a fat, split lip and a swollen black eye. I could barely recognize her, but the blouse and suit she was wearing I'd seen a few times. The guard handed Nicky her passport back and waved her through. She slipped the sunglasses back on her face, turned away, dropped out of the bottom of the frame and vanished.

"She'd been hurt?" I asked, aware too late of the concern in my voice. But if DS McCoy noticed it she didn't let on.

"Looks that way. But more to the point, these photos confirm Ms. Hale left the country, using her British passport, early on Monday the fourteenth—the same day you came to us."

"So where did she go?"

"We've traced her as far as Charles de Gaulle airport, but after that . . ." She shrugged, as if there was nothing more she could do. "Before these pictures were taken the money—your money—was transferred to an offshore account in the Cayman Islands, and almost immediately transferred out again, and we can't track that down either."

I shuffled through the photographs again, as if something in them might have changed since the first time I'd looked at them. Then I realized something had.

"You said 'her British passport.' Does that mean she had another one?"

"Ms. Hale had dual nationality," said McCoy. "English-Brazilian. Chances are she travelled on from Paris using her Brazilian passport. The UK has an extradition agreement with Brazil, but first they'd have to find her, and we don't even know if that's where she went." She leaned back in her chair in a way that suggested sympathy and regret and the closure of the case. "She hasn't been abducted, Mr. Maguire," she said. "She stole your money, and she fled the country. There's nothing more we can do, and there's no point in you running around interrogating her acquaintances. That's it. I'm sorry."

I noticed the way she said sorry. She'd guessed it wasn't just the money I'd lost. Sitting there it felt like I'd been clubbed with a crowbar again. I hadn't wanted to accept Nicky could have fleeced me—I'd refused to believe it. I'd wanted to find her, to ride to her rescue, avenge her, even . . . All just futile, idiotic teenage fantasies. I'd been shuttling back and forward like a bluebottle butting its head against a window because it's too stupid to see the glass.

"Anyway, we felt you were entitled to know," said McCoy. "And if that phone does turn up, you can return it to her husband. Sooner rather than later, I'd suggest."

I was so dazed I barely noticed her get up to leave. It was like she and her sidekick were tiptoeing out to avoid upsetting me any further.

"Yeah, no, thanks," I said. My scalp was throbbing and wouldn't let up, right now I was glad of the pain.

# five

A uniformed PC took my statement about the car-park brawl, very slowly and methodically. He was a southpaw and wrote with his hand hooked over the top of the pad. I could imagine him spending hours after this interview reading my words aloud while a bored typist who couldn't make out his handwriting transcribed it onto the police computer. I envied him all the same, because bad as his scrawl was, mine was so terrible even *I* couldn't make it out. The PC seemed a bit irritated when I insisted there had been three attackers, because the cops had only arrested two—presumably Sean and the apprentice legbreaker or whatever he was. I got the impression recording the fact that Dean had been present but had got away would mean loose ends and more work for the cops, so the PC tried his best to write Dean out of the story by muddling him up with Sean. Who, apparently, was in another interview room saying nothing to anyone about anything. The hired help he and Dean had brought along couldn't speak English, or wouldn't, and the police were still trying to figure out what language he was refusing to answer questions in.

Asked if I wanted to press charges, I said no. I had no lawyer, and I was sure that Sherwood retained someone to look after his chimpanzees. By the time he or she had finished plaiting the facts into decorative knotwork it would look like I had laid into two big-hearted blokes who had been washing cars for charity. The legal system wasn't there to establish the truth, I knew, just to bang someone up and be done with it, and I wasn't going to risk that someone being me. I didn't check the statement over, of course. I just scrawled a squiggly line at the bottom so I'd finally be free to go.

As I stepped out of the nick and down its wet steps into the night, an ice-cold breeze sliced into me. I had no idea where the hell I was or which direction was home, but a long squint at a map in a nearby bus shelter gave me my bearings, and I pointed my feet east and started to run.

OK, so I'd been wrong—Nicky had left the country and taken my money with her. But why? The cops didn't seem to think that part was important. Who exactly had split her lip and blacked her eye the night she left? She had been thumped in the ring that morning, yeah, but with blows to the body, and she'd been wearing a sparring helmet. The last time I saw her face it was as pretty as it had always been, if a little pale and tense. She hadn't fled the country of her own free will—she'd been frightened out, and whoever had done that to her had screwed me in the process.

I wondered if McCoy had asked Nicky's husband Harry Anderson about his wife's battered face. Anderson would have denied knowing anything about her injuries, I was sure, and that would be that. Even those photographs didn't constitute enough evidence to charge him, if the witness, and the victim, wasn't around any more. But I didn't need the same standard of proof as the cops. Maybe I should interview Anderson my own way.

It might not get my money back, but I really wanted to have a go at somebody, and Nicky wasn't here, and he was.

It was late at night and the suburban streets were broad and dark and silent as I ran east. Eventually I began to recognize a few landmarks: the spires, parks and crossroads that had once marked the villages on London's fringes, before the city had sprawled outwards, submerging and drowning them in a flood of dirty yellow brick. Buses blazing with cold blue light rumbled past, empty but for wilting shift workers and scruffy students who had run out of drinking money, and I let them all pass me, and kept running.

The gym doors were unlocked, and although I was breathless and sweaty I took the stairs two at a time, half expecting to find Dean and another bunch of hired knuckleheads trashing the place. But the place was empty and silent and neat and tidy, and the floor had been mopped. I saw Delroy emerging from the direction of the kitchen, weary and demoralized, like a big old bull nosing around a meadow for shelter and rest.

"Delroy?"

"Finn, hey. I thought those bastards would keep you locked up all night."

"Thanks for earlier. That was one hell of a punch you laid on that guy."

"Ach, he was out of condition, and all over the place. Boy learned his fighting off Hollywood movies." But for all his bravado there was a sad and bitter edge to Delroy's voice that I had never heard before. I tried to lighten the mood.

"You've done a great job cleaning up. I might have a lie-in tomorrow."

"We both can, I think," said Delroy. "It's about time." He was moving from workout machine to workout machine, pretending to wipe them down, and avoiding my eye.

"Del?" I said. "You OK?"

"I never said thank you, Finn," said Delroy. "For the chance to get back to work. I really appreciate everything you've done and all. Thing is, I can't do this no more." I saw his broad shoulders sag in defeat, and I thought, *Not you, Delroy, not now . . .*

"Delroy, you can't pack it in—I can't run this place without you. I'm nothing at coaching."

"Neither of us can run this place, Finn. It was a stupid idea, and it's cost you way too much."

"Don't worry about that—"

"One of us has to worry about it. This is money you'll need to live on. I should never have encouraged you—you're just a kid, your folks have gone, I should have tried to set you straight—"

"Look, to hell with Sherwood, OK? We've seen him off once."

"Finn, please," he begged. "Listen! We can't keep this place going. Sam and Daisy have quit. Half tonight's clients have cancelled their membership, they're not coming back. And if just one of them claims for the damage to their car—"

"That wasn't our fault!"

"That won't matter! We'll have no turnover to pay Sherwood his money—"

"But that's just what he wanted! That's just why he did this!"

"Then he's won, and it's over. Long as this place stays open it's vulnerable and anyone in here is vulnerable. We have to shut this place down, before you lose all your money and someone gets hurt bad."

"No. No way—"

Delroy flung down his cloth in frustration at my stubbornness. "It was never going to work. What do you think the insurance people would say if they'd found out I am the only qualified first-aider in the place? I can barely walk, for God's sake. Someone is injured, I can't even help you move them—"

"We've managed so far! We just need to hire new staff, qualified—"

"I'm not hiring anyone to put them in harm's way. We been lucky, Finn, and we had fun, but it's over. I'm done here."

He shuffled towards the door. My words were making no more impression on him than my fists used to when we sparred.

"Close this place, sell it to one of the big chains, put the whole thing down to experience. You're young, you're smart, you'll find some way to make a living. Hell, you have that place in Spain, you don't even need to make a living."

"I can't do this without you, Del."

"Then don't. 'Cos I'm not doing it any more. I'm going home. Lock up after me, and keep them doors locked."

He limped past me towards the stairwell, his crutch clanking, and I heard him slowly make his way downstairs, step by step, as I stood there grinding my teeth with frustration, alone in that chilly empty barn of a place. I was furious with Delroy, and with myself, because I knew he was right.

Sherwood had won this round.

Delroy's clean-up had been mostly symbolic and he had missed the corners, but then he probably had been leaning on the mop as much as swinging it. I finished off, wiped the kitchen down again, scrubbed the toilets and trudged down the stairs to lock the doors. They swung open before I was halfway down, and when I saw Nicky Hale walk in and look up my heart leaped, till I realized it wasn't Nicky, of course.

"Hi, Finn," said Susan. "I was hoping I'd catch you at home." She pulled at her hair as if she was ashamed of something she'd done and was scared to look at me. "The police came to see me today," she said.

"Yeah, me too."

"I'm sorry, I didn't mean to get you into

trouble, I just thought it would be better if I admitted I'd spoken to you—"

"It's fine. Don't worry about it."

I stood there on the stairs while she lingered self-consciously at the door. She clearly thought I was pissed off with her, so although I really didn't feel like company I said, "Do you want a cup of tea or something?"

"Or something would be nice," she said. "Have you got any gin?"

"We've got some surgical spirit."

"Er . . ."

"Stick a slice of lemon in it, you can't tell the difference."

"Seriously, have you got anything to drink?"

"Tea," I said.

Among the bits and pieces I'd taken from the old house before I rented it out was my bedside light, but here there was nothing to stand it on, so it lit my attic from the floor upwards. The effect under the sloping ceiling was weird but still cosy somehow. Susan seemed at home, anyway, as she draped her jacket on a dining chair and sat back on my ripped and bulging sofa. I hoped no broken rusty spring would poke through and scratch her—she'd probably need a tetanus shot.

"They showed me some photos of Nicky at border control, leaving the country."

"Using one of her passports," I said.

"Oh yeah. She has family in South America."

"And you don't?"

"Half-sisters," she said.

"Yeah, right. Sorry, I keep forgetting, you're so . . ."

"Alike, I know, it's weird. Sometimes I think about dyeing my hair or having a nose job."

"Na, don't, fair hair suits you."

"You like it?" She ran her fingers through her blonde bob and looked at me, and suddenly I realized where this was going, or might be. The same thought seemed to occur to her, and take her just as much by surprise. She looked away, suddenly self-conscious.

"Her dad was Brazilian. German-Brazilian. I used to say he was a Nazi on the run, just to wind her up. He left our mum when Nicky was two. Mum married again, had me, but Nicky was always her golden girl . . ." She tried to make it sound light-hearted, but I could hear the edge in her voice, and I knew how she felt; finding out your mother preferred someone else to you could kind of take the shine off your childhood. "My dad left when I was ten. We never heard from him again. Nicky was still in touch with hers . . . went over to visit when she was eighteen or so, worked there during her gap year, and again after she got her first from Oxford. She never told me anything about her other family, or even where they lived in Brazil. São Paulo or somewhere, I think, but . . ."

Her words trailed off. She stared into her cup as if to divine the future from the leaves, but I'd used teabags so we had no future.

"It's late," she said. "I suppose I should go." She stood, carefully, so as not to bang her head, and I fetched her jacket from where I'd draped it over the back of my chair.

"Do you feel relieved?" I said. Susan frowned. "I mean, now we know she's safe and well and spending other people's money?"

"I don't feel much of anything any more," she said. "Do you?"

"I feel bloody furious," I said as I offered her her coat.

She didn't take it. "I'm sorry, Finn," she said, and she reached for me, and this time I knew exactly where this was going.

Or I thought I did.

I went in with my guard down, expecting her to offer consolation, but when she sank her teeth into my lip I realized Susan was just as angry as I was, and I was way outclassed. I might have been half as heavy again with twice her reach, but I'd never faced an opponent who gouged, scratched and bit with such abandon, and she had me on the ropes while I was still trying to figure out the rules. But I'm a quick learner, and I soon grasped the concept—there were no rules. She kept coming at me like a title contender, grabbing handfuls of my hair at the temple and swinging on it, but she relaxed her grip when I seized her wrists and pinned her back against the cold gable wall. The battle was hot and frantic and ferocious and fun, and not for a minute did I stop wishing it was Nicky driving her nails into my shoulders.

Sitting in a café in Kew the next day I could still smell Susan on my skin, and I wondered if anyone else would. She'd stayed till two, then borrowed a shirt of mine—the blouse she'd arrived in was no longer in one piece—dressed quickly, and threw her leg over me where I lay in my unmade bed. She said nothing, just leaned down, grabbed my face and kissed me so hard she nearly split my lip. She smiled, but it wasn't a satisfied smile—it was wistful, as if she'd been aware what I'd been thinking, but understood. When I came downstairs with her to let her out she whispered in the dark, "Thanks, Finn. See you." She made our encounter sound so casual, almost accidental. I felt a twinge of guilt, tinged with resentment, that she'd seen through me and didn't care for what she saw.

"Hey, Finn. How's it going?"

Zoe pulled out the chair facing mine and slipped off her jacket. Wandering aimlessly in my thoughts I hadn't even noticed her enter the café, though the place was pretty small, and empty apart from me and the monosyllabic old lady behind the counter listlessly making up sandwiches ahead of the lunch-time rush. I stood to say hello, not sure whether Zoe would let me hug her, but she wrapped her arms around me and kissed me on the cheek. Her full, firm body felt familiar against mine, and I hugged her back—a little too long, because I felt her tense, and knew she'd noticed the scent of another woman on me.

"Thanks for coming, Zoe," I said, and she grinned brightly, and the tension passed. Why the hell was she being so possessive anyway? I wondered. Zoe had kind of dented our friendship when she sold me out to those child traffickers who'd done a tap dance on my kidneys. I'd forgiven her, but we both knew she owed me a favour—to say the least—and I supposed that was why she was here.

She ordered a cappuccino, and while we waited for it we made small talk about her move to a college up north to study IT. "Don't you know all this anyway?" she said. "You've been following me on Facebook."

"I only look at the pictures," I said. She knew why that was. The photos on her virtual wall told me all I needed to know. Although she was the same age as me, with no parents to tut or cluck or tell her off, she was already living the life of a student. That meant lots of drinking and parties and gigs and festivals, and every photo she posted seemed to show her in the middle of a crowd of blokes. Meeting her again, that didn't seem so surprising. Now that she'd eased up on the eyeliner and put on some weight she looked more healthy and happy and normal, and less like a frazzle-tempered druggie with a sharpened steel comb under her coat. All the same, I'd noticed, her status read "not in a relationship" and for some reason I was pleased, though her status was no concern of mine.

"What about you? How have you been?" It was nice of her to pretend we were here to catch up, when my online message to her had been so brief and impersonal. But she knew everything I wrote was brief and impersonal because it took me hours to tap out a sentence.

I filled her in on recent events. She looked suitably aghast when I told her about Nicky, and angry when I told her about Sherwood and how he'd shut down my gym, and at last we came to the point.

"What are you going to do?"

"I'm going to find out what happened," I said.

"I thought you knew what had happened."

"Yeah, but I don't know *why* it happened," I said. "And I want to. I trusted Nicky. I didn't think she wasn't the sort of person who'd shaft me like that." I saw Zoe stifle a bitter grin of regret. "Not without being forced to anyway," I said. "And I'd like to know who forced her."

"What are you going to do, fly out to Brazil and start asking around? How's your Portuguese?"

I pulled Nicky's smartphone out of my pocket and slid it across the table. Zoe looked down at it, then up at me, and she didn't pick it up.

"There are some emails and texts on there I need to trace," I said. "I thought you, or maybe one of your geeky mates, could help."

"Why would they do that?"

"I'm sure you can think of a way to persuade them," I said, and I wished I hadn't when I saw the hurt in her eyes. I had forgiven her, and I didn't mean to keep milking her mistakes, but I needed to know. "Please, Zoe. You're the only person who can help."

She sighed, reached out and picked up the phone. "Which ones do you want me to trace?"

"You'll know them when you see them.

Don't switch it on in here—soon as it logs onto the network the cops will know, and they might come looking for it."

"Why don't you let them?" asked Zoe. "Get them to trace these messages."

"They already tried, a few months back, and they got nowhere. Half the time the police can't trace people who leave them a bloody name and address—they wouldn't have a hope with a phone. Even if they did manage, it would take them months, and I don't want to twiddle my thumbs that long."

Zoe slipped the phone into her handbag, glancing around the room as if to check for concealed surveillance cameras. With good reason, I reflected. She picked up her cup but saw the last dregs of her coffee had gone cold and put it down again.

"Want another?" I said.

"No thanks," she said, and checked her own phone for emails, though I guessed she was really checking out the time. "You called her Nicky," she said.

"That's her name," I said.

"I mean, she doesn't sound like your lawyer. She sounds more like a friend," she said.

"She was," I said. "She came to my mum's funeral."

"You told me nobody came to your mum's funeral," said Zoe, and she looked oddly upset.

"Hardly anybody. I didn't really know her then." And what the hell's it got to do with you? I thought.

"Some friend. You never really did know her, did you?"

"Obviously not," I admitted.

"I worry about you, Finn. You seem to put your trust in the wrong people."

*Like you*, I wanted to say.

"I'm learning," I said.

"Who are you seeing these days?"

"No one in particular." It was almost the truth. I'd met Susan maybe three times, and slept with her once, and even for me that hardly counted as commitment. But Zoe's expression hardened as if I'd lied to her face, because I *had* lied to her face, and for a moment I thought she was going to take out Nicky's phone and fling it back at me.

"And do you trust her? This woman you're not seeing?"

"I don't trust anybody," I said. "That way I'm never disappointed."

Zoe pushed back her chair. "I'll talk to the head of my department, see if he can find out their IP," she said. I must have looked mystified, because she explained, "Whoever sent these messages, they'll have an IP address, an Internet address. They'll probably have tried to hide it or fake it, but that can be cracked if you know how."

"That would be great," I said. "Thanks."

"You're welcome," said Zoe. "Was there anything else?"

"I'll walk you to the station," I said.

"I'm not headed that way," said Zoe, but she didn't say what way she was headed. Then she seemed to soften, as if she was ashamed of sounding so much like a sulky teen. "Thanks for the coffee, Finn. It was good to see you. Take care, yeah?"

She leaned down and kissed me, and her lips were soft and full, and gentler than Susan's, and I felt a sudden pang of something, loss or regret. But feelings like that have never got me anywhere except in trouble.

"Cheers," I said, and I let her go.

As I paid the bill I pondered whether I could afford a tip. I couldn't, but I left one anyway. I emerged from the café, turned north and started to run.

It wasn't hard to figure out why Susan had jumped me, I thought. She had been angry at Nicky for skipping town for ever without so much as a goodbye, and she'd wanted to get her rocks off, and I'd happened to be there. I wondered now if she'd got it out of her system or whether she'd be back for seconds. I kind of hoped she'd come back, and I kind of didn't, because I knew that really it was Nicky I wanted. I'd wanted her for a long time, and Susan might be closer to my age but she didn't have Nicky's wit or her laugh or the turn of her head. Also, Nicky had my money. And she kept her nails shorter . . . Those welts in my back had stung in the shower and they were smarting now as I picked up speed and ran towards Kew Bridge.

A scrawny young mum shoving a stroller and dragging a fractious toddler along by the hand jerked back in alarm as the Merc convertible swerved towards her, bumped up on the pavement ahead of her and shot into its off-street parking space. She glared at the driver like she intended to give him a steaming earful when he got out, but he didn't get out, and she pushed her buggy on down the street, swearing under her breath.

Sherwood was still on the phone when he emerged, looking grim and lugging a slim leather attaché case that probably held nothing but a porn mag. When he saw me walking towards him from the door of his office where I'd been lurking he looked grimmer still and hesitated, maybe pondering whether he would be safer getting back into his car. Which was I more likely to dent, his bodywork or him? I'd expected Dean to be babysitting, since Sean was either still in prison or in plaster, but there was no sign of him. Little wonder Sherwood looked worried.

"We had an agreement, Mr. Sherwood," I said. "How am I expected to make my repayments if those jerks on your staff drive away all my customers? Or is that part of the service too?"

"The agreement you proposed was predicated on your providing collateral," said

Sherwood. I guessed he was lapsing into financial jargon because he was scared. "But you don't own the title to that property."

Interesting, I thought. Few people apart from Nicky would have known that. "Who told you?" I said.

Sherwood licked his lips. "I spoke to the sellers."

That answer was plausible, although it didn't sound like the truth.

"No, I don't own the building," I said. "So don't bother sending any more goons around, unless you like visiting people in hospital."

Sherwood clutched his briefcase in both hands like he planned to use it as a shield. "The contract your friend Delroy signed is still valid," he said.

That was the point of trashing the gym—not to put the squeeze on me, but on Delroy. I was itching to stick Sherwood's face through the windscreen of his flash car, but it wouldn't help. Delroy needed a lawyer. Sod it, I thought, I can find another one—I'd get Vora out of retirement if I had to.

"You're not getting Delroy's house, you

prick," I said. "Take him to court and see how far you get."

"Well, I prefer to explore other avenues first," he smirked. His eyes flicked over my shoulder, and when I turned to follow his look I saw a traffic warden patrolling the street nearby, casting sideways glances at us as if he could smell the adrenaline from across the road. Sherwood was probably hoping to goad me into taking a swing at him in front of a witness.

Leaning down close I kept my voice as soft and gentle as I could.

"You go anywhere near Delroy, and I'll be exploring your avenues. With a broken bottle."

His smirk got smirkier, and I decided to leave before I lost my temper and thumped him anyway. We both knew my threats were bluster. Delroy had signed a loan agreement, and I wasn't in a good position to negotiate— I'd just have to wait till Sherwood's representatives got in touch. Then I'd negotiate their teeth in.

But Sherwood would have a special goon fund for situations like this, I suspected, and his money would generate infinite heavies coming at me in waves until it felt like I was trapped inside some urban combat video game with a dwindling supply of pound coins.

I'd been banged up in a young offenders' institution when I was way too young, and even though I'd deserved to be there, it was a hell-hole. That's where I'd learned how two plastic knives taped together could make a blade hard enough to puncture a lung, that boiling tea with sugar in could scar someone's face like napalm, and that if all else failed you could hang yourself with the plaited pages of a magazine. But back then what really kept me awake at night were the rumours that the place had been declared overcrowded, and that some of us would be transferred to Dalston Prison.

Dalston was an adult nick in North London, a decrepit Victorian cesspit that should have been shut down and demolished years ago but was always being reprieved. The politicians needed the cells because they were trying to show everyone how tough they were on crime, arm-twisting magistrates into locking more and more people away for dodging their TV licence or carrying a pinch of blow. It was notorious for being run not by the management but by the prison guards, who on a whim would lock the prisoners in their cells for twenty-three hours a day, only opening the doors to cart away the corpses of lags who had topped themselves in despair.

As I entered HMP Dalston that afternoon and those black wooden gates and six-metre-high walls closed around me, it wasn't the acrid tang of cheap bleach, the clammy overheated air, and the stench of sweat and fear and misery that made me tense. It was the smell of the fake ID burning a hole in my pocket. As I joined the queue for the security desk I could feel the palms of my hands tingling with perspiration.

A mate of mine—Jonah, far more bent and vicious than I ever was—had pulled this stunt years ago when he'd come to visit me. He wasn't there to cheer me up—he was convinced I was hiding another stash of free drugs—and he'd proudly shown me the ID card, complete with photograph and official stamp, he'd used to get in. It had been issued by the Royal British

Archive, just across the river from our hunting grounds, and it looked totally kosher, because it was. The Archive staff would issue an ID card to anybody who claimed to be researching historical records for schoolwork, and it was easy to give them a fake name. I had gone there myself after seeing Zoe, and found the same system in place. Nobody checked that you were actually there to look up records or archives, or even that you could read, which was just as well for me.

The prison guard on the visitors' admissions desk looked at the ID card, looked back at me, flipped the card over and peered at it, then handed it back. I very gently breathed a sigh of relief, but I wasn't in the clear yet. He slid his finger down a clipboard until he found the name I'd used when I'd phoned the prison to arrange a visit. He ticked the column beside it with blue biro, promptly forgot I existed, and nodded at the next in line to approach his desk.

Then it was the security cordon. I'd left everything metal at home—watch, phone, coins, even my belt buckle. The prison provided lockers for your valuables, but you might as well have spread your stuff out on a table marked with a notice reading STEAL ME. A bored guard who looked like he ate chips three times a day waved a metal detector in my general direction and nodded me through to the visiting area.

About two dozen tables were laid out in rows, and I was suddenly reminded of all the examination rooms I'd been in, and all the exams I'd so spectacularly failed. Here and there tetchy, fractious kids perched on the wooden chairs swinging their legs while Mum filled Dad in on what was happening at home, trying not to make life outside sound too interesting. I took the table as close to the prisoners' entrance as I could manage; I wanted to see the guy I was visiting before he started looking around for the son he expected. He was not going to recognize me, and there was a real chance I wouldn't recognize him either. The newspaper archives I'd found online were a few years old and his picture had been a standard full-on mugshot with no human expression. But I had only just sat down when a prisoner who looked very much like James Bisham entered. I immediately stood up again and called out, "Dad?"

Bisham saw me and hesitated. I beamed at

him with my broadest, warmest smile, and I saw doubt cross his face, then curiosity, and when he at last smiled cautiously and approached me I knew I had cleared that last hurdle. I held out a hand to shake before he reached the table, in case he thought I'd want to hug him or something. He gripped it firmly and shook, grinning broadly as if he was delighted to see me, when he didn't know me from Adam. Out of the corner of my eye I'd been watching a prison guard watch us. Then I sensed his attention flick to two four-year-olds who had decided to chase each other up and down the rows.

"You've changed a lot, son," said Bisham. "I'd hardly recognize you." He pitched his voice low and kept his posture relaxed.

I pitched my voice even lower. "Mr. Bisham, my name's Maguire," I said. "Your wife told me you were banged up in here. I had to use Gabriel's name to get in. I was hoping I could talk to you."

"I'm listening." He was curious, but distant too, and I knew I would have to tread carefully, because he could still drop me in the shit if he wanted to. It probably wouldn't be very deep shit—impersonating a kid to visit his dad in prison hardly counted as depraved and violent conduct—but the staff might accidentally scrape my face along a few brick walls before they threw me out, just for showing them up.

"A friend of mine left the country in a hurry," I told Bisham, "because she was getting threatening messages, emails and texts and tweets. Your wife said she'd been getting a lot of messages like that too."

Bisham rolled his eyes, but he smiled ruefully. He'd heard this stuff before, I could tell. "And she told you I'd sent them?" he said. "Yeah, everybody's issued with an untraceable phone when they come in here, free unlimited calls and texts. It's like a holiday camp."

"I wondered if it was a well-meaning friend of yours," I said.

"What friends?" he said. "I had all the same friends as her, until she screwed me over. Cleaned me out, had me banged up. You one of Gabriel's mates or something?"

"Sort of," I said.

Bisham nodded. "You've never met him, have you?"

"I have, actually," I said. "He seems like a nice kid."

"He was, before my wife got hold of him," he said. "She's why he never comes to see me."

"I could try and get a message to him, if you like," I said. Bisham blinked, and I sensed that he was almost tough enough to bear years of confinement, but losing touch with his son was really pulling his guts out. But then that's how prison works.

"Not sure there's any point, now," he said. "You wouldn't believe what that bitch has told him about me."

"I know she says it was you who torched that old pub."

"That's not the worst part. Gabriel wouldn't have cared about that."

"Then what?"

I saw him hesitate, wondering if he wanted to blurt all this out to some yob he'd only just met.

"It was Messy, the cat," he said.

"What happened to Messy?"

"Someone soaked her in lighter fuel, put a match to her. Made it look like I did it when I was drunk. Little Gabe was catatonic, traumatized. You can bet the wife brought that up at the divorce hearing."

"But it wasn't you?"

"Of course it wasn't me! *I'm* not the god-damn nutter—*she* is!" He'd raised his voice, and I was worried that we'd attract the attention of the guard, but I guessed plenty of families squabbled during these encounters, because no one seemed bothered. Bisham took a deep breath and calmed down again, but the way he'd lost it to start with half convinced me he was telling the truth. "It was her bloody lighter fuel—I found the can hidden in her car . . ." It sounded hideous, but I couldn't see what a tortured cat had to do with Nicky, so I cut across him.

"Have you heard of a woman called Nicky Hale?"

"Yeah, she was Joan's lawyer. Nice enough, but the silly bitch should never have taken Joan on. Cross my wife, you end up soaked in petrol. Or in here."

"Nicky was the friend of mine getting the obscene messages," I said.

"Then she shouldn't have given Joan her contact details," said Bisham.

I was here under false pretences; nothing Bisham told me could ever be used as evidence. He knew that, and I'd kind of been counting on him knowing that—hoping he'd boast about what he'd done, or at least deny it unconvincingly. But he'd convinced me; everything he said about his wife and her mental state sounded pretty much on the money, from my encounter with her. And that meant I was back where I'd started.

"Thanks for your help," I said.

"We've still got twenty minutes," said Bisham.

"What would you like to talk about?"

"Know any jokes?"

"I know one about a pig with a wooden leg."

"Nah, not that old one." He looked down at his hands, steeled himself, and asked, "How was he? Gabriel? When you saw him?"

"He's big," I said, mentally fishing for some compliment that wouldn't be a transparent lie. "Looks smart. Plenty of courage too. Was willing to have a go at me when he thought I was overstaying my welcome."

"Good," he said. "He was always a bit of a mother's boy."

"Do you want me to give him a message?"

Bisham took a deep breath, then shut his

mouth, as if he had too much to say to fit into the time we had left. Or as if what he had to say to his son couldn't be entrusted to a stranger.

"Tell him I said hi." He suddenly reminded me of my dad, and how I'd taken him for granted, and how as a teenager I'd stopped even listening to him, and how one day I'd come home and found him murdered, and it was always going to be too late to fix that. I'd get past Gabe Bisham's crazy mother somehow, I decided, and shake the pasty little runt till the teeth rattled in his head, and tell him to go and talk to his dad while he had the chance.

I stood, and offered Bisham my hand again. Bisham took it, and there was warmth in his grasp. "Thanks for coming," he said. "Seriously. It's so bloody boring in prison you wouldn't believe it."

"I would, actually."

He smiled to recognize a fellow old lag. "Come again, yeah?"

"I'll try," I said, and we both knew what that meant—that I would sooner peel the skin off my leg with a blunt knife than walk in through those gates again.

\* \* \*

Dalston Prison was on the other side of the city from my gym and I went back the way I had come, by train, through the bleak hinterland of North London, with its railways sidings and decaying brick tenements dotted with weeds on their facades and parapets. The wheels of the carriage didn't even have a reassuring clickety-clack, they just rattled and banged over endless points, and the thoughts rattled and jostled in my head the same way. So the Bishams loathed each other and their kid was caught in the middle? I'd heard that story a hundred times. At least when my mum had walked out I'd been left with one parent who loved me enough to put up with all my attitude. I knew a few kids who had ended up wandering the streets all night, seething with rejection and humiliation, because their folks couldn't agree whose turn it was to feed them. Gabe Bisham's mother might be bonkers, but she loved him and was there for him, and I knew in that respect at least he should count himself lucky.

What I still didn't know was who had sent those threatening messages to Nicky.

# six

The estate where Delroy and Winnie lived was a huddle of bright modern houses, clean and cheerful and green; the local playground was full of kids screaming with glee as they spun around on the multi-coloured whirligigs mounted on thick rubber matting. When I had been a kid around here the playground surfaces had been mostly broken tarmac glittering with fragments of glass and dotted with dog shit, and the climbing frames and seesaws were always vandalized with such painstaking effort you wondered why the punks who did it couldn't get a well-paid job in demolition.

My dad had hated nostalgia—he said his childhood had been rotten weather and worse food, and anyone who got sentimental for the past was a fool. You had to learn to enjoy the now, he said. He had a point, but I kept remembering how I'd played on those swings, and how he used to stand behind me, pushing me higher and higher while I squealed in fear and joy. Afterwards I'd ride home on my noisy plastic tricycle, asking impossible questions he'd always try his best to answer.

Winnie opened her door wearing her big flowery apron, and insisted on giving me a huge hug. Her embrace smelled of soap and furniture polish and hairspray, and from inside the house wafted the scent of spiced meat. I followed her into the kitchen, stomach rumbling, to find she was making gungo peas soup—in enough quantities, as usual, to feed a small Caribbean island. While I filled the kettle she drained the water from the pigs' tails she'd been salting overnight and explained that Delroy had gone to the Benefits Office for tests to see if he was still disabled or had somehow been miraculously cured of his massive stroke.

"These days," said Winnie, "if you can stand upright for two minutes, they declare you is fit for work, doing what the good Lord only knows, holding up a sign saying 'Car Wash' or some such nonsense, but Delroy so proud he'd rather agree with those . . . numbskulls before he admit he need help."

"I should never have come to him with that idea for reopening the gym," I said. "I'm really sorry, Winnie."

"Lord, it's not your fault. Delroy big enough and ugly enough to make up his own mind. It's just a shame it didn't work out, that's all." She slid chunks of yellow yam from her chopping board into the pot that was just starting to boil. "And you know, maybe it's for the best. You too young to spend your life slaving away in that place. And Delroy too old, he need to be taking it easy, his time of life." I frowned. I knew Winnie was trying to put a good spin on it; everything she was saying now contradicted what she'd said when we'd first opened. "Maybe we should go home," she said. "Sell this place, we could live OK back in Jamaica."

If Sherwood lets you, I thought.

"Winnie . . . have you heard anything else from that moneylender?"

"That man . . ." Winnie scowled. It didn't suit her.

"Has he been around? Or sent anyone?"

"That creepy little guy who took our TV, one who look like Elvis. He came here, tried to tell us Sherwood was going to take our house, but Delroy told him to take a hike."

"Seriously?"

"I been to the Citizens' Advice Bureau, talked to the lawyers down there. They say that man Sherwood can't take our home, he don't have a leg to stand on. We repay that loan in our own time, he just have to lump it."

"I'll pay it off, Winnie, I promise," I said. "Soon as my money's sorted out."

"Oh, that money!" Winnie flapped her hands. "Just goes to show the truth of the Good Book. All that money's brought nothing but trouble."

She had a point. Life had been a lot simpler when I'd been working in that greasy chicken sandwich joint, running for fun and spending evenings at home with my dad, both of us wrapped in blankets to save on the gas bill. But simpler doesn't mean better, and I'd actually started to enjoy having money, and all the possibilities it offered . . . until Nicky disappeared with it. That was what had brought us all this trouble, I thought, not the money.

There was a rattle of keys and a clatter at the front door which I knew signalled the arrival home of Delroy, stumbling over the front step on his crutch.

"Damn it, something smells tasty! Is it you, Mrs. Llewellyn?"

I saw Winnie's face break into a huge embarrassed and delighted smile. As she heaved her creaking joints out of her chair and waddled out to meet her husband, I caught a glimpse of the girl Delroy had met on a beach in Jamaica and had followed home and had pestered continuously until she agreed to marry him. Forty-something years later they were still together, still devoted, still sniping and bickering at each other. I wondered if I would ever find someone I could share my life with so completely, and was startled when the image that came to mind was of Zoe in the café in Kew, stirring sugar into her coffee. The girl who'd told me—taught me—never to trust anyone.

"Finn!" barked Delroy. "Sitting there with your gut filling up my kitchen! Fetch some glasses, boy!"

* * *

Delroy finished one bottle of rum and started on another, despite Winnie's tutting and head-shaking. He barely bothered to dilute it, determined to tie one on, presumably to wipe out the humiliation of having to parade his disability and weakness for some hack government doctor ticking boxes on a form. I was glad to learn he hadn't demonstrated on the examiner the one physical action he could perform perfectly—a right hook—although if he had I wouldn't have blamed him. But there's only so much watery rum I can take, and I took as much as I could before I kissed Winnie's cheek, clapped Delroy on the shoulder and headed home at a run, my head hazy and my belly sloshing like a water bottle with every step.

Maybe it was the alcohol, or the prospect of another night by myself, or maybe I'd stopped missing Nicky whenever I saw Susan, but when I got home I picked up my mobile and called Susan's number. Her voice was pleased to hear me, like she'd been waiting for my call, but her words didn't match.

"I can't make it this evening, sorry. Can we do it later this week?"

She made it sound like I was her personal fitness trainer, and I realized suddenly she was trying to hide me from whoever she was with. It figured, I thought; I was an illiterate bit of rough about seven years her junior, and she was an educated posh bird whose friends and family had money. She wasn't likely to be taking me to dinner parties any time soon, unless it was to amuse the other diners by drinking wine out of the bottle or maybe peeling bananas with my feet.

"Yeah, sure," I said. "Call me." I slung down the phone.

She wouldn't call me. She'd only stuck around to find out what had happened to Nicky, and now she thought she knew, and she didn't care about the reason why Nicky left, any more than the cops did. I was the only one who gave a toss.

I cleaned my teeth, pulled off my clothes and went to bed.

I woke at five the next morning feeling like a dog turd someone had stepped in, and my mouth was parched and sticky. I wasn't good at drinking—that had been my dad's field of expertise—and I never wanted to be. I was about to slip into my old routine and start cleaning the gym, when I realized the gym had closed, and I was effectively unemployed. I decided to go for a run to burn the alcohol out of my system, and managed ten kilometres before I had to spew into the Thames.

It worked, though. Back home, after a shower—that was one expense of refitting the gym that I didn't regret—I started to feel human again. I climbed the stair back to my room, towelling my head, and my eye fell on the box files still cluttering my table. There was one client of Nicky's I hadn't spoken to yet. Maybe there was no point any more, but I had nothing else to do.

The place I was looking for was once a cosy café in a bustling parade of shops until the North Circular ring road had carved its way through the street, slicing it in half like an earthworm. Except earthworms can survive being sliced in half, while the two ends of this high street were slowly writhing in their death throes. The only businesses clinging on were betting shops and grubby grocers selling bruised fruit and dented tins. At this time of the morning the bookies were closed, and the busiest shopfront was the one I was headed for. A succession of shambling, scruffy figures, some of them clutching greasy sleeping bags, some of them without even that, came through the open door into the steamy welcoming warmth.

If anyone noticed me, or thought I didn't belong in a soup kitchen, they didn't say so, but then homeless and hungry people come in all shapes and sizes. I spotted Reverend Zeto, the kamikaze motorist, right away although he wore no dog-collar. This morning he was in jeans, a T-shirt and a stained cotton apron, which he was using to lift a stack of heated soup bowls onto a counter near a big vat of watery porridge. Two other volunteers bustled around behind the counter, slight women barely into their twenties with their hair pinned up and discreet golden crosses dangling from chains around their necks. They beamed at the punters lining up for breakfast, as if they were privileged to serve them, and their sincerity was touching. I'd never really intended to join the queue, but as I watched the shuffling customers pick up their plastic cutlery I remembered my own circumstances and wondered if I'd be joining them soon.

"Hi there, what are you having?" Zeto beamed at me. I held back, guilty about taking food meant for the homeless, when I wasn't— not yet anyway. I grinned inanely, and saw Zeto's glance flick up and down, and his smile widen. "Haven't seen you in here before," he said. "The porridge is better than it looks, believe me."

"Are you Reverend Zeto?" Zeto's brilliant smile dried up and crumbled to dust. He was in his mid-thirties, at a guess, with fine cheekbones and a youthful mop of blond hair. He looked fit, if scrawnier than in his photos—but then getting drunk and nearly killing a score of motorists while failing to kill yourself would motivate anyone to lose a few pounds. I was surprised no one had ever tried to sell "Screw Up Your Life" as a weight-loss regimen—some dieters would try anything.

"Do you want any porridge?" he snapped at me, as if I hadn't addressed him by name.

"Actually, I was hoping to have a chat with you," I said.

"Sorry," he said. "This food is for people in need, so if you're not in need you shouldn't be here."

"About Nicky. Nicky Hale," I said.

Zeto hesitated, as if I'd muttered a code-word, then changed his mind. "Whatever it's about, I can't help," he said. "Next!"

"I can wait," I said. "It's not a problem. I was a client of hers too. I'm just trying to find out what happened to her."

"I don't know what happened to her," said Zeto. His voice was distinctly lacking in Christian warmth. "I can't help you, sorry—you can hang around all day if you want. Next!"

The guy behind me didn't need to be told again. He walked round me, elbowed his way in front and handed his bowl to Zeto, who slopped a big ladle of grey porridge into it and passed it back. "Sugar's over there," he said, and pointed. Then he turned and looked straight through me. "Next please!"

You must be the rudest bloody vicar I've ever met, I thought, as I went to sit down at one of the long laminated trestle tables. I was hoping maybe Zeto would relent when the crowds eased off, and maybe come and talk to me, but as the morning wore on he carried on grimly slopping gruel and ignoring my presence. After an hour or so, when the line started to thin, he picked up a rack full of dirty dishes and disappeared into the back room. I kicked myself; I saw now I should have volunteered to help out, instead of marching in and demanding an interview like some arrogant copper. I'd blown it, and Zeto wouldn't talk to me now if I joined his congregation, served on the altar on Sunday and made a pilgrimage to Jerusalem on my knees. I stood up and got ready to go: it probably didn't matter anyway—Zeto might be sour and short-tempered, and lethal behind the wheel, but it was hard to imagine a vicar who volunteered in a soup kitchen sending obscene text messages to Nicky or plotting her disappearance.

But as I turned to the door another man entered and I did a double-take. The new arrival saw me staring and he stared back defiantly, maybe expecting me to look away or gag. He was hard to look at: the left side of his face was a mass of scar tissue and his left eye a sightless white ball twitching under warped and rigid folds of skin. His woollen hat was pulled down low over his head—I guessed that was to hide his missing left ear and wrecked scalp with its mocking wisps of hair.

Deciding to ignore me, he headed over to the counter for breakfast, and I saw the smile falter on the face of the volunteer with the porridge ladle. Then she forced herself to look him in the eye and grin, and I knew he had seen it too, and I imagined how hard it must be to face that mixture of revulsion and pity every day.

Tray in hand he finally made his way to a seat, and I moved to take the chair opposite. I made sure I faced him full on and held my look to his one sighted eye.

"Excuse me, but is your name Leslie?" I said. "Alan Leslie?"

"What do you want?" Leslie grunted, his mouth full.

"My name's Finn Maguire. I saw your picture in the paper . . . I wanted to ask you about what happened."

"What happened when?" he snorted. Some food fell from the left side of his mouth, through his stiff lips. Nerve damage, I guessed, and I wondered how often he bit the inside of his cheek and didn't know until he spat blood.

"You were sleeping rough in a building that burned down," I said.

"Got burned down," he corrected me. "It wasn't spontaneous bloody combustion."

"Got burned down," I said. "I'm sorry about your friend Martin."

Leslie took another forkful of food. I wondered how many times he'd told this story, and hoped it wasn't often. If finding someone willing to listen to—and look at—him was rare, there was a better chance he'd open up to me.

"He wasn't my friend," Leslie muttered.

"Wasn't he? The media must have got it wrong."

"He was my lover. We were together." He stared at me as if daring me to laugh at the idea that this wreck of a face would ever have been attractive to anyone of any sexual orientation.

"Jesus," I said. "I'm sorry. It must have been a horrible way to lose someone."

Leslie shook his head and blinked. His one

good eye watered, and I wondered if he was trying to weep, but couldn't any more.

"That bastard of a barrister made out we started it," he said. "On purpose, to keep warm!"

He seemed to realize he was ranting, the same rant he'd ranted a hundred times before, that nobody ever cared about, and he clammed up.

"What did happen?" I said.

Leslie stared at me, wondering if this was a wind-up. "There was a report, a fire brigade report—they said the fire started at the foot of the stairs—why the fuck would we . . ." His voice trailed off again.

"Did you tell the court that?"

"I wasn't at the trial. I was still in the burns unit."

"Bisham went to jail for it, though, didn't he?"

"Six to ten for arson? It was murder, he should have got life."

"But if he didn't know you were in there . . ."

"The hell he didn't know—the bloody door was screwed shut."

"Screwed shut?"

"Yeah. Bisham drove screws through the door into the frame, that night, before he torched the place. I know—I'd used that door earlier—but they never read my statement out in court. Nobody picked up on it, because we're street people and nobody gives a damn."

"How did Bisham start the fire? Petrol through the letter box?"

"Anyone could have done that. It started at the bottom of the stairs, about ten feet from the letter box. The prick had keys, he let himself in."

"Bit sloppy, for an insurance job. No wonder he got caught."

"It wasn't an insurance job. He wanted us to burn. Me and Martin both."

"But why?"

"To frighten any other homeless people who wanted to try it on, is why." Leslie dropped his fork and stared down at his plate as if his appetite had vanished. When he started talking again his voice was so soft I could barely hear him. "Martin had no enemies. He was the gentlest guy you'd ever . . . He died in front of me. Fell through the floor. He was still alive when the fire . . ."

"Jesus," I said.

"Unless you're praying for Martin," said Leslie, "stop using the Lord's name. He hears you." I thought he was being ironic, but his voice had hardened again—he was deadly serious.

"Who does?"

"The Lord hears you!" snapped Leslie.

"Oh, right, sorry," I said. "Are you one of Zeto's . . . ?"

"What?" Leslie snapped, a bit defensively, I thought.

"Congregation," I said.

"Oh." From what I could read of Leslie's face he looked a bit sheepish. "I go to his church, yeah."

"What did you think I meant?"

"Forget it." He picked up his fork again to chase a scrap of scrambled egg round his plate.

"Thanks. For talking to me."

Leslie shoved his plate away. "What's it worth?" he said.

I fished out my wallet and opened it. All I had left was a tenner.

Leslie snatched it. "That'll do nicely," he said.

For all his God-bothering, I guessed he'd spend any money I gave him on booze or drugs. But with a face like that, he was welcome to it. He needed all the narcotics he could get.

I had planned to go straight home, but when I emerged from the railway station I found myself heading south towards the river instead. Not for the scenery, but because Nicky's house was that way.

A cop—Zoe's father, in fact—once told me that when someone was murdered the prime suspect was always the one who reported finding the body. Nicky wasn't dead, but her husband, Harry Anderson, was the last person to have seen her, and it was time to visit him again, to find out what else he knew. Talking to Nicky's clients had been getting me nowhere; maybe I could rattle Anderson somehow, get him angry. I could mention his coke habit, I suppose, to imply I knew more about him than he'd like me to. I knew he'd helped to make Nicky miserable—he'd told me himself they'd argued the night she walked out—and I wondered again if it was Anderson who'd beaten her, and if that had been the final straw. I'd ask him to his face, and hopefully he'd claim that it was loveplay, and that Nicky had liked it rough. It would give me an excuse to show him the same sort of affection.

Running all the way it only took me five minutes to get to Nicky's house, and when I got there I paused on the other side of the street as if I had a stitch and needed to catch my breath, in case anyone watching thought I was casing the place for a burglary. But there was nobody about except the postman trundling his overloaded trolley towards me, music pumping through his headphones. From his tanned legs I guessed he was one of those posties who wear shorts all year round to show everyone how outdoorsy they are. Nicky's chocolate-box house looked empty, however—the sleek Beemer was missing from the driveway. I cursed. It was the middle of the day, after all—I should have known Anderson would be at work. It occurred to me that maybe I *could* case the joint . . . start by knocking on the door, see if I could spot an open window. Then I remembered the intruder system I'd seen during my short and sour encounter with Anderson, and scratched that idea. As the postie approached, leaned his bike against a gateway two doors down and disappeared up that drive, another approach occurred to me—just as illegal, but much less risky.

I braced my leg against the curb and rubbed my calf as if I was massaging out a cramp, and surreptitiously watched as the postman re-emerged, wheeled his bike up to the gateway next door to Nicky's house, flicked through the presorted bundles of letters on top of his mailbag, chose one and went to drop it off.

The essence of daylight robbery is timing and decisiveness. There's an element of per-formance too—to anyone watching you have to make your actions appear unconscious and unremarkable. In two seconds I was by the postie's bike, in another half-second I had grabbed the next sheaf of letters from his delivery pile, and one second after that I was jogging down the street with Anderson's correspondence stuffed up my shirt. Luckily I wasn't really sweating much. I just hoped that the slim bundle I had snatched actually had letters for Anderson and not just spam from pizza joints and dodgy cab firms.

I paused by a post box two streets away and checked through the bundle. It took me a minute or two, but I found three letters for Anderson and one for Nicky. I posted the remainder, stuffed the others back up my hoodie and ran on. North of Kew Bridge the traffic was static as usual; it gave me a lovely smug feeling to run past the drivers sitting fuming in their cars like a thousand sardines, each festering slowly in its own tin.

My mobile buzzed noisily on my table. I checked the name that appeared on the screen, thought about it, then hit "answer."

"Hey, Finn, it's me, Susie."

"I know it's you, your number's in my contacts."

"I wondered if you wanted to meet up."

"When?"

"Now would be good."

"Thought you couldn't make it till later this week?"

"This is later this week."

"I'm kind of busy right now."

"I could come to you." Part of me liked that idea, and it was easy to tell which part.

"OK. I'll be in all evening."

"Good, because I'm downstairs. Why don't you have an entryphone?"

When I opened the door she pushed her way in like a copper on a raid, grabbed my hair and pulled my face down to kiss her. Well, I thought, no long awkward pauses wondering if the other night was a one-off misjudgement. As she climbed the stairs ahead of me, my eyes level with her swaying ass, I felt the scratches tingling on my back in anticipation, and as soon as she made it to the top floor she turned and seized my shirt. It was just as well I hadn't got round to replacing the broken furniture.

An hour later, sweaty, panting and newly bloodied, I lay face down on the rumpled wreck of my bed while she wandered around the room in a shirt of mine that barely covered her finely toned ass.

"What do you do for a living?" I said.

"I coach tennis. It doesn't pay very well, but

I have some money saved up, from when I used to play professionally."

"That would account for that very fine ass you have."

"Thank you. I'm told it's good, I've never seen it myself."

She noticed the mail lying opened on my table and reached for them with the easy familiarity of someone I'd just slept with.

"You have an AmEx card?" she said. She sounded vaguely surprised. Then she clocked the address on the statement. "This is Harry's," she said. She looked shocked, and at the same time thrilled—as if I was a cat burglar who had lifted a diamond tiara from a yacht off Monte Carlo, rather than a West London hoodie who had robbed a postman's bicycle. "What are you doing with it?"

"Checking him out," I said. "Did you say he worked for a bank?"

"Hennessey's—one of those private banks you never hear of unless you're loaded. Very classy, very exclusive. He's always dropping hints about how his latest client is a rock star, or a Premiership footballer. Nicky got fed up telling him to be more discreet. I think he just doesn't want people to know how boring he really is."

"He's not that boring," I said. "I mean, for a bank manager. He's not boring enough."

"You talking about the coke?"

That took me aback. I thought Anderson snorting cocaine would be a big deal, given his position. "It's practically a rite of passage in his business," Susie went on. "I mean, all the young fund managers do it. For those guys, not snorting coke is like being a vegan or something."

"Actually, it's not the coke," I said. I clambered out of bed, wrapping a towel round my waist to stop the draughts from the crooked windows getting to my vitals. Picking up the credit card statement I pointed to three transactions I'd underlined. "See those?" I said.

"For ten thousand pounds?"

"Each. Don't you think that's odd? That he withdrew exactly ten thousand pounds three times in the space of two weeks?"

"Yes, but . . . those could be for anything." She checked the payee. "Fine Times Ltd?"

"They're some sort of financial services company. I Googled them."

"Well then, it must have something to do with his work."

"Why would he use his credit card to get cash from one of his clients?"

"I don't know, Finn, I'm not a City banker, and neither are you."

"He went over his credit limit twice last month," I said. "If you were a Premiership footballer, would you want a coke-addicted spendaholic managing your account?"

"Harry's a creep," said Susie, "but he's not a coke addict. Nicky would never have put up with it."

"Maybe that's why she left," I said.

Susie tossed the statements back on the table. "What are you going to do about it?" She turned back to me and raised her hand to stroke my face.

"Dunno yet," I said. "Sleep on it, I suppose."

"Not tonight," she said. I flinched as her fist clenched in my hair.

# seven

Susie left at dawn, sashaying up the street in a way that would have had me chasing after her if I didn't feel as if I'd just done ten rounds with a garden shredder. It was a beautiful summer morning, but the air wasn't as fresh as it could be. Some passer-by had been smoking one of those cheap cigars that smell like burning hair, and the stink was still lingering. I couldn't understand how anyone could smoke so early in the day, but then I couldn't understand why anyone had invented smoking in the first place.

The archive crate holding Zeto's files was still sitting on the table, and I wished Susie had stuck around to help me plough through the reams of notes and interviews Nicky had collected. Why was there so much material anyway? I knew Nicky was thorough, but it seemed way over the top for a straightforward drink-driving offence. I picked up the psychiatric report. At two pages long, it wouldn't take me more than fifteen minutes to read it.

It took me half an hour and at the end I was no wiser. There was a lot of waffle about depression and loss of affect, but nothing specific—it looked as if Zeto hadn't cooperated with the shrink supposed to be helping him. Did he want to be convicted? If he did, why not just plead guilty?

I tossed the report back in the crate and lifted out the mugshot of the case officer, DS Lovegrove. Why did Nicky have his photo on file? Her memory for faces can't have been that bad. I flipped the photo over again and found the phone number.

"Traffic unit."

"Hi, I was looking for Detective Sergeant Lovegrove?"

"Speaking." His voice was gravelly, brisk and impatient.

I should have got my story straight beforehand.

"I'm, er, a colleague of Nicky Hale," I said. "Colleague" was vague enough not to get me into trouble, I hoped.

"Of who, sorry?"

"Nicky Hale. Acting for Reverend Zeto, the drink-driving charge?"

"Zeto . . . OK." There was a pause and scuffle at the other end as if he was settling into a chair and grabbing a pen. "You say you're a colleague of Ms. Hale?"

"That's right. The name's Maguire."

"I understood Ms. Hale was no longer representing Mr. Zeto. That she'd left the country."

"Yes, but we still have some case files here, and there's something . . ." How would a lawyer put it? "There are outstanding issues we need to address. Perhaps we could meet up?" That was a crap idea—I'd have to borrow a suit. And an office.

"How come you have his case files? I thought Zeto was being handled by a different firm."

I tried to sound casual. "We just need to sort out these, em, anomalies first."

There was a brief silence, broken by a soft snarl. "Who the fuck is this?"

I hung up.

I'd known I was winging it, ringing the case officer. I'd expected to be stonewalled or challenged, but even that way I thought I might learn something from their reaction. I had— it felt like I'd poked a pile of straw and felt something huge, vicious and hungry lurking underneath. I wished I'd remembered to withhold my phone number.

Zeto was working the late shift. I could just about make him out through the steamed-up windows of the old café, his fair hair dank with perspiration as he wrestled an empty pan caked with remnants of lasagne out of the rack under the glass counter. Where else would he go? I thought. Suspended from his parish, separated from his family, what has he got to do but this? I suddenly realized that the same logic applied to me.

It was a soft cool summer's evening. The sinking sun made even this dead-end street look picturesque and peaceful, and the semis whistling along the North Circular nearby were already lit up like fairground rides. I could have been down by the river, making a fool of myself chatting up some girl, and instead here I was standing in a disused bus shelter in North London, staring through the windows of a soup kitchen at a washed-up vicar washing up. I didn't even know what I expected to find—I just knew that there was more to his story than anyone was saying, and that DS Lovegrove was a scary creep. I suspected Nicky had sensed that too. And Nicky had vanished.

As had Zeto. I suddenly realized I couldn't see him any more, and that the only figures shifting behind the misty glass were those slight, cheery Christian girls I'd met the other morning. I cursed inwardly—I'd checked the rear entrance when I arrived, and found rubbish piled up against it, so I'd presumed it was disused—but what if that was the wrong back door, and Zeto had sneaked out that way? I had thought of going into the old café, keeping my hoodie pulled up, and tailing him from there, but with my build Zeto would have spotted me easily. Now I wished I'd taken that risk—I'd slogged all the way up here and lounged around for hours for nothing. I was poised to cross the road, go inside and ask for him—say I was a former parishioner, trying to track him down, maybe. They might think I was some hack journo sniffing around for a story, but what did that matter?

Then the wooden gate sealing the alleyway next to the café slowly shuddered and scraped open, and Zeto emerged, pushing a bike ahead of him. He still wore his sweaty T-shirt, but he'd changed into knee-length shorts, and the knotted muscles on his calves told me I was in trouble. I'd known he'd lost his licence and couldn't drive—I'd been counting on it— but I'd presumed he'd walk home, wherever home was now, or maybe catch a bus. Then it would have been simple to follow him. I tried to merge my bulk with the bus shelter as I watched him clip LED lights to his bike, switch them to flash, and strap on his helmet. His bike was old, with deep scratches in its blue paint, but it was light and sleek—a road bike, and it looked fast. He's a bloody vicar, I thought; he should be riding one of those cast-iron pushbikes with a basket on the front, the sort that can only do two miles an hour.

Zeto took his phone out of his pocket, unlocked it and checked the screen. I couldn't tell what he was looking at, a text message or a missed call, but his face registered a sort of sick resignation, like he'd been expecting bad news and had finally received it. He stood there a moment, clearly deciding what to do, then slowly dragged his bike around so it pointed the other way, threw his leg over the saddle, stood on the pedals, and bumped down from the pavement onto the road.

I'd planned to give him a twenty-metre lead if he'd been walking. By the time I'd decided what to do, and took off after him at a jog, he already had a twenty-five-metre lead and was pulling away. He wasn't going to be competing professionally any time soon but he was already pedalling nearly as fast as I could run.

At the end of the street was a four-lane highway with a railing running down the middle to separate the streams of traffic. I turned the corner in time to see Zeto glance over his shoulder, cycle over to a crossing thirty metres away, turn right across the far two lanes and disappear up a leafy avenue. I barely had time to check oncoming traffic as I picked up the pace and tore after him, heading straight across the road and vaulting over the railing in one movement. The car approaching in the near lane was far enough away and I kept running, but the semi overtaking it on the inside was going faster than I'd calculated and the driver punched his horn, nearly deafening me, but barely slowed down. As I leaped for the far curb the stink of diesel filled my lungs and I felt the whirling turbulence of the air the HGV displaced as it roared past, horn still blaring, missing me by inches.

Still running I turned into the avenue, clocking almost unconsciously the signpost announcing it was a cul-de-sac. I kept looking around as I ran—where the hell was Zeto? Row after row of fat, shiny redbrick houses on either side, with neatly trimmed privet hedges and the occasional plume of pampas grass in their front gardens. Spotless brick driveways leading up to mock-Tudor garages too small for modern cars. No people, no bikes, no vicar. My breath was starting to burn in my lungs, and at the end of the road was a long blank stretch of hedge, but I pushed myself to keep going, and saw as I covered the distance that the hedge concealed a park, and that there was a rickety kissing-gate at one end that Zeto must have gone through. He would have had to dismount, I thought, and that would have slowed him down—just for a minute, but it might be enough.

Past the gate and through the hedge the park opened up into a wide vista looking south over London, a grimy pile of bricks in a puddle of smog just starting to twinkle as the city switched its lights on. Paths led off in four directions, right and left, with a fork straight in front of me. I saw a cyclist on the right-hand path in the middle distance, and the flashing of his rear light matched Zeto's, or close enough—he was the only cyclist I could see anyway. I sped after him. He was following the path as it curved around the park, so I sprinted straight across the grass to head him off, but he was cycling downhill on tarmac at full speed, and he vanished round the corner while I was still halfway across the open space.

I kept going, cutting my speed and steadying my pace so I could maintain it for longer. But when I came to the corner there was no sign of Zeto. Two dog-walkers were enjoying the last of the twilight, and a bike heading in my direction wobbled as the old man riding it pumped his way steadily uphill, panting.

My heart sank but I ran on in the direction I had seen Zeto take, rejoining the path that converged now with three others, just inside a park gate opening onto a quiet side road. No sign of Zeto anywhere. Flagging, I staggered to a halt, taking gulps of breath, too exhausted even to curse myself for such a comprehensive waste of time and effort and Tube fare. I stood upright, pondering whether to head back towards the refuge where I'd started, or whether to look for a bus stop nearby that might at least head in the right direction.

Somehow my wobbly legs found the energy to straighten up and walk towards the gate ahead, and as I approached it I noticed a bike chained to the park railings—a dark blue road bike with deep scratches in its paint. Zeto's.

Near the entrance was a stout square redbrick building that had once been a public toilet, and I checked that out first. But it was long since locked up and the windows covered over with metal screens. So where was he? I took shelter behind a tree at the junction of two paths and surveyed the road. There were no parking restrictions along there, from what I could see, so the street was lined with empty parked cars, some of which had been there for months, judging by the layers of bird shit and dust and dead leaves. I scanned each parked car one by one, trying not to be conspicuous, and saw a shiny new saloon just up from the gate, with someone in the front seats. Zeto, in fact. He was in the passenger seat, listening to a bloke behind the wheel—a thickset man whose jowls bulged over the collar of his shirt. I moved closer, keeping the bushes by the park gate in the line of sight so neither of the men in the car would see me approach.

The guy talking to Zeto was the copper in charge of his case, Lovegrove. Whatever he was saying, Zeto looked utterly miserable— ready to climb out and throw himself under a bus, if there had been any buses passing. The two of them must have been discussing the up- coming trial—what else did they have to talk about?—but a car parked in the street seemed an odd place for a police officer to be inter- viewing a defendant. Even if I couldn't hear what they were saying, I could grab some ev- idence of the meeting, I thought, and slipped my phone out of my pocket. The video footage it took would be grainy and soft, especially in this failing light, but if it registered Zeto and Lovegrove that would be enough to make it useful.

The lens picked them up OK, although the focus went a bit wonky when leaves of the bush concealing me got into frame. I lifted the phone higher, and suddenly there they were, Lovegrove and Zeto, clear and sharp on my screen. And then Zeto bent over out of sight, with his head in Lovegrove's lap, and Lovegrove tilted his head back and closed his eyes like he was listening to rapturous music.

*Holy crap.*

I remembered all the blokes in shabby over-coats who used to slip into the toilets at the back of the snooker hall where those scrawny smackhead teenage boys hung out. I never saw what went on in there, but my mates explained it to me. And what they'd described was this.

"Reverend?"

Zeto had just finished unlocking his bike, and straightened up in surprise with the bulky chain in his hand. I kept my distance: he didn't look like the type who would take a swing at me, but then the Reverend Zeto was proving to be full of surprises. I threw back the hood of my sweatshirt so I'd look less threatening, and kept my hands relaxed by my sides. But anger and guilt and fear still fought in Zeto's face, as he tried to figure out where I'd come from, how long I'd been there and how much I'd seen. Then he recognized me from my visit to his soup kitchen, and relaxed slightly.

"You again," he said. "Look, I've already told you, I don't know anything about Nicky Hale or where she went. I'm sorry, I really can't help you." He fumbled with his bike lights, his hands shaking too much to mount them on their clips.

"That's too bad. Maybe I should ask DS Lovegrove." I saw the colour drain from Zeto's face, and he stopped messing about with his bike lights. I pretended to look for the sleek saloon that had sped off into the dusk a few minutes earlier. "Oops, too late, he's gone. I'll have to give him a call at the station."

Zeto's lips moved but no words came out.

"It's a pity Nicky's gone missing," I said. "If you're being interviewed by the police, you really should have a lawyer present. Don't want them putting words in your mouth." *Don't want them putting anything in your mouth*, I was going to add. But Zeto was wilting now like a dried-out plant, and I was starting to feel like a bully, and I hated bullies.

"You didn't—I wasn't—" he started to protest feebly.

"Look, Reverend," I said, "I don't give a crap if you're gay. It's nobody's business but yours—"

"It's not like that! I'm not gay!" His voice was choked with fear and anger.

"OK," I said. I don't think I sounded convinced.

"I'm not. He takes advantage, of my . . ." He stuttered to a halt, then blurted, "I found myself in an unfortunate situation . . . it was a simple misunderstanding, that's all. And he's exploiting that."

"Did you tell Nicky Hale all that?"

"Of course not! Why should I? The question never arose!"

But she suspected something, I thought. That's why she kept digging, gathering evidence. The reaction of the squatter with the burned face, when I asked if he was a member of Zeto's congregation, made sense now. He thought I was taking the piss, asking if he and Zeto had ever been lovers. He had known the truth about Zeto, even if Zeto himself didn't want to.

Now Zeto had grasped that I wasn't there to hurt him, he let himself get angry, tugging his bike upright and swinging it round. Well, he was going for angry, but it just came across as petulant. I took a few steps forward to stand in his way, and he nearly ran his front mudguard into my crotch.

"What exactly was this unfortunate situation?" I said.

He glared at me, trying to look fierce. "I don't want to talk about it."

"I noticed," I said, and reaching out gripped his handlebars and held them. I hated bullies, true, but Nicky had clearly tried being nice to him, and got nowhere. Zeto glared at me some more, and I stared back at him, and he blinked and looked down.

"There was a boy in my parish—not a boy, a teenager . . . about your age. He was from a—problem family. He came to me for advice, for counselling, but he wouldn't listen to anything

I said, kept insisting it was me who was— confused, not him. And when I suggested he seek help elsewhere, he . . ."

"Took it badly?"

"He said he'd expose me. Slander me, say I'd assaulted him."

"Could he prove anything?"

"He didn't have to." Zeto's voice trembled, and I sensed the black despair that had sent him the wrong way down the motorway. "Nothing improper occurred," he insisted lamely. "But— once an accusation like that is made, a man in my position . . . people assume the worst."

"Mud sticks," I said.

Zeto nodded, I think because he couldn't talk. After what I'd just witnessed happening in Lovegrove's car, I didn't entirely believe Zeto's version of events, but it didn't matter. Zeto seemed to believe it. I was willing to bet that even if this kid had produced a high-definition video of whatever it was Zeto had got up to, Zeto would go on denying the truth, claiming it was all CGI and fancy editing. But that part wasn't important any more.

"And you didn't tell Nicky any of this?"

"She asked me to undergo psychiatric

evaluation." He sounded almost offended. "But why would I talk to a psychiatrist about someone else's sick, ridiculous fantasy?" That explained the empty report.

"And Lovegrove found out?" I said.

"He interviewed me right after—my motorway accident." The suicide attempt, I wanted to say, but Zeto was so determined to deny everything it would have been like waking a sleepwalker. "It was totally improper, I was in shock," went on Zeto. "There was no lawyer present. I confided in Lovegrove, and . . ."

"He took advantage?"

"He offered to straighten everything out. Arrange to misfile the blood test results, to speak to the boy who'd made the accusation, and I thought—I thought it would all go away."

"Obviously he was lying."

"My wife somehow found out, about the boy's accusations, and she left. And Lovegrove keeps asking to meet me, to discuss the case, claims there's a problem that needs to be dealt with, and it always comes down to—"

Rape, I thought. Maybe not the exact legal definition of it, but ultimately that's what it was: sex by coercion. By the sound of it Lovegrove was locked in the closet, just like the reverend—he was getting off on the power he had over Zeto, and forced blowjobs were his way of demonstrating it. And Zeto was so scared of the truth—of everyone else knowing it, of knowing it himself—that he had been going along with it.

I took my hand off the handlebars and stood aside. Zeto stood there like he was waiting for me to give him permission to leave, and I felt a twinge of shame at being one more big thug he had to placate. In the dim distance what sounded like a cracked church bell started ringing.

"That means they're locking the gates," said Zeto.

"We'd better leave, then," I said. "Don't want to get stuck in here all night, never know what sort of pervs we'll bump into."

He didn't laugh—maybe he thought I was serious—but he seemed to loosen up a bit. He wheeled his bike towards the gate and I walked alongside him.

"Did Nicky say anything to you about Love-grove?" I said.

"She didn't like him very much," said Zeto.

That didn't surprise me—I'd never met the guy, and I loathed him. "I know she was asking questions about him, about his record."

That would explain the photo of Lovegrove in Zeto's file. At the same time it occurred to me that if Nicky had been asking questions about Lovegrove, maybe Lovegrove had got to hear about it. He had had as much to lose as Zeto if the truth came out—more, since he was a copper. Yeah, the Met was supposedly all diverse and inclusive these days—if you believed their PR—but Lovegrove's little sideline would almost certainly land him in prison, where tolerance for gay ex-coppers was in extremely short supply.

I wondered where Lovegrove had been the night Nicky left the country, and whether her black eye had been a parting gift from him.

Zeto hesitated before climbing onto his bike. "I'd be grateful if you didn't mention anything that happened this evening to anyone," he said hesitantly.

I'm sure you would, I thought. I had no intention of telling anybody, but I didn't say that, because I'd just remembered something else that had been bugging me.

"Can I ask how Nicky came to be your solicitor anyway?" I said.

"I was her vicar for a while. In fact, I married her and Harry," Zeto said, with a touch of pride that sounded odd in the circumstances. When I said nothing he went on, "She came to me for counselling." I still said nothing. Zeto was getting worried, I realized, because I hadn't promised to keep his secret, and it seemed the less I said the more eager he was to volunteer.

"She had a, a relative," stammered Zeto, "with a drug problem."

You mean a husband, I thought. But this little lie was Zeto's way of convincing himself he hadn't betrayed a confidence. I still said nothing.

"He was a gambler too," said Zeto, "and got badly into debt."

He finally clammed up, clearly feeling he'd given away too much and got nothing in return. I didn't speak, this time because my mind was racing—Anderson was a gambler? Those transactions on his credit card statement, thirty grand in less than a fortnight—they must have been bets, or purchases of chips from a casino.

"And when all this happened," went on Zeto, "Nicky was the first person I thought of. I found it hard to believe she'd simply walked out like that."

"So did I," I said.

"I mean, she seemed so reliable. So hard-working, so . . . discreet." He fastened the strap of his helmet, avoiding my eye, but I knew what he was getting at.

"I liked her too, Reverend," I said. "Everything you've told me, it's just between you and me and DS Lovegrove. I promise."

He nodded, still not meeting my eye. I suppose he was trying to calculate how much my promise was worth. Then he threw his leg over the saddle of his bike and set off without another word.

I watched his lights flash and fade into the distance and vanish. Damn, I was miles from home, soaked in sweat, and I had no idea where the nearest Tube station was, or even in which direction. I decided to go back to the one nearest the soup kitchen, and that if I ran it would warm up my clammy clothes and help me figure out what to do next.

# eight

As I walked into my room my mobile twitched in my pocket and started to ring. I took it out and answered it without checking the caller's ID.

"Yeah?" I said.

"Are you ever going to get a proper entry-phone?" said Susan.

There were no apologies or explanations; she didn't even stop to ask how my day had been—she just pounced on me. My heel snagged on the rug and I went over backwards and instantly she was on me like a crazed animal, and my shirt buttons went flying, and moments later so did hers.

\* \* \*

Night had fallen by the time we called a truce, but there was just enough light trickling through the curtains for me to make out her shape in the darkness. She was lying face down, hugging her pillow, and I felt rather than saw the thin sheen of perspiration on her soft smooth skin.

"Who were you with?" I said. "When I called that time?"

"Friends," she said. "I do have some."

"Any of them your boyfriend?" I said. She snorted softly, and I didn't know whether she was laughing at me, or at the term "boyfriend" or at the whole idea of commitment.

"I'm not sure that's any of your business," she said.

"I'm sure it isn't," I said.

"I'm on the rebound," she said. "He was a total bastard."

"But not in a good way?"

"In a married way."

"Ah."

"Does that bother you?" she said. It sounded like a trick question. Was she asking me to pass judgement, or trying to find out if I cared? I didn't know how I felt about it, but should I admit that, or would she rather hear some re-assuring lie? I felt way outclassed again; fighting was straightforward compared to this.

"Sounds complicated," I said finally, and thought, Whew, dodged that bullet. But the way she tensed in the dark suggested I hadn't dodged it at all, that in fact I was bleeding profusely and just didn't know it yet.

"It wasn't that complicated. I wanted him, but he wanted a mistress. To go with his car and his expense account and his place in France." She sounded deeply bitter and I wondered how often she'd flayed herself like this. "It's over now anyway." She didn't sound relieved.

"Has it been over before?"

She lay silent so long I wondered if she was going to get up, gather her clothes and walk out. But she finally spoke, so softly I could barely hear her.

"A few times. I never want to go there again."

Then don't, I thought. But I didn't say it. I wasn't in any position to tell her what to do, when it was my daft crush on Nicky that had helped get me into this mess. Both of us were lying here for pretty screwed-up reasons, but saying that out loud would only have blown the moment. When you've nothing to say, say nothing, my dad always told me. Everyone will suppose you're deep and thoughtful even when really you don't have a clue.

"What was your day like?" Susan said. It was a clunky way to change the subject, but I could hardly blame her.

"Interesting," I said. I was calculating how much I could say without breaking my promise to Zeto. Even if I wasn't sure he'd keep quiet about me, I wasn't going to wave his dirty laundry just to impress Susan.

"That picture in Nicky's files, of the copper in the drink-driving case," I said. "I'm pretty sure he's on the take."

"Seriously?"

"And I'm pretty sure Nicky knew about it."

"You think he might have been the one who threatened her, sent her those messages? So she'd leave the country?"

"It's possible, yeah."

"If he knew she was on to him—could he find out who you are?"

I hadn't thought of that. It occurred to me now I should have made Zeto make the same promise as me—that he wouldn't tell anyone about our conversation. The only person he'd be likely to tell, of course, was Lovegrove, and a guy as desperate to keep his secrets as Zeto might decide the copper was the nearest thing he had to a friend. Lovegrove had as much at stake as he did, after all. Maybe Zeto didn't know much about me, but then I had called Lovegrove this afternoon and asked questions, and even a traffic copper can put two and two together, given the right motivation.

"We'll see, I suppose," I said.

Susie's hand covered mine, and her breathing slowed, and the darkness crept over both of us, and the rumble of the night buses in the streets below faded to a sound like the sea.

It was the bitter smell that woke me up, catching at the back of my throat. Burning hair, I thought, and I opened my eyes. It was still dark, but something had changed about the texture of the darkness—it seemed to billow and shift like ghosts were hovering over my bed. And it wasn't just a smell in the air—the air itself was rancid and sour in my mouth, and in the distance I heard a window breaking and a whump like a huge heavy blanket being flapped, and suddenly I knew what was happening. I grabbed Susan and shook her.

"Susie. Susie—!"

I saw the outline of her head as she raised it from the pillow. She looked around sleepily and coughed.

"There's a fire," I said. "The building's on fire—!"

She scrambled out of bed while I fumbled for the switch of my bedside lamp still lying on the floor in bits. When it flickered into life my guts turned liquid with fear. Black smoke was billowing under the door and seeping through cracks in the floorboards, and every mouthful was like acid. I suddenly remembered the second-hand furniture store on the ground floor, a hotchpotch of old vinyl armchairs and sofas packed with polyurethane foam, materials that had been banned years ago because of the toxic fumes they gave off when they caught fire. And now all that plastic was blazing below us, and we were in a gas chamber twenty metres above ground level with a wooden floor that was already growing warm under my bare feet.

Susan had tugged on her jeans and the nearest T-shirt she could find and was pushing her feet sockless into tight boots, swearing under her breath, and I could hear her voice tremble. I too dressed as quickly as I could, pulling on trainers, picking up a jumper and then throwing it aside when I realized it was acrylic. If—when—acrylic catches fire it melts onto your skin, and when they take it off your skin comes with it. I found a woollen jumper full of holes and smelling of old sheep, tugged it on, and turned just in time to see Susan reach for the door handle.

"No—!"

The handle was already hot, and she snatched her fingers away. But she tugged her sleeve down over her hand and reached for the knob again but I pulled her back from the door.

"Don't open that door! We'll be dead in seconds!"

I realized I was shouting now, that the distant roaring had grown closer, and was now punctuated by the tinkle of windows exploding outwards and falling in fragments down to the street.

Dragging her by the hand I rushed into the bathroom, fumbled the plug into the plughole and turned the taps on full. The towels hanging off the back of the door hadn't been washed in a few weeks, but that hardly mattered now. I grabbed them and threw them into the tub, calculating that soaked in water they would seal the door of the bathroom and keep the toxic fumes out for a while at least. But even as I pushed the towels into the water I saw the door wasn't going to be the problem. The bathroom floor was covered in vinyl, but the air in the room was already hot and sharp and stung the eyes. I looked around and saw that smoke was seeping—no, gushing now—from around the bath. The floor directly underneath the tub, I realized, must have been bare boards, and the smoke from below was coming up through the cracks.

I tugged my mobile from my pocket and pushed it into Susan's hand shouting, "Call nine-nine-nine!" As she stabbed the keys, blinking back tears of pain, I dashed to the window and unscrewed the latch. I knew there was nothing out there but a twenty-metre drop to the concrete pavement below, and only Spider-Man could get out that way, but the fire brigade might have a ladder that could reach us—presuming they got in here in time. I heard Susan trying to talk into the phone, but coughing so badly she could barely speak, and that made me realize I'd been holding my breath. I tried to take air in slowly, through my nose, but my eyes immediately flooded with tears and the smoke seared my lungs. I stuck my head out of the window, but that didn't help—flames were surging through the window frame directly below and the heat rising up was blistering the paint on the windowsill outside our bathroom.

Susan shoved the phone back at me, screaming something, but I couldn't make out what she was saying, and from the look of terror on her reddened, soot-smeared face I guessed what she had said hadn't made much sense anyway. I dragged her over to the bath, grabbed a soaking towel and wiped her face with it. She stopped coughing momentarily, but now I could see she was crying with fear, and I hugged her close.

"Here," I shouted, grabbing the soaking hand towel, wrapping it round her face, and fumbling to tie a rough knot at the back. "It'll help you breathe," I tried to shout, but my mouth and throat were so scorched with fumes I could hardly get the words out. I grabbed a wet flannel from the bathtub and clamped it over my mouth before turning to the door and touching the handle, praying it wouldn't sear my hand. It was hot, but bearable, and I grabbed it, turned it and yanked the door open.

My bedroom was now so full of black smoke I could hardly see across it. The sodium light from the street lamps and the flames refracted from below lit black pillars of fumes that coiled and seethed like fat snakes writhing in a pit. The room was filling with toxic gas from the ceiling downwards, and the light from my bedside lamp was fading and faltering as the lethal black smoke crept closer and closer to the floor. Susan resisted as I pulled her through the doorway, as if she wanted us to turn back and lock ourselves in the bathroom, but I knew there was no hope for us in there. I had planned to try the door to the stairs again— maybe I had been too quick earlier to assume the stairwell was on fire. But without opening the door I knew that if I'd been wrong then, I wasn't wrong now. Smoke wasn't just pouring under and round and over the door—it was leaching from the door itself. I could feel the heat coming off the wood in waves, and knew it would burst into flames at any moment.

Susan was sobbing through her towel, and her nails were digging into my arm again, in terror rather than passion. I stood there, lost, my head spinning, and I turned to look around, and I cracked my head on the sloping ceiling and cursed. And suddenly I knew what I had to do.

I dropped the wet flannel that had been over my mouth, threw off Susan's arm and punched the plaster panelling in front of my face. It was as solid and unyielding as brick and it nearly broke my hand. I yelled in frustration, then realized I had been panicking—for Christ's sake, think straight! I moved my aim a little to the right, and punched again, and this time felt the plasterboard flex under my fist. My first blow had hit a hidden rafter, but now I threw punch after punch, like it was my last stand, determined to go down all guns blazing, though by now my lungs were burning and my eyes streaming and the strength was fading from my arms. Through the darkness and the thick, oily smoke I felt Susan push past me and start to pull at the edges of the hole I'd knocked in the plaster, bringing down cascades of ancient filthy dust and cobwebs that fell on our faces and got into our eyes. I clenched my eyes shut and clamped my mouth tight as I scrabbled too, ripping away horsehair padding and rotten felt until my fingers felt rough wooden battens running horizontally, and beyond them cool smooth slate. I slammed my fist into the slates and felt the thin stone shatter like glass even as it split my knuckles. But one hand was out, clawing in the cold clear air above the roof.

Frenzied now, we snatched and pulled and pushed and ripped, ignoring the dust and the splinters and the razor-sharp shards of slate, feeling the viscous, poisonous heat in the room gush past us into the night, as hungry as we were for oxygen. The draught grew stronger and stronger, sending the dust we had dislodged flying upwards until it felt like we were wedged in the chimney of an incinerator. I could feel the hairs on my legs curl and singe, and the skin scorch, but I pulled back from the hole in the roof, grabbed Susan and shoved her upwards. The towel round her face snagged on the broken battens and she tugged at it. I grabbed it, pulled it up and free of her head, and manhandled her out into the night—only to see her sliding downwards, screaming hoarsely.

I scrambled after her, somehow gripping the roof's rough edge with my stomach, and unthinkingly flinging something towards her—the damp towel she had worn over her mouth. She grabbed it with both hands, her knuckles turning white, and waited, eyes shut and face turned upwards, as I climbed after her, through the hole, one hand clenched on the towel, the other fumbling upwards to the ridge tiles of the roof. Now I could make out sirens boiling to a frenzy as the fire engines pulled up in the street below. The racket mingled with the roar of the inferno and the peal of shattering glass, and the tongues of flame in the smoke around us merged and fought with the flickering blue light of the fire trucks like demons at war. Finally my left hand grabbed the ridge of the roof, and my right gripped the towel so hard my nails dug welts into my palm, and I folded my body together somehow, slowly pulling Susan up from the sagging gutter towards me. Ten centimetres from the apex she threw a hand out and grasped the ridge tiles herself, and her smooth-soled boots somehow managed to grip the slate, and she pushed herself upwards to straddle the roof.

We were more than twenty metres above the street, with nothing between us and the drop but a short slate ramp slick with moss, and we could feel the heat underneath us and the judders of the building as the inner walls tumbled and crashed through the blazing floor into the cauldron of molten plastic below. And Susan smiled at me, coughing, because now we could breathe, and we had won maybe sixty seconds before the roof we were perched on would start to burn. But sixty seconds was enough. We could creep like scorched slugs along the ridge towards the eaves, where the blank wall dropped two metres to the flat roof of the building next door.

And that's what we did.

\* \* \*

I've never liked hospitals at any time of day, but on this particular morning the local accident and emergency unit was empty, apart from a frazzled young couple fretting over a fat bald two-year-old who seemed perfectly happy to me. A nurse wearing spectacles held together with the traditional Band-Aid—he told me a drunk had knocked them off his face the night before—patched up the cuts to my hands, fed me sips of water and gently sponged me clean of grit, soot and scorched crumbs of slate. I sat there in a daze, gazing upwards through the skylight at dawn creeping through the sky, dissolving the stars and diluting the black to a pale, peaceful luminous blue.

The curtains around my cubicle were pulled back, but instead of the strung-out skinny doctor who'd checked me out earlier, Susan appeared, in a flimsy hospital gown that left little to the imagination. It seemed incongruous to get steamed up at the sight of a girl so soon after we were nearly barbecued, but I'd heard it was a common reaction to near-death experiences. It seemed to be true in my case, and hers, because she slid her arms around my neck and her tongue into my mouth almost before the nurse had time to make a retreat. My arms went round her slim, firm waist, and I pressed her body against mine, and a shudder of desire ran back and forward through both of us like an electric shock. She pulled away and looked into my eyes. I never know which eye to look in when a girl does that to me.

"Thank you, Finn," she said.

"No. Thank you," I said. "For an unforgettable evening."

"Will you do me a favour?" she said.

"Right now, anything."

"Will you stop chasing after Nicky?"

I hesitated, not sure I'd heard her right.

"You know that fire can't have been a coincidence. Nicky obviously found out something she shouldn't—maybe about that policeman—and she ran. She's not a coward, and she's not stupid, but she left, and she doesn't want to be found." She grabbed my face with her hands. "Please, let her go, forget about her. You'll get your compensation, you'll get your life back. Keep asking all these questions—I'm scared you'll lose everything."

She kissed me, and the electricity ran tingling through my body, and it went on and on, and I let it. When she pulled away her eyes were full of tears.

"Susie, I can't," I said. "Nicky was a friend of mine, and someone hurt her, and I'm not going to let that go. I have to know who did it—maybe it was Lovegrove, maybe it wasn't—and I have to know why. Nobody else is going to try, so . . . I'm sorry."

Her face showed a tumult of emotions—anger, exasperation, fear, and something else that I thought might be jealousy. And I could think of no way to persuade her to feel otherwise, so I didn't try.

"I'm going to get dressed," she said, turning to leave.

"I'll see you later," I said.

"No, Finn, you won't." With a bitter glance over her shoulder she pushed through the curtains and disappeared.

You rarely see burned-out buildings in London, so you don't realize how much mess a fire makes, or how that mess is made a million times worse by the oceans of water firefighters pump onto it. My home and my business was now a blackened shell, and I could see the sky through the charred timbers of the roof where Susie and I had felt so safe a few hours earlier. Long tongues of grime licked upwards from every window opening, and the empty frames were charcoal. Through them you could see the ground floor where my gym equipment was steaming gently—a scorched, worthless mess of metal tangled up with blackened sofa springs and flaps of wet leather. Burned plaster had been washed over the pavement into the gutter and across the road. It crunched underfoot, and it stank, with an acrid odour of rot that went right up my nose like a rusty bedspring.

The road nearest the gym had been closed, and red and white plastic tape cordoned it off from pedestrians. The Saturday morning traffic was beginning to build up, drivers parping their horns and saluting each other with single fingers as they jostled for precedence. They barely threw a second glance at the wrecked building where I and Susan had nearly burned alive.

"Sorry, mate, you can't go through there," said a lanky red-haired firefighter, as I ducked under the cordon tape. He was wearing one of those dusky pink fire-resistant overalls and carrying his helmet under his arm. I wondered if male firefighters miss the huge yellow helmets and black woolly coats they used to wear. Surely they couldn't pull the same number of groupies wearing gear that made them look like glorified plumbers?

"I lived here," I said. "Top floor."

"Oh, that was you?" he said. "How's the girlfriend?"

"Not impressed."

"She should be. You're both bloody lucky to be alive."

"Don't think it was luck," I said. "I think it was you guys."

"You're welcome. Made a change anyway—we haven't had a good blow-up in weeks."

"Can I take a look?"

"Long as you don't get too close. There's not much to salvage, if that's what you're after. Sorry."

Someone called his name and he turned away. As I crunched over the muck and cinders that littered the tarmac, the other firefighters ignored me and carried on rolling up their hoses and sweeping the crumbs of wreckage into soggy black piles. Even now I could see wisps of smoke and feel the heat from the embers through the soles of my trainers, and I suddenly realized that I too could have been inside that incinerator, a charred heap of bones and teeth mixed in with all that tortured metal and damp ash.

Of the four tenders I had seen hosing down the inferno when the ambulance took me and Susan away there were only two left, and now one of them was revving up its engine. I watched it move off with a quick ear-piercing burst of siren to cut a hole in the traffic. Nearby, a chunky four-wheel drive vehicle was parked half on the curb, splashed with the hi-viz red livery of the fire brigade, with some writing on the side. I didn't bother to read it—I guessed it was the officer whose job it was to establish the cause of the fire. In fact, I could see him now, stooping at what used to be my doorway and taking photographs with a standard digital camera. On the tarmac behind him was another heap of rubble, and something glinted in it, something that didn't look as if it had belonged either in my gym or in the furniture store. I picked it up and peered at it: it was a circle of gold wire with a few purple beads on it. I scraped at them with a thumbnail.

"Could you keep your distance please—this building's not safe." The fire officer had turned from the door and noticed me. I slipped the wire into my pocket. "In fact you should be on the other side of the tape, sir."

"I used to live here," I said.

"I'm sorry about that, but you will have to retire to a safe distance." He was short and stout with neatly clipped hair, and I guessed he spoke that way because instead of a personality he had a health and safety manual. What was he like at home? I wondered. Did he disinfect his lips after kissing his kids?

"Have you found out what caused it yet?"

"It's far too early to reach any conclusions, sir. Now if you don't mind—"

Maybe I could have been a fire safety officer, because I had already reached a preliminary conclusion using standard issue equipment—namely my nose. Even now, hours after the fire, I could smell the sharp chemical tang of petrol. The front doors that had opened onto the staircase were bulging and sagging on their hinges, but they were still tightly shut. They seemed almost fused into the doorframe and the threshold. The fire safety officer had opened his arms to shoo me away like I was a stray dog trying to steal his sandwiches.

"I think someone was trying to kill me," I said.

"Sorry, sir, we need to keep this area clear. I can't discuss any of my findings at this stage."

"That's why they screwed the doors shut, so I wouldn't be able to get out," I said. That shut him up, and I knew my guess had been right. The same trick had been used by whoever had torched the old pub where Alan Leslie had taken shelter with his boyfriend. I could have ended up like one of them—scarred for life, or mixed with landfill.

"Sir," insisted the fire officer. "If you don't clear the area I'll have to—"

"Yeah, yeah, I got it," I said. I walked away with my hands in my pockets, fingering that bent beaded piece of wire. I remembered now where I'd seen it before, but I wasn't about to tell that pompous jerk of a fire safety officer about it—not just yet.

This had nothing to do with Detective Sergeant Lovegrove.

As I crossed the road and headed east towards the Tube station I checked my phone. Fourteen per cent charge left. All my phone chargers were melted lumps of clag now, of course, at the bottom of a smouldering brick pit. And suddenly I realized everything else was in there too: my laptop, my paperwork, my family photos . . . and Nicky's copied files. All of it had gone for ever, leaving me just the clothes I stood up in. Even the tired anorak I was wearing had been donated to me by the hospital—I hadn't wanted to know where they'd got it from. And only now, looking back at the gaunt blackened shell of the place where I'd lived, did it occur to me to wonder where I would sleep that night.

But as my dad would have said, look on the bright side. I still had my mobile, and all the information on it. I picked a number from my contacts, and pressed "dial."

"Zoe, hi," I said. "Yeah, I know how early it is. How are you getting on with that phone?"

# nine

It had started raining by the time I got to Bisham's house, and water was running down its front wall where the guttering had fallen away. I jogged up to the door and huddled in the shallow porch. That's what it meant to be homeless, I saw now; if I got soaked or filthy, I'd have nowhere to dry off and no clean clothes to change into. But that mattered less to me at that moment than getting the truth out of that demented Bisham.

When she opened her front door her face registered plenty of annoyance but not a trace of fear or guilt. Then again, anyone nuts enough to murder by arson wouldn't react like a normal human being. My own face must have registered plenty of anger, because she stepped back to slam the door, only to have it bounce off my foot as I stepped inside the hall. Ever helpful, I took hold of the door and slammed it for her.

"Get out of my house," she said.

"I think this belongs to you," I said. I held up the bent golden wire with the scorched purple beads. Where my thumbnail had cut into them they gleamed blue, the same shade as the beads she'd been wearing last time I called. Bisham looked confused and tried to snatch the earring from me, but I pulled my hand away. "I found it near the front door of my home," I said. "Or what's left of my home. Next time you torch a place, don't wear clip-on earrings."

"What?" she said. "Piss off!" She actually managed to sound indignant.

"Is that what Nicky found out?" I said. "That you burned that pub down and killed that squatter, and made it look like your husband did it?"

"You're talking bull!" she spat.

"Who did you send to scare Nicky into leaving," I said, "when those obscene texts and the sick tweets and the threatening emails didn't work? Do you have someone on the company payroll for jobs like that?"

Cornered now, Bisham came back at me, snapping in my face like a rabid dog. "I said, piss off! I never sent her any texts or twitters or whatever the hell it is you're talking about—"

"I had a friend check, an IT expert," I said. "The IP address of the sender resolves to this house—"

"The IP what?" For the first time she seemed rattled.

"The address of your Internet connection," I said. "It leads right back to you, just like this earring does."

"How did you get hold of that?" Bisham came back. "That was a present from my—"

Abruptly she clamped her mouth shut, and stared at me. I could see calculation cross her face, as if she was working out whether to placate me or get rid of me or try to bribe me somehow. That was when I knew I had her wrong. In the kitchen a glint of blue light from the wireless camera caught my eye, and from outside I heard the faint bong of a footstep on a metal staircase. I turned and bolted back out the front door.

Bisham's son had scurried unseen down an ancient fire escape at the back of the house, but he wasn't headed for the front gate—he was running for a corner of the muddy overgrown garden. I guessed there was a hole in the fence among the bushes, a way out his mother didn't know about, but he never made it that far, because the podgy little bastard couldn't run to save his life. He had barely reached the hedge when I brought him down hard, flat on his face into the rotting leaves and chipped bark. He yelped and screamed incoherently as I dragged him upright and hopped him, with his arm halfway up his back, towards his mother's house.

Joan Bisham stood white-faced and shaking with shock in her disgusting kitchen, while Gabe Bisham sat at the table sulking. He seemed insulted that he'd been caught by someone he considered a moron, but then he probably considered everyone he knew a moron, compared to him. Underneath his bratty screw-you defiance was a smugness, like no one would ever believe he was guilty. Maybe he was right—if he hadn't tried to run I'd never have guessed that this pasty, obese slob was a killer.

It was clear his mother had no idea how her son liked to spend his spare time, but I did—I'd read the threats and insults he'd sent to Nicky, and to his mother. The sewers of the Internet were full of paranoid hate-spewing wankers, and Gabriel Bisham was one of them.

"Where's my blue earrings, Gabe?" His mother wanted to sound calm but her voice was stretched tight as a drum skin ready to split. "The clip-on pair you bought me for my last birthday. Gold with blue beads."

"Uhuhuh," said Gabe, shrugging. I recognized the teenage term for "I dunno." I'd used it myself on my dad when I didn't want to talk, and now I knew why it had always infuriated him.

"I've been all through my jewellery twice: they're not there. I was wearing them the other day." She was appealing to her son for any explanation less awful than the truth.

"He's hidden the other one," I said. "It would have turned up when the police came to search this place." I took the twisted golden wire from my pocket and tossed it onto the table. "This one still has your DNA on it, and that would have been all they needed to charge you with arson and murder."

Gabe looked at me with a sneer. "Why would the police even search this house?" He was trying to snarl but it came out like a whine.

"Because you'd tip them off," I said. "With an anonymous message. You're good at those, but not that good. What do they call guys like you, copying hackers' tricks off the Internet? Oh yeah—script kiddies."

"Fuck off," snarled Gabe. Now we were getting closer to the real him.

"Gabe!" his mother cut in. Christ, I thought, she's worried about his language? She really hasn't thought this through.

"It wasn't your husband who sent those texts," I said. "It was your little boy, Gabriel."

"But why? Gabe?"

"Because he gets off on it," I said. "He's been manipulating both of you for years. He got your husband sent to prison, and you would have been next, and he would have been free." Social Services wouldn't have had a hope of controlling him, I knew. They would have had no idea what sort of creep he was—any more than his mother did, even now.

"I'm sorry, Gabriel. I'm sorry if I wasn't there for you. I'll get you help, I promise."

The way she talked it was as if I'd caught him shoplifting chocolate. He doesn't need help, I thought. He needs sedation and a home where he can't sneak out at night and burn people alive while he watches, fondling himself.

"Mrs. Bisham, it was Gabriel who burned down that pub. Where that squatter died. He tried the same stunt again last night, and I only just made it out alive."

"It can't have been Gabe—he's only fifteen, for God's sake—"

When I was fourteen and coming up for trial I'd been assessed by psychologists, and now I remembered all the questions they had asked.

"When Gabriel was young, were there any unexplained fires at your home?"

"No," she said. "Nothing out of the ordinary."

"What about the cat?" I said. "The one that got doused in lighter fuel?"

Bisham's hand flew to cover her mouth, but her son merely giggled.

"He's accused me of murdering someone, and you're upset about that stupid cat? Priceless."

She looked at him in disbelief, as if she'd given birth to a baby that was inside out but still alive somehow. Then she steadied herself, and tidied her clothes, and stood up straight. I realized the veneer of the hard-nosed businesswoman was all that was holding her together. She was pretending to herself that this had been a particularly challenging human resources problem, but now the issues had been identified we could address them and move on.

"Thanks, Finn," she said. "Would you let me deal with this?"

"How?" I said. I didn't say, *Your son's a psychopath. They set fires, torture animals, and from there they graduate to murder. You can't fix this by grounding him.*

"I'm going to call the police," she said. "And we'll face them together." She actually put her hand on her son's shoulder to reassure him.

245

Gabe had stopped smirking, I noticed, and wore the expression of a kid lost at an amusement park.

"I'm sorry, Mum," he said. "I never meant to hurt you, or anyone." It was the least convincing performance I'd ever seen, but it seemed to satisfy his mother.

"Where did Nicky Hale go?" I asked him.

He smiled at me and sighed, as if he had genuinely liked her. "Who gives a toss?" he said. And I thought about Nicky, and the torrent of crap he had sent her way. Gabe Bisham had tormented her as if she had been a small animal, but at a safe distance—if he had tried anything face to face, Nicky would have crippled him. It wasn't Gabriel who had hurt her physically, or any friend of his. I doubted he even had any real-life friends . . . although he'd probably make a few in prison.

The phone in my pocket shivered and started to ring. I'd thought it had died hours ago. I answered it, my gaze locked on the brat.

"Finn Maguire," I said.

"Hello, Mr. Maguire." It was a woman's voice, soft yet brisk. "We've been given your name as next of kin."

"Sorry—who did?"

"There was a road traffic accident this morning, involving a Mr. and Mrs. Llewellyn?"

I was miles from home—not that I had a home any more—so I caught a passing bus, but it moved more like a hearse. At every stop some parent got a baby buggy jammed in the door, or some pensioner had to root for a bus pass at the bottom of their tartan shopping bag, and before long I was wishing I'd tried running all the way. Eventually the hospital loomed ahead, the same grey hodgepodge of concrete boxes I'd been so glad to leave that morning after Susie said goodbye. As yet another teenage mum wrestled her buggy and brats and her shopping towards the doors I dashed in front of her and hit the pavement running.

I didn't stop to try reading the signs in the hospital grounds, but headed straight back to casualty. It wasn't empty now: it was late morning on a Saturday, and the waiting room was packed with crippled weekend footballers and amateur DIYers who'd drilled holes through their hands. Eventually I learned that

Winnie and Delroy were upstairs in the HDU, whatever that was, and I ran for the lift.

Like the bus the lift seemed to stop at every opportunity to slowly empty and refill with overworked staff and confused punters. I tried not to curse under my breath every time someone pushed the "door open" button to let extra passengers aboard. The doctor who'd called me on my mobile had been vague, and I wasn't sure what I was going to find, but my sense of dread grew deeper as the lift stuttered slowly upwards.

HDU was on the seventh. I checked the sign facing the elevator as I stepped out, and paused to work my way through the wording. High, Dependency, Unit. Male wards to the left, female to the right. I looked around for a nurse or a workstation.

Delroy was sitting by Winnie's bed, his crutch lying on the floor by his chair where he had let it fall. He held Winnie's right hand in both of his, and his head was bowed, and his lips were moving. If he was praying, it was bad, because he'd sworn Winnie would never catch him praying. But for now his wife was unconscious and perfectly still, lying on her back with her hands loosely by her sides and a clear mask over her nose and mouth. Breathing gear hissed and clicked by her bedside, and machines with digital numbers glowing green pumped plasma and colourless liquid into shunts in her left arm. When I looked at her my throat tightened, because her face was horribly discoloured and swollen where it wasn't concealed by bandages or the oxygen mask. Delroy's left wrist was in a cast, I saw, when I reached out and touched his massive right arm.

"Delroy, hey."

He looked up at me, and tried to form a smile, but it was too much effort. The paralysed left side of his face looked like someone had taken a cheesegrater to it. He said nothing, and I didn't ask how Winnie was doing because it would have been a stupid question. I looked around for another chair and dragged it over, its rubber feet squealing loudly in protest until I lifted it the rest of the way.

"It was an accident," Delroy mumbled at last. We'd been sitting there five minutes, or maybe ten, watching Winnie doing nothing, listening to the life support machines hiss and click. "I was walking her to the bus stop. On my way to the club where I do my therapy. We heard the car behind us but thought nothing of it until we realized it was right on top of us." He shook his head. "Driver had mounted the pavement—must have been tuning his radio or God knows."

"Did he stop?" I said.

Delroy shook his greying head, and rubbed his face with his uninjured hand like he was trying to wash the horror away.

"Did you get a look at the car, or the driver? Did anyone?"

Delroy shook his head again and stared at the floor.

A hit and run? What sort of a rat would . . . ? A dark thought seeped into my mind like some foul fluid.

"Delroy? You're sure it was an accident?"

He winced and sank his face into his hands. How the hell would he know, I thought, if the car came from behind, and didn't stop?

All afternoon the machines hissed and clicked and every so often beeped, and nurses would materialize to check Winnie's charts and change the drip bags. They brought us cups of tea that sat and went cold, and murmured to each other outside the curtains in medical-speak about volumes and liver functions. Time had slowed to a crawl. There was a window nearby but the lower half was frosted and the upper half showed a sky so overcast and grey it was impossible to tell where the sun was or what hour it might be. My phone had finally died, but there was nobody for me to call anyway; the only people who mattered were here with me at this moment. Delroy and Winnie had relatives in Birmingham and more in Jamaica, I knew, but when I asked Delroy if I should contact them, or a member of Winnie's congregation, he just shook his head, as if he couldn't cope with anyone else's presence right now.

Eventually I needed a piss, and went to find a loo; the first one I found had a sign that read "Staff Only" but no members of staff were around, and I didn't particularly want to wander through the hospital in search of an officially permitted peeing place. I pissed, washed my hands and shook the water off, and for good measure stopped by one of the antibacterial gel pumps that were dotted around the ward and squirted a splash of that onto my hands. As the alcohol in the gel evaporated, chilling my skin, I heard two nurses at the nearby desk talking in a language I could understand for a change.

"Are those policemen coming back?"

"Don't think so. They said he had given them enough to go on for now, that they needed to find more witnesses."

"What did this guy say?"

"The husband?"

"No, the driver, when he stopped he said something, apparently."

"I thought it was a hit and run?"

There was a sudden harsh, short buzz from under the counter.

"That's Ling, in five—BP's dropping—"

They hurried from their workstation, their rubber-soled shoes squeaking urgently, away from where I stood listening against the cool corridor wall.

"Delroy?"

"Do you think she needs a drink? She must

be thirsty. She's been here so long, not even a glass of water . . ."

I glanced at the fluids oozing down the pipes, keeping Winnie hydrated. Delroy understood what they were for as well as I did; he just felt helpless, and wanted to do something.

"No, Del, I think she's fine."

"She's so still . . . I wish she'd wake up, even if just to nag me, you know?"

"Delroy . . . what did the driver say to you? When he stopped?"

"He never stopped. It was an accident."

"I know he stopped. What did he say to you, Del? Why won't you tell me?"

For the first time in ages he looked at me. His eyes were bloodshot and weary but full of fight.

"I know you, Crusher. You'll think you have to set things right, go picking fights out of your league. Winnie wouldn't want that. Violence begets violence, she'd say."

"Yeah, and you used to say, they come at you hard, come back harder."

"In the ring, Finn, not in the real world, for God's sake—"

"What did he say, Del? The guy who ran you and Winnie down?"

Del was about to answer when one of the machines—I wasn't sure which—started to beep, and then another, overlapping in a deafening, tangled electronic racket, and Winnie opened her eyes.

I knew immediately that this parting wasn't going to be peaceful or poignant. Winnie was terrified. She seemed to be choking, and her eyes bulged in terror. She didn't know where she was or who was with her or what was happening. Delroy squeezed her hand and tried to talk to her, but she stared at him in confusion and fear like she was sinking into a mire of chaos and darkness and pain.

I stood there, useless and helpless, until I was pushed aside by one nurse, then another, and now an army of nurses in scrubs descended, shouting statistics and readings at each other, and one tiny Chinese nurse ushered us all the way out of the room, murmuring reassurance, while the curtains closed around Winnie. The nurse pressed Delroy's crutch into his hand and hurried back in, shutting the door behind her. As I watched through the wired glass the frantic activity around Winnie's bed seemed to slacken, and I saw the lead nurse glance at her watch. I caught her grim look to a colleague and the tiny shake of her head, and saw them slipping on that emotional armour medics use when they've fought twenty rounds and lost.

Delroy wasn't watching any of this. He had slumped into a chair and was staring into space as if he no longer understood what he was on this earth for or what he was meant to do. But I knew what I was there for, and what I was going to do.

"What did he say to you, Delroy?"

"Finn, let it go. You'll do something stupid, wind up back in prison, and everything you've achieved, everything your father gave you, all that will be for nothing."

"It was Sherwood, wasn't it? Just tell me."

"I didn't hear him, I'd banged my head, I was looking around for Winnie—"

"Del, for Christ's sake—!"

Delroy's shoulders drooped. "'Mr. Sherwood says hello,'" he whispered.

The door of Winnie's room reopened gently and a nurse emerged—a doctor, I realized, when I saw the DR on her name badge. She was twenty-something, ash-blonde and beautiful, with skin as smooth and perfect as a doll's, but her face was set in a solemn professional mask.

"Mr. Llewellyn? I'm very sorry."

Night had fallen by the time I left the hospital. Saturday night, I remembered, when I saw and heard drunks in the distance hooting at each other as they staggered from one pub to the next.

Delroy had wanted to stay with Winnie until the undertaker came, but I couldn't do that. He made me promise to go home, and I said I would, but I didn't tell him that I had no home any more, so I couldn't go home if I'd wanted to, and I didn't want to. I didn't suppose Sherwood would be in his office at this time of night, but I'd wait for him until he turned up, however long that took. His office was only forty minutes away, if I ran at my usual pace.

I made it in just over thirty.

# ten

I'd already decided that if Sherwood wasn't in, I wouldn't wait—I'd break in somehow and find his home address and hunt him down. If I had time and no alarms went off, I'd shit on his desk too, before I torched the place. I was going to find that prick, and no matter how many Neanderthal bouncers got in the way I was going to hurt him, permanently. For the rest of his miserable life he'd wake up every morning and see in the mirror what I'd done to him and wish he'd picked another line of work.

The alley beside the old snooker hall was empty and stank of cat piss and cheap cigars. Sherwood's car was parked up in its private parking space, so maybe he was around after all, but I wasn't going to lurk in the shadows and wait for him to come out. I walked up to the alley to his office and raised my foot and kicked one door, hard. It burst open like it hadn't been properly locked, banged off the wall and bounced idly back. The stairs beyond stretched up towards Sherwood's moodily lit landing, but no one came down to challenge me. Just as well for them. From above I could hear Frank Sinatra belting out some old song about moonlight and romance, so loudly no one upstairs could have heard me. I stepped inside, let the door swing shut behind me and pounded up the stairs, two at a time.

The landing was deserted and the door at the end was ajar. That's where the music was coming from, and I paused to listen, to get an idea of how many people I might have to deal with inside. My eye fell on that classical painting of a hay cart fording a stream I had noticed on my first visit, and I suddenly understood why it looked so out of place. It had come from Nicky's house—it was part of that set hanging in her library. Anderson must have borrowed from Sherwood too, and fallen behind on his repayments, and Dean and his boyfriends had confiscated it the same way they had taken Delroy's telly.

I couldn't hear any conversation or movement beyond Sherwood's door. Was there even anyone there? I felt sure there was, or that someone had only just left—but why leave the place open like this? Now I noticed a smell too, slightly foul, like a toilet that hadn't been flushed, mingled with something else, something stale and salty. My cold fury started to subside, and I found myself wondering if Delroy had been right, and I had rushed into something I couldn't handle. Hell with that, I thought—I'm here now, let's dance. But I tugged my sleeve up over my hand before I reached forward and pushed the office door fully open.

Sean the Wardrobe was the first thing I saw, lying face down on the floor, his head towards me, one arm trapped beneath him and the other flailed out sideways with its palm upwards. He had been clutching his belly when he fell, like he'd been shot or stabbed. Now he was staring at the carpet with a sightless bloodshot eye and his nose was squashed flat into the pile like someone had stamped on the back of his head. No sign of Dean though, not yet.

On Sherwood's big shiny desk a briefcase perched at an angle that suggested Sean had been about to pick it up before being rudely interrupted. It was shut, but one catch had been flipped open. I reached for the other— it would take only a squeeze of my thumb to pop it, so I could lift the lid and see what was inside. But I held back. Something told me it was full of money, and I had stopped believing in Santa Claus a long time ago. The cheesy swing music came to a roaring crescendo of brass and then stopped, and in the brief pause before the next track started I heard dripping, from the cupboard or toilet or wherever that door behind Sherwood's desk led to. Then the next Sinatra track kicked in, all jaunty and cheerful: love was here to stay, apparently. As I crept forward I noticed the odour getting thicker—a smell of shit mixed with mouldy vegetables, and under that an odour that reminded me of that shop in the high street my mum used to take me into sometimes on the way home from school . . . the butcher's shop.

The music was coming from a CD player on a sleek smoked-glass unit near the door. By now Frank was making my ears hurt so I hit the power switch with my elbow. Silence fell, broken only by that faint dripping, and the buzz of a bluebottle that flew past my ear and through the door ahead of me like it was hurrying to a party. I shoved the door open with my toe and looked in.

It was a bathroom, but a huge one like a showroom display, with a shower cubicle filling one corner and beyond it a glass basin mounted on a plinth under a mirror surrounded by LEDs. Beyond the basin was the loo, and on it sat Sherwood in one of his designer suits, tilted forward on the seat lid, staring down with a look of surprise. Someone had tied him there, wrists behind his back, with a thin wire that looped up and round his throat. Then they'd slit his belly open, so his guts spilled into his lap and overflowed down the legs of his blood-sodden trousers.

I hadn't eaten all day and it was just as well because I would have spewed everywhere. As it was I bit back the bile in my gullet and swallowed it. Sherwood had been alive when this had been done to him. This was way beyond revenge—this was delight in pain, joy in horror. It was how traitors had been executed in medieval times. Whoever did this was preserving an ancient art form—disembowelling as public entertainment.

Through a daze of shock I heard electronic whooping in the distance: an emergency vehicle on its way to some drunken pile-up. My mind ran backwards and forwards like a rat in a maze with no exit—who had done this to Sherwood? A debtor, driven too far? No, Sherwood had always picked on the weak and helpless—whoever did this wasn't one of his clients. A rival loan shark? That cop, Lovegrove—but did he even know Sherwood? The hit-and-run driver . . . ? No, that guy had been sent by Sherwood; he told Delroy as much.

Except . . . Sherwood never signed the bricks his people flung through windows. He was never that obvious.

The siren was getting closer. Now there were two of them—three. I could see now that someone had set out to kill or maim Delroy and Winnie, and point the finger at Sherwood.

They must have hoped I'd get to hear about it and come galloping after Sherwood like a rabid Rottweiler, and that's exactly what had happened. I'd been played. Sherwood had been tortured to death, and a suspect with an obvious motive and an arm-long history of violence was standing over his corpse, too stunned to run.

Voices from below in the alley, lowered and urgent. Car doors slamming and a burst of radio chatter, muted too late. The police were right outside—I had to move. I backed out of the bathroom, suddenly aware I might have trodden in Sherwood's gore and be leaving a trail of bloody footprints. But no, nothing visible. Where were the exits? Sherwood's punters would have been angry, desperate people with little to lose, and there must have been times when he'd needed another way out. There were no windows as such, apart from a domed skylight set into the sloping roof, but that was too high to reach. Sherwood wouldn't have relied on it. There was another door in a recess beyond the loo entrance that looked like a stationery cupboard. I didn't know if I'd left any prints or DNA on the way in, but I'd sure as hell leave some going out, unless . . .

A buzzing from Sherwood's desk, echoing on the landing outside. Sherwood had an entryphone, I remembered now, but I'd never used it. I probably had about twenty seconds before the cops sledgehammered the door.

Gloves. Sean's outflung hand was bare. Stooping by his body I gingerly inserted one finger into the pocket of his leather jacket. I felt a rubbery bundle, like two gloves rolled together, and abandoning caution for a moment reached into Sean's pocket. I pulled out the gloves, tugged them apart, stood up and put them on.

Hurrying to the recess I turned the handle and pulled. The door opened onto darkness. My gloved hands groped at the wall beside the door, found a switch and flicked it. Halogens sprang to life revealing a dead-end corridor lined with shelves, with a window halfway down on the right. On the shelf nearest the door was an electric fan. I grabbed it, wrapped the flex round and round the handle of the door I'd just come through, knotting it with the plug, then grabbed the fan, stretched the flex tight against the upright metal strut of the shelf, and wound it round and round. The fan's casing bashed and clanged against the metal shelving and my skin crawled at the racket I had made, but I kept going, more carefully, finally letting the fan fall and dangle. The shelving was screwed to the wall, so that lash-up would slow the cops when they pulled at the door and buy me a minute or two at least. I hurried to the window.

It was barred on the outside. The window was a sash type with a lower half that slid upwards but there was no point trying—I'd need to be an anorexic supermodel to squeeze through the bars beyond. I thought about turning back, but now I could hear boots clattering up the stairwell. I hurried to the dead end and saw there was a fire door with a pushbar on the left, recessed into the wall where it couldn't be seen. Wouldn't the cops be coming up the rear fire escape by now? I had no choice. I leaned on the bar, shoved it down, and pushed the door open. A bell burst into life right by my ear—a nerve-jangling, teeth-rattling racket designed to scare off burglars with its very volume. I barged through the door, stepped outside onto an iron gantry and backed against the door to shut it behind me. The alarm kept going—how soon would the cops realize it wasn't them who'd set it off?

The night outside was warm and smelled of beer. I was high above the ground, level with thrumming air conditioners sucking stale booze-soaked air out of some nearby pub and blasting it up into the night. The fire escape ran straight ahead of me for ten metres along a brick wall before turning back and downwards towards street level, where the pavements and alleys would by now be crawling with uniforms. They'd soon get bored of waiting for me to come to them, and then they'd start trying the rear gateways in the hope of finding a way upwards. Out here on the fire escape the clamouring of the alarm bell was less strident, muffled by the constant rumble of traffic and the music thumping upwards from the bars all around and the general bawdy racket of a boozy Saturday night.

Trying all the same not to make the iron platform under my feet announce my presence like a gong, I hurried halfway along, then stopped to check out the parapet two metres above. I couldn't go downwards, but I couldn't leap that high either—unless I stood on the handrail to my left. It was slightly rounded on top, and only half a hand's-breadth wide. If I slipped it was a four-metre drop onto concrete and steel bins full of broken glass. Adrenaline was gushing through my system and I forced myself to stay calm, to remember all that Delroy had taught me about distributing my weight; he'd even rigged up a tightrope once to teach me balance. No time to think about how this could go wrong. Throw your leg over the handrail. Pull your knee up. Balance, keep it steady. Pull up the other, slow steady, now . . . both feet on the rail, and . . . push.

I was standing upright, the empty air at my back. Laughter and music and girls screeching somewhere, miles below, maybe cheering, maybe crying.

"POLICE! Do NOT move!" The shout came from ground level, and I ignored it. They were obviously talking to someone else.

"You, up there! DO NOT MOVE!"

OK, they were talking to me. But that suggested they still hadn't found a way to get up here and catch me. I focused on my balance and fixed my eyes on the lip of the parapet, now only an arm's length above my eye level. I bent my knees into a half-crouch. And I jumped.

Empty air, then rough cold concrete under my fingers, my folded hands the only thing supporting my weight as I swung from the parapet, my knees scraping the brickwork, my feet searching in vain for a toehold between the bricks. Bracing my arms I pulled myself up, slowly, knowing I would have only one go at this, that it had to work, and when my chin was level with the parapet I flung my right arm over, pulled harder and swung my right leg up after it, rolled my body over the concrete lip, and fell half a metre onto fibreglass roofing, my ass landing in a puddle that immediately soaked into my jeans. I wanted to stop and congratulate myself, but there was no time—I jumped up into a crouch and hurried along the rooftop, down to a corner that turned away from the direction of the fire escape and ran parallel to the main drag, until I hit another corner and was forced back away from the street. There was another low corrugated roof below me, and beyond that another.

I straddled the concrete parapet again, turned and lowered myself down until my trainers touched the rippled metal below. Slowly I let the corrugated iron take my weight. If I went for the apex where the roof would be strongest I would be too visible against the skyline. I had to stay lower down. I tested the metal roofing with my feet—it flexed, but held. I decided to run for it as if I was racing over ice and hope that forward momentum would see me to the far side.

It worked, for most of the way, but a metre short of the far end the roof under my foot didn't flex, but burst, and my leg went straight through, scraping half the skin off my shin. My forward momentum dissipated as I fell, and the metal screeched and tore and my other leg went through, waving in space, and as I slid backwards I clutched in vain for a grip and finally dropped, landing two instants later flat on my back with a bang and clatter, onto a heap of wood and metal struts and mildewed cloth.

I lay there for a minute, trying to figure out where the hell I was and how badly hurt. The dusty darkness throbbed with thumping music. Was that blood on the ass of my jeans? No, just stagnant water from that puddle I'd dropped into earlier. My back ached and my shin burned like fire, but that was it— everything else seemed to be working. I looked around, trying to work out where I'd fallen. For a moment I thought I was back in the derelict pool hall, but this place looked as if it had never been used except for storage. Light was seeping in from some misted high-level window that was flickering with refracted laser dots and rattling in time to the beat of music beyond.

I had landed in a storeroom—one that hadn't been visited in ages, by the smell of it. The mildewed cloth and metal struts were parts of parasols that had once been used in a pub garden, and I had mangled them utterly beyond repair by landing on them. I could just make out that the walls of the storeroom were bare cobwebby brick, and the floor was heaped with ashtrays, bar towels, broken optics and other obsolete pub crap so densely packed there was nowhere even to place my feet. I clambered over the rubbish towards something that looked like a door. Luckily it was bolted from my side. The rusty knobs of the bolts bit into my fingers as I worked them up and down and slowly pulled them free. There was no handle that I could see so I tugged at the bolts until the door opened just wide enough for me to get through.

It was dark on the other side too, but here the air smelled of sweat and booze and perfume and cosmetics. A laser reflected from a mirror ball danced and flickered over packed clubbers dancing in their finest pick-up outfits. As I pushed through the crowd—no point apologizing, when the music was too loud to make myself understood—a few clubbers stared, and I realized they were wondering why the hell the bouncers had let in someone wearing ripped jeans, a woolly jumper that smelled of smoke, and an anorak from a charity shop. I smiled and waved, as if my outfit was the latest casual wear from New York. Yes, this time next year you'll all be dressed like hobos who've been savaged by dogs.

I jostled, shoved and fought my way to the front door, determined to get there under my own steam before any bouncer did notice me and made a big scene about throwing me out.

If I could get onto the high street upright and unmolested I had a better chance of mingling with the Saturday night crowds and disappearing. One chair I pushed past had a leather bomber jacket draped over the back. I discreetly grasped the collar and slid it off without looking down or back to see if I'd been noticed. I felt sorry for the poor sod I'd ripped off, but shortly I'd need that coat more than he ever would. I let the charity shop anorak slide off my shoulders in the crowd and felt it fall to the floor behind me. Sean's gloves I tugged off and bundled into a ball.

A bunch of heavyset guys—rugby players, judging by their thick necks and broken noses—were milling by the entrance, and from the way they were staggering and fumbling with their jackets it looked like they'd been here for quite a while and were now off in search of hotter girls and colder drinks. I'd never understood the point of pub crawls—if you were enjoying yourself, why up sticks and leave?—but then I'd never been into drinking anyway. As I attached myself to the departing knot of jerks—several of them as tall as me and most of them heavier—I shrugged on my stolen leather jacket and helped one of them on with his coat, grinning like an idiot. He didn't notice me slipping the gloves into his pocket.

Then I followed them out, pretending to listen to a long and incoherent anecdote being told by one guy about the time he had shat himself while wearing white trousers to a mate's wedding. His pals were all groaning and laughing, and I groaned and laughed too, and stepped aside politely to let three beefy uniformed cops rush past us into the pub, looking incongruous and overdressed in their stab vests and peaked caps. Tugging up the collar of my newly acquired bomber jacket I contrived to look as detached and uninterested as the lads I'd latched onto, and as they bumped about on the pavement debating which boozer to hit next I stuffed my fists into my pockets and moved off down the street, trying not to limp and hoping the blood leaking from my shin wouldn't soak through my jeans.

Coppers were running along the street, craning their necks downward to shout into their lapel radios. From the way they were scattering in every direction it was clear they had lost my scent. By now I was heading back towards the street that ran past Sherwood's office, and that felt right, because the cops would be looking for a guy running in the other direction. I watched the police activity openly, because that's what most of the Saturday night drinkers were doing—it was like the plods were providing free street theatre to give the revellers something novel to talk about. Coming to the junction with Sherwood's street I saw two police cars halfway down blocking the road off, while a junior PC in a hi-viz jacket ran blue and white incident tape from lamppost to lamppost to form a cordon at the entrance to Sherwood's alley. A knot of girls in tiny skirts and skimpy tops looked on, giggling loudly and speculating how the young PC would look with his shirt off. Two other blokes loitered casually at the cordon, and one of them flicked a Zippo to light his cigarette.

It was Dean, Sherwood's in-house Elvis impersonator. He took a long drag and threw his head back to blow fumes out of his nose. As I moved closer, hugging the shadows, I caught a whiff and recognized that smell, the one that had been haunting me—cheap cigars. It was Dean who'd been hanging around my gym the other night, and I'd smelled that same stink outside Sherwood's office a few minutes before. Dean must have helped to set me up, and now he was waiting to see if I'd be frogmarched out in cuffs or dragged out in a body bag. Clearly he'd changed employers; I wondered if he'd simply watched, trying not to puke, while his new colleagues had slit Sherwood's belly open—or had he mucked in, to show them how willing and adaptable he was?

The guy he was talking to now was tall, muscular and totally bald, with a shining scalp and a long thick moustache. I could see him rubbing his chin thoughtfully, his fingers glinting with rings. He jerked his head at Dean and they turned and walked away down the road, as if they were bored with observing the chase and now it was time to catch their bus. I strode after them, wincing when I put weight on my barked shin but trying to look casual, while watching from the corner of my eye the coppers on duty outside the murder scene. They barely glanced at me.

Dean's new boss walked straight across the next street without even checking the traffic, as if any truck that hit him would bounce off. Dean jogged at his heels like a spaniel puppy trying to match the strut of a mastiff. I paused at the corner in case they looked back, but they walked straight on towards a sleek black Merc with tinted windows parked nearby with the engine running. When Dean and his new friend jumped into the back I broke cover to cross the street, but with no idea what I would do if I caught up with them—jump on the roof of their car and hope they wouldn't notice? Grab the bumper and hang on? I told myself there might be a sticker or something on the window, or a car dealer's name on the number plate, and if they would only stay parked for fifteen minutes I might have time to read it. But before I could come close the driver tossed some litter out the window and pulled away from the curb, and the Merc sped off with a muted roar of power, its rear lights quickly merging into a million others.

I was homeless and hungry and alone on the street, wearing a stolen jacket and wanted for murder. Dean and Baldy had screwed me over nicely, and I'd never find them before the cops found me. Where was I going to hide out? Delroy and Winnie's?

The memory of Winnie, thrashing with fear and pain in that hospital bed while Delroy tried in vain to comfort her, filled me all over again with cold and bitter fury. I stood in the spot where the Merc had been parked and looked around—for what, I had no idea. I checked for CCTV cameras covering the street, knowing that London was dotted with them; the operators liked to supplement their rubbish pay by flogging off footage of drunken couples shagging in doorways. But the only camera I could see now was pointed in the opposite direction, monitoring a 24/7 bus lane.

Where the Merc had been parked a paper coffee cup was rolling around in the gutter— the litter the driver had thrown out of his window. I picked it up, feeling like an idiot—what was I going to do, ask the cops to take prints off it? Analyse the coffee grounds? Inside the cup I could feel a few inches of coffee sloshing about, and something solid tapping the sides. I prised the lid off and saw floating in the dregs a cigarette butt and a twisted wad of paper. I took the wad out, tossed the cup back in the gutter, shook the coffee off the paper and untwisted it.

I could just make the logo of a chain of roadside cafés. The rest of it was a mass of faint grey figures and numbers, hard enough to decipher even before that milky coffee had soaked in. Charms. Sauces? Church-something. Churchfield . . . Chelms . . . ford. Churchfield Services, Chelmsford. 2 x reg latte, £4.90.

Chelmsford was in Essex, fifty miles out the other side of London. Yes, the cup had come from Dean's car—but what did that signify? They'd stopped at some services to buy coffee, but so had a hundred thousand other people, all headed somewhere else.

As a lead it wasn't much. In fact, it was practically nothing. But it was all I had.

# eleven

There are few sounds I find more depressing than the rattly rumble of a wheeled suitcase being dragged along a pavement. It always puts me in mind of someone stumbling through life lumbered with crap too heavy to carry. There were dozens of those cases being trundled around the smoky strip-lit caverns of Victoria Coach Station by knackered, grumpy travellers too broke to catch a train. I queued at the travel counter—I hate reading off ticket machine screens while a queue builds up behind me, sighing and tutting—and paid my fare with a tenner and some odd coins I'd found in the pocket of the jacket I'd stolen. I felt bad about it, yeah, but I'd already taken the jacket, how was I going to give the owner his spare change back? Before leaving the counter

I asked for directions, and trudged past a long line of waiting coaches before I came to the right bay for the Chelmsford service.

The weather had turned cold and I shivered as I curled up in a seat towards the back, keeping an eye through the tinted windows for police. I doubted they'd be looking for me here. Catching a late-night coach to Chelmsford made very little sense, and that was what clinched the decision for me. The only other option was to chuck that coffee receipt into a litter bin, head to Delroy's to beg a bed for the night, and to lie awake waiting for the police to pitch up on the doorstep.

Dean's new friends had gone to a lot of trouble to set me up, which suggested I'd been getting too close to the truth. But what truth? I'd been rattling a lot of cages—which one held the nutter who'd turned Dean and had Sherwood gutted? Who was that bald guy with the rings? Thinking about it, I couldn't believe Sherwood had been sacrificed just to screw me. He must have been a loose end, a liability, so that killing him and framing me had been two birds brained with one stone.

Harry Anderson's gambling addiction had

left him in debt. If I was right about the painting, he'd borrowed money from Sherwood, and he couldn't pay it back, and he couldn't afford his bosses finding that out. But Anderson was a banker, not a gangster—he could never have arranged the bloodbath I'd just seen. The only man I'd ever met capable of that sort of sadism was the Guvnor, and he wasn't even in the country . . . was he?

The coach engine revved to a roar, the doors beeped for a minute before hissing shut, and we backed away from the parking bay. Only a handful of passengers had boarded so I had room to stretch out, though the stiff seats with their locked-down armrests seemed designed to keep travellers sitting rigidly to attention like crash-test dummies. Muzak started leaking from the sound system, never rising above a vaguely tuneful burbling as the coach roared and swayed through the heart of London, past tall buildings that had once been crammed with servants and were these days crammed with desks and filing cabinets. As the coach's air conditioning circulated warm germs I felt my eyelids starting to droop, and I let them; I hadn't slept, and I'd eaten nothing except a stale bean salad wrap since the fire had woken me up beside Susan twenty hours ago.

I dozed for a while, vaguely aware of London flickering past, a maze of dark streets, lonely night-time walkers, and gleaming rivers of sodium light. I closed my eyes completely somewhere in the East End and when I opened them again I was miles from anywhere, thundering along a dark divided highway, and the bright square shapes of buildings had given way to the vague soft outlines of trees against a hard black sky. I panicked briefly, wondering if I'd slept through a stop, but when I looked around I saw no new faces among the passengers and nobody missing. The late-night coach wasn't an express service, but took its passengers on a rambling mystery tour of Essex, with three stops before it reached Chelmsford. The second stop, I'd been told, was Churchfield Services, so I wouldn't need to ask anyone else to read road signs for me.

The first stop was some commuter town where an old lady had stepped gingerly down and waited for the driver to manhandle her huge suitcase out of the luggage compartment on the side of the coach. We drove off and left her standing there in the dark like we'd stranded her to die on an ice floe. Churchfield Services took another forty-five minutes.

The coach nosed into a space in the parking lot and pulled up with a grunt and wheeze like a clapped-out carthorse. When the driver cut the engine, silence rushed in with the chill night air, broken only by the hum of cars passing on the distant road. "Fifteen minutes," he bellowed to the passengers, before opening the doors, climbing down and scuttling away in the direction, I assumed, of a bathroom. A kid who looked like a student followed him; I clambered down and headed in the other direction, towards the fuel station, wondering what the hell I was doing in this godforsaken dump in the middle of the night. Hopefully it would take less than fifteen minutes to get nowhere, then I could travel on to Chelmsford and use the return half of my ticket. Even though it was the wee small hours three or four customers were browsing the filling station's racks of sweets and crisps and chocolate, all different forms of sugar and starch cooked up by one huge global conglomerate that probably owned shares in dental clinics and diabetes treatments too. The two servers at the counter were Asian. I knew those guys worked 24-hour shifts sometimes, and I hoped I hadn't caught these ones at hour 23. But either they hadn't been in the country long enough to understand what I was asking or they were too knackered to care. They might have seen a black Merc—they saw a lot of black Mercs, none today though, yes they had, no, that was the day before. Did you want any fuel with that, sir?

It was every bit as hopeless as I'd thought it would be, and I headed for the hot food section to find something edible, hopefully with a vitamin in it. The waitress wiping down the counter looked vaguely Slavic, with high cheekbones and pale green eyes, but when she opened her mouth to talk she was pure Essex.

"What you looking for?"

"I dunno, a BLT maybe?"

"No, I mean, a car, I heard you asking."

"Er—yeah. A big black Merc. Expensive. I was wondering if it filled up here, you know?"

"Late reg? Like, this year?"

"Yes, I think so." I hadn't clocked the year, which was stupid, because it would have been the middle two numbers, and even I could have managed that. But it had looked pretty new.

"There's one just like that, comes here for a jet wash every week."

"Seriously? Do you have the registration?" I had no idea what I was going to do with it—I hadn't thought that far ahead.

"No. But I know where the driver lives. Young guy, doesn't speak much English?" She picked up her tongs. "Did you actually want a BLT? We might have one out back."

"What? No, forget the BLT—I mean thanks, but—did you say you knew where to find it, the Merc?"

"There's this big house down the road from here"—she gestured with her tongs—"used to be a stately home, then it was a loony bin or a special school or something—anyway someone's moved in, a whole bunch of blokes. I seen that car pull into the drive when I was headed home, that's how I know."

"How far down the road?"

\*   \*   \*

The gateway was unremarkable—two concrete pillars set wide apart with black steel railings on either side and matching gates that didn't look as if they'd been closed recently. No signage or post boxes, though the wooden posts standing about two metres back from the gates must have supported a notice board at some point. No CCTV either, which suited me. After walking for forty-five minutes along the hard shoulder of a dark wet divided highway I didn't fancy cutting across fields to find a side entrance to the house or mansion or stately home or whatever I'd find in there.

Dawn was starting to leach through the clouds, and as I passed through the gates I quickened my pace, feeling exposed and vulnerable. The long tarmac drive stretched away into the night, dotted with potholes and bordered on either side by gloomy, dense, dark green shrubs.

After about half a mile there was enough light to make out the road ahead dipping downhill and curving off to the left, where tall brick chimneys poked up among a copse of scraggy firs. Now I left the road and walked over the grass, which hadn't been cut in months. The dew soaked through my trainers and up the legs of my jeans, so my feet soon squelched and my calves froze under the wet flapping denim. I barely noticed; I focused on what I hoped to find—the reason all this was happening, and who I had infuriated by trying to discover what had happened to Nicky.

Nothing grew beneath the scraggy firs surrounding the house and my soggy shoes made no noise on the thick brown bed of pine needles underfoot. I could make out the walls of the mansion now, pale grey stone and render. It was an ugly, institutional building, set in a hollow, with lots of rippled glass at ground level to stop its inhabitants looking out. I could guess what it was like inside—dark, airless, cold, damp and gloomy. It certainly looked as if it had been a mental hospital at some point. If the patients weren't insane when they got here, they'd have soon ended up that way.

Nearer the house the fir trees thinned out and thick holly bushes took their place, their rubbery thorns ripping at my skin as I pushed through them. The forecourt was a broad expanse of grey gravel bordered by flower beds, or rather beds of empty clay dotted with weeds, and the black Merc was parked there, between an anonymous silver saloon and an unmarked box van that had once been white but was now a dingy grey. The silver saloon was parked with its nose facing outwards, and the hood was dented as if it had collided with something heavy . . . *Winnie?*

I could see no lights and no movement. If I'd done it on purpose I couldn't have arrived at a better time. This was the hour when babies were born, and police squads kicked your doors in. I surveyed the ground-floor windows, trying to recall some of the housebreaking tricks my fellow hoodlum, Genghis, had shown me. I'd never burgled anyone's house back then, I'd just been the lookout. At the time it had made me feel less guilty about what we were doing; now I knew I'd been lying to myself.

But my youth hadn't been totally misspent— I spotted a small sash window in a corner that wasn't fully closed. Not too small for me to get through either, as long as I didn't have to smash it. I walked as softly and swiftly as

I could from the shelter of the holly bushes across the gravel to the side wall. The gravel barely crunched, as if it was too soggy or tired to make the effort. I checked out the window from close up; as I thought, the frame had warped and the window didn't shut properly. There was a screw-down latch on the bottom of the upper section that was supposed to sit in a U-shaped catch on the top of the lower section, but it didn't quite reach, and someone had simply flipped it into position and left it.

I worked my fingers into the tight gap between the window frame and the lower sash and lifted gently. It didn't budge. I tried to rattle it in its frame, but it seemed the whole window was so warped it might have been jammed like that for years. I gritted my teeth, dug my fingers in further, shook the frame and pulled, and abruptly the whole pane shot upwards so hard I thought it would fall out of the frame and shatter. It hit the top with a muffled bang, but the sound seemed to die away almost instantly. The room beyond smelled of damp and the magnolia paint was peeling. Apart from a metal trolley behind the door with a wheel broken off, and a plastic chair gathering dust in the corner, it held no furniture.

I clambered over the sill and lowered a foot to the floor, hoping there'd be no grit or glass to crack underfoot, but all I heard was the faint squelch of my wet trainer. Turning back I tugged at the sash and it slid back down to the almost-shut position it had started in, making barely any noise. Best to leave as few signs of my presence as I could. I crept over to the door and tried the handle. It turned, and gently I cracked the door open, and listened.

Voices down the hall. Talking, arguing, laughing. Three men, by the sound of it— what the hell were they doing out of bed? But it didn't sound like anyone was keeping watch in the corridor, so I pulled the door open wider and I craned my head round it. The long hallway was harshly lit by neons screwed to the cracked ceilings. Their light washed what little warmth there was out of the yellowing beige paint on the walls and doors. A threadbare carpet ran down the centre of the floor, over parquet flooring missing plenty of blocks. The interior was even more dismal than I'd expected; dawn had broken properly now but only the most feeble daylight penetrated the fir trees and holly bushes crowding round the house.

The voices were coming from a large room with double doors about three metres away. Opposite the doors a wide staircase led upwards, curving off to a landing I could not see.

"I tell you now, don't play."

"I'm in."

"You have no money left."

"The big man owes me two weeks' money. Deal."

"No credit." More laughter.

I recognized one voice anyway. Dean was playing cards, and losing. His opponent had a deep gravelly voice and an accent that sounded Mediterranean—Greek, maybe? His voice was good-humoured and amused right now, but something told me you didn't want to be around when he stopped laughing. I suspected that was the big bald guy with the moustache and the rings. There was a third man in the room who seemed younger, with a high-pitched giggle that somehow sounded foreign as well.

"Look, here, right, it's a Rolex, all right? Deal?"

"I have watch."

"It's a fucking Rolex, it's worth six grand!"

"Not to me. Is worth maybe one."

"Hell, fine, deal!"

From what I could hear Dean would soon be reading the time off his mobile phone, if he managed to keep hold of that. I moved out quickly and tiptoed down the hall in the other direction from the voices, keeping clear of the carpet. Walking on it would have muffled my steps, but my sneakers might well have left prints or damp marks.

The first door I came to was open, revealing a narrow staircase heading downwards, to a cellar or an old scullery. I wasn't sure about going down there; chances were there'd be no other way out. Then again, it wasn't likely anyone would be sleeping in the cellar. I might have more chance to look around without being caught.

The staircase was solid and barely creaked under my weight. I expected to see low-ceilinged rooms piled high with junk or papers or maybe rows of wine racks, but instead

I found myself in another long corridor. This one looked newly decorated, with vinyl flooring and a row of doors off one side, each with a window at eye level glazed with wired glass. Every door, I noticed, had a bolt on the outside, although none of them were bolted right now, as far as I could see. On the wall by each door was a light switch.

I glanced into the nearest room, a small bare cube with pale green walls and a ventilator but no window apart from the one in the door. It reminded me too much of a room in my old youth detention centre—a sink, a plastic chair, a single metal bed with a quilt rolled up at the foot of a thin mattress. I could guess what that bucket in the corner was for. The wired glass in this door had crazed where someone inside had rammed something hard into it—the leg of a chair, I guessed. Maybe this place had once been a special school, but even the grimmest special schools didn't have cells in the basement—these features were a recent addition to the house. It looked more like a prison, waiting for a fresh crop of inmates. But where did they come from, and where did they go?

I was about to turn back for the stairs when I

noticed one door at the far end of the corridor was still bolted shut. Jesus, I thought, there's someone locked in here? That was bad news. I had no idea how I was going to get out of this place, and if I tried to help anyone else we'd both be caught. Should I run for it, get help? But I knew that wasn't really an option. I crept up to the door and pressed my face to the wired glass.

The only light in the cell came from the hall where I was standing, and it was hard to see anything beyond my own reflection. I could just about make out a figure asleep in the bed. This cell wasn't as bare as the others; a track-suit lay folded neatly on the bedside chair, and there was even a TV on a little table, plugged into a DVD player, although there seemed to be more books scattered around than DVDs. After staring very hard I realized the prisoner was a woman, small and slight, with blonde hair that hadn't been washed in a while . . .

I scrabbled at the bolt and nearly slammed it back before I remembered where I was and eased it home softly instead. Turning the handle slowly I opened the door, glancing over my shoulder before I crept inside, terrified now of getting caught. The room was stuffy and smelled of stale breath and piss, but the woman slept on. I reached out to touch her shoulder, and her eyes opened, and she scrabbled backwards in the bed as if I had come to kill her. I couldn't risk her crying out, so I clapped my right hand over her mouth, and she twisted her head and sank her teeth into the heel of my right hand. I gritted my jaw and bore the pain, whispering urgently, "Nicky—Nicky, it's me! It's Finn!"

Either she heard what I was saying, or she recognized me from the taste of my blood, but Nicky finally heard what I was hissing at her, and I felt her relax. When she opened her teeth I tugged my hand away, and she flung herself at me, her arms so tight around my neck I nearly choked. But I could feel the fear and relief in her slender body, and I gave her a moment to realize that I was really there and that she wasn't dreaming. I knew that at any minute Dean or one of his friends could come downstairs, but I sat there and held her for as long as I could, because I'd wanted to take her in my arms long before I'd lost her.

Finally she pulled away, but before she could

speak I raised a finger and held it to her lips. I had as many questions as she did, but explanations could wait. She flung the bedclothes aside, grabbed the sweatpants from the plastic chair and pulled them on. I ducked down and felt under the bed for shoes, and found a pair of expensive trainers—the ones she was wearing when she was abducted, presumably. Nicky snatched them from me and tugged them on while I checked the corridor to see if anyone had heard us.

The starkly lit passageway was still empty. When I stepped outside Nicky followed me, wide-eyed, and tense as a wound spring. I raised a hand to indicate she should wait a second, then ducked into the cell next door, where I grabbed the pillow from the unmade bed. There were no other props I could use, and no time to set up anything more elaborate anyhow. While Nicky stared at me, clearly desperate to run, I returned to her cell and stuffed the pillow under the blankets, hastily arranging them to try and make it look like Nicky was still asleep, curled up and facing the wall. The finished arrangement would barely have fooled a two-year-old, I thought, but it was better than nothing.

I rejoined Nicky outside the cell and slid the bolt home on her door. I felt her hand slip into mine as she led me stealthily up the corridor towards the stairs, but although I could tell how frantic she was to escape I couldn't let her lead the way. I knew the simplest way out would be the way I had come in, and that she couldn't know that. At the foot of the staircase I tugged her hand to slow her down, moved past her and led the way up the steps, holding my breath, expecting every moment a creak underfoot that would betray our presence.

I had left the door at the top of the stairs ajar, and now I pulled it open a little further and listened. I couldn't hear Dean any more, just what sounded like the guy with the rings having a discussion with the younger guy in some language I didn't recognize. The double doors of the room they were in hung slightly open.

I beckoned Nicky to follow me, stepped out into the hall and tiptoed up the corridor to the door I had entered by. That's when I heard a chair pushed back, and footsteps approaching, and a foreign expression used in a way that sounded very much like "see you later." I was two-thirds of the way to the second door, and there was no time to turn back.

I dashed forward, praying my soft footsteps would be lost under those of whoever was coming. I made it to the second door, stepped inside, and pushed it nearly shut just as I heard him emerge from the large room and close the doors behind him. I prayed Nicky had had the presence of mind to step back inside the doorway that led to the cellar stairs.

She hadn't.

I could tell, because the young, dapper guy who had just appeared paused by the room I was hiding in, looked down the corridor towards Nicky and smiled. He was tanned and fit, with eyes so brown they were nearly black, a smart blazer and jewellery that made him look like a talent-show host. He said nothing, but ambled towards her, and I knew I only had seconds before he called out to his big mate with the rings to tell him what he'd found. Maybe I could take both of them, I thought, but I didn't know how many other men were in the building. I opened my door again and silently stepped out into the corridor behind Talent Show Tony.

Nicky was staring at him like a rabbit with its leg in a trap would stare at a fox, but in one glimpse I knew that she was standing like that to distract him, because she didn't even glance past him towards me. Talent Show Tony had raised a finger and was waving it from side to side, like he was about to say, "Ah ah ah, naughty," when my arm snaked round his neck and my other hand clasped the back of his head. I squeezed his throat, hard, and pushed his head forward. He grabbed at my arm and started to claw at my face, wriggling and thrashing, but I screwed my eyes shut, braced my feet and leaned back. I had so much height on him his own feet barely touched the ground, and I held my own breath while he struggled for his. Stop fighting it, I thought, don't kick anything, don't make a bloody sound. He tried all of that, and when he realized I was too strong for him he tried to kick the walls and stamp to summon help, but he'd left it too late. He was too weak, and growing weaker by the second.

Nicky was watching him, wide-eyed and motionless. I caught her eye, glanced down and jerked my head. She frowned, not comprehending. "Feet!" I hissed. By now Tony's body had sagged and his head was lolling. I grabbed him under the armpits and hauled him backwards while Nicky seized his ankles and lifted his feet high enough not to drag on the carpet. The three of us staggered along, still trying not to make a noise, but when I reached the side room and backed into the door it flew open and banged on the abandoned trolley. I kept going, dragging the unconscious Tony inside—he seemed to weigh a ton now—while Nicky grabbed the door and shut it, turning the handle so it clicked home almost silently.

I bent my knees, lowered Tony to the floor on his side, and finally let myself breathe, straining to listen beyond my own gulps for footsteps in the hall or a voice calling for him. We waited like that for ever, it seemed, but no sound came. Just the two of us breathing.

Shit—it should have been three. I knelt and laid my forefinger on Tony's carotid. No pulse.

"Damn," I murmured. I rolled him over onto his back, laid my left hand on his heart, and braced my right behind it, before Nicky grabbed my shoulder, and shook her head. I couldn't believe what she seemed to be saying—that she wanted me to let him die? I frowned at her, but her face was set, bleak and merciless. I realized she was right—if I did bring him back, he'd only raise the alarm—but I'd never meant to . . . I looked up at her again, searching for pity or a spark of compassion, and saw neither.

The decision had been made; no time now to agonize. I started to go through Tony's pockets. He was still warm, and I pushed to the back of my mind the thought that he would soon grow cold and rigid. His trouser pockets held a smartphone and a bunch of keys on a ring with a fat plastic fob bearing the Merc logo. Of course—he was the driver of the Merc. It was him who'd thrown that cup out the window after picking up Dean and the bald guy near Sherwood's office.

I offered the keys to Nicky—I still hadn't learned how to drive—and she took them while I checked his other pockets. The wallet in his rear trouser pocket was stuffed with twenty-pound notes and held a European driving licence; I stuffed the notes into my pockets and dropped the empty wallet beside the body. His smartphone was brand-new and top of the line, but pressing the power button revealed it was locked. I kept it anyway. When it rang I'd know they'd started looking for him.

I turned to the window, flipped up the latch, and eased the pane upwards. Fresh air billowed in, cold and damp. Poking my head out I looked both ways, but saw no one. When I turned to urge Nicky through I saw she had picked up the plastic chair that had been lying in the corner and was wedging it under the door handle. It was a good idea; it would at least slow down the discovery of the body. I'd always admired the way she kept her head under pressure, and seemed to think two steps ahead of everyone else.

I went first, then helped Nicky clamber out through the window and down; her grip was still strong—she hadn't been locked up long enough to lose her muscle tone—and immediately led the way towards the front of the building where the cars were parked. The gravel under our feet seemed to crunch more loudly now than when I'd arrived, but

I guessed she was deliberately walking with firm, loud strides, rather than wasting time and raising suspicion by trying to sneak across the car park unheard. I followed her, mimicking her brisk but relaxed footsteps. As we approached the Merc she flicked the remote and I heard the locks click open. We both slid inside at the same moment, not even glancing back at the house. She slipped the fat key into a slot on the dashboard—it was one of those all-electronic keys—and turned it. The engine fired up instantly, and she reached for her seatbelt. An electronic chime sounded and I squirmed, looking around for the source—was it an immobilizer or something?—but Nicky just murmured, "Seatbelt, Finn."

Sheepishly I pulled my belt across and clicked it home while Nicky found a button on the side of her seat and moved it forward. Power seats are all very well and flash, I decided, but they're no help when you're trying to make a snappy getaway. However, Nicky seemed completely unflustered; when she had the seat where she wanted it she adjusted the rear-view mirror, pulled the gear lever back, threw her arm over the back of my seat, looked over her shoulder and reversed out as smartly as if we were leaving the car park of her local supermarket. She slipped the car into drive and moved off, sending up a spray of gravel as we pulled off the forecourt and onto the driveway, but that was pretty much how Talent Show Tony would have taken off. He too would have weaved and swerved like this to dodge the potholes in the gravel—he'd liked to keep his Merc spotless.

"Are you OK?" Nicky asked me after a few moments. Her eyes flicked between the driveway ahead and the rear-view mirror.

"Me?"

"About Tony."

"Who's Tony?"

"The man you just . . ." She glanced at me.

"He was really called Tony?"

"What?"

"Never mind," I said. "Yeah, I'm OK, I think. It was him or us."

"Yes, it was," said Nicky. "He and his friends would have done the same to you if we'd been caught. He was a thug, Finn. Just yesterday he was boasting to me how he'd run down an old couple on his boss's orders. He actually laughed about it."

Old couple? I thought. *Winnie and Delroy!* My blood ran hot and cold at the same time, and I felt an insane urge to tell Nicky to turn back, so I could revive Tony and kill him again—properly this time, so he'd know what was happening to him and why. Maybe I'd been wrong to kill him, maybe it wasn't what Winnie would have wanted, but when I searched my conscience all that bothered me was the thought that the others might have discovered Tony's body already and be closing the gates before we managed to reach them.

But at the end of the drive the gates lay open as wide as when I'd arrived, and the divided highway beyond was empty and silent in both directions, like in one of those zombie-apocalypse movies. All the same Nicky slowed at the exit and checked for traffic before joining the nearside lane, even indicating before moving smoothly off. Then she floored it, the acceleration pushing me back in my seat, until she hit seventy-five. From that point she eased back on the pedal and held her speed steady, still glancing in her rear-view mirror every few minutes to ensure no one was pursuing.

"I'm sure this thing can go faster," I said. Dad had explained to me about back-seat drivers, and I was trying to be tactful.

"We don't want to get stopped by the police," she said.

"We don't?"

"Not until we're far enough away. Tony said they'd bought every cop for miles."

"You think he was telling the truth?"

"No, but I don't want to risk it. Oh God, oh God, that place!" Her voice was suddenly shrill and I saw tears in her eyes. "I thought I'd never . . ." Her knuckles were livid on the wheel, and I realized just how much terror and tension she had been keeping bottled up.

"Hey, Nicky, it's OK. You're safe now. Relatively, anyway."

That worked, and she laughed, despite herself. She shook the black thoughts out of her head and took a deep breath.

"Thank you for coming, Finn. I hoped you would. I can't believe you actually found me."

"It was mostly dumb luck," I said. "You want to tell me what happened?"

"They snatched me off the street. Not off the street, from the park near my house. I'd been running, late. I should have avoided that park—it's always so dark and deserted . . . I thought they were going to kill me. Rape me first, then kill me."

"Who were they? What were they after?"

Nicky thought for a while. "Honestly, Finn," she said at last, "the less you know the better."

A sign flashed by, way too fast for me to read, but I knew it would be a long time before we hit London, and after all I'd been through on her account I wasn't going to settle for a pat on the head.

"Those threatening emails and tweets you'd been getting on your phone," I said. "They were from Gabriel Bisham, Joan Bisham's kid. He's a deeply sick little fuck. It was him who torched that old pub, burned that man alive. He let his dad go to prison for it and was planning to do the same for his mother."

Nicky tore her eyes away from the road and the mirror long enough to look at me in disbelief.

"But I think he was trolling you for kicks— he had no connection to Tony's crowd."

"Finn, how the hell did you . . . ?"

"And that copper, DS Lovegrove? You were right about him being bent. He'd promised your friend Reverend Zeto he'd screw up the trial evidence, in return for blowjobs in the front seat of his cop car."

"Jesus Christ," she said. "You got hold of my client files?"

"Vora was worried about what had happened to you," I said. "I was worried about what had happened to my money."

"I'm sorry," said Nicky. "They made me do that after they grabbed me. Transfer the client account to the Cayman Islands. I didn't want to, but then I thought, maybe you'd come looking for me. Asking questions like you did after your dad died."

I would have looked for you even if you hadn't taken the money, I thought, but I didn't say it.

"I thought once I'd done that, they'd kill me. Instead they took me to—that place."

"What were all those cells for?"

"They bring in girls from all over Europe. Auction them off on video over the net, like cattle. Some tried to escape while I was there.

Tony brought them back . . ." She made an effort to steady her voice. "I think they're buried in the grounds somewhere."

"Jesus. We have to tell the police."

"Not yet. I have to get home, warn Harry, before he pays the ransom."

"Ransom? That's why they were keeping you alive?"

"They said if he didn't, they'd hand me over to the boss."

"I saw him," I said. "The big guy with the rings."

"That's Kemal," said Nicky. "He's not the boss."

"So who is?"

Nicky checked her rear-view mirror again. "I don't know his name," she said finally. "They called him the Turk."

*The Turk?* The new face Sherwood had talked about, and DS McCoy? I fell silent, thinking. Something stank about this. If Harry had been worried sick about his kidnapped wife, but hiding it while he got a ransom together, he deserved an Oscar for his performance. Maybe he'd only been snorting that cocaine to soothe his nerves.

"Nicky . . ." I said. "The women who came through that place . . . did any of them look like you?"

She frowned. "They brought a girl into my cell, not long after I arrived. To see if she was my height, my build. I never figured out what that was about."

"They needed a decoy," I said. "They gave her your passport and sent her to Paris, so me and the cops would stop searching for you."

"But she didn't look that much like me."

"They beat her first. That way the border guards wouldn't look too closely at her face."

"Oh God," groaned Nicky. "I hope she got away. I mean, properly, so those men can't find her again."

"Yeah," I said. "But that's not the point. How did they get hold of your British passport?"

Nicky glanced at me, unwilling to follow where this might be leading. "They must have stolen it." But her voice was tinged with doubt.

"Nicky, I know about Harry. About the gambling, and the coke." By now nothing I said seemed to surprise her.

"He's getting help," said Nicky.

Harry owed Sherwood money, I thought.

Sherwood sold the debt to the Turk, and boasted about it. The Turk cut him open to shut him up. And to frame me, because I knew about Harry.

"Is he?" I asked. "Getting help?"

"I told him if he didn't, I'd talk to Hennessey's. The bank where he works."

Jesus, I thought. That was why the Turk's people had snatched her.

"Who knew?" I asked. "Who knew you'd gone running in the park?"

She shook her head as if that would stop her hearing what I was saying, but I persisted. "How did the Turk know you were going to be there, that night?"

"Finn, Harry's my husband. Yeah, we have problems, but he'd never—that's just insane." She was staring hard at the road ahead, as if unwilling to meet my eye.

"But you were going to leave him, weren't you?" I said. "You were going to stay with your sister."

"Susan?" she said, perplexed. "Who told you that?"

"Susie did," I said.

"Susan's mixed up in this?" She seemed incredulous.

"She was worried about you," I said. "She helped me with the files . . ." I couldn't believe how my face was suddenly burning, like it wanted to give me away, but Nicky didn't seem to notice.

"Susan would never have me to stay," said Nicky. "She hates my guts."

It was my turn to look perplexed. "But you're sisters," I said. "I mean, half-sisters, but—"

Her laugh was brief and bitter. "Oh, right," she said. "You're an only child, aren't you?"

"But you're so alike," I said.

"We didn't used to be," said Nicky. "She had surgery, dyed her hair, just so she'd look more like me. I know how screwed up it sounds, but . . . she hates me and she wants to be me. Everything I've ever done for her, she's resented. Everything I've ever had she's wanted for herself."

*Including me?* I thought.

"If she was helping you look for me," said Nicky, "it was probably to make sure I was dead."

Suddenly I didn't know what to believe. I was confused and exhausted and I just wanted to crawl into a hole and sleep.

We had reached the eastern fringes of London without my even being aware of it, just as the city was starting to stir into life. Buses and commuters were heading in, huge articulated trucks heading out after stocking up the supermarkets. Nicky killed her speed, driving slowly and steadily to avoid drawing any unwelcome attention. The black Merc, I knew, was the sort of flash car that was always getting pulled over by London cops, especially if the man at the wheel was black. Some coppers couldn't grasp the concept of a black guy driving a motor like this and not being a drug dealer or a car thief . . .

"Shit," I said.

"What?"

"They'll have fitted a tracker to this car," I said. "We need to dump it, quick."

Without a word Nicky indicated, turned deftly into a cul-de-sac, pulled up on a single yellow line and killed the engine.

"We can take the Tube from here," she said. "Have you got any money?"

"I have enough," I said.

# twelve

The nearest Tube station was a short walk away and I used a lump of Tony's wedge to buy Nicky and me single tickets across the city. Out in the hinterland at this time of a Sunday morning there were plenty of empty seats, and we found ourselves a double bench facing forwards. We sat staring into space, as wordless as one of those married couples who have run out of things to say to each other, while we tried to make sense of everything that had happened. If I'd been wrong about Susan, maybe I'd been wrong about Harry. Maybe he was planning to rob his own bank to pay the ransom . . . but surely as soon as he paid up, this Turk would kill him and Nicky both?

And why had Susan been helping me if she and Nicky hated each other that much? Because they're still family, I thought. Then it occurred to me that I of all people should know the cruelty families are capable of.

As the ancient Tube train rattled and banged through the gloomy cuttings the carriage slowly filled with Sunday workers and nervous tourists clutching flimsy maps and checking the Tube diagrams every three minutes. One girl with wavy blonde hair still wet from her shower glanced at me and turned away. I realized I'd been staring at her hard enough to make her uncomfortable, but I honestly hadn't been ogling her. It was just that seeing her made me long for a shower—I couldn't remember the last time I had washed. I abruptly became aware of how badly I smelled, of dirt and sweat and violence and death. Oh well, I thought, at least it will stop the tourists crowding my space.

If I did stink it didn't seem to bother Nicky. It must been a long time since she had bathed too. She looked as dazed and shell-shocked as I felt, which was understandable after all that time locked in a windowless box wondering if any moment she might be violated and murdered and dumped in a pit. Yes, she was free, but then I'd said those things about Harry. She must have been wondering now if it was even safe to go home. And I couldn't help her—I had no home to go to. The last haze of days had been all about finding her or finding out what had happened to her, and now I had, it didn't seem to have fixed anything or solved anything or answered any questions.

The clatter of the train's wheels as it dived deeper into the tunnel rebounded and echoed inside the carriage until it was almost painful to my ears, but somehow I still felt sleep creeping up on me. I lost all track of time, the way you do in dreams, and I felt myself falling into a pit, and as the floor rushed upwards I knew it was strewn with the bones of others who had fallen before me, tangled with the entrails that had burst from their bellies on impact.

Nicky touched my hand, and I woke with a jolt. We were at Embankment station, where the darkness and thunder were displaced by the blue glare of striplights and the tramp of travellers' feet and the squawking electronic burble of platform announcements. Semi-comatose I followed Nicky past the bustling bodies through the warren of stairs and elevators onto yet another Tube train, until we finally emerged onto the concourse of Waterloo, Nicky leading me through the ticket barriers onto a platform for the next overland train to West London. Beyond the station roof I could see cheery blue sky and innocent white clouds cavorting miles above our grimy crowded circus.

As we waited I noticed a copper staring at us—not a real copper, I realized, but a ticket inspector, or revenue protection officer, or whatever they were called—clearly trying to decide whether Nicky and I were fare-dodgers who'd been sleeping on trains for a week or just seriously partied-out lovers. But when the train pulled in Nicky walked right past him and her air of blithe self-assurance seemed to change his mind about challenging us. Maybe she'd teach me that trick someday.

As the train carried us rocking gently across the Thames the sunshine gleamed off the wrinkled grey river below, dazzling us both so much we turned away, shading our eyes. Heading out of the city this early on a Sunday the train was almost empty, and only the cheery chime of the doors at each station and the hiss of them sliding open and shut again marked our progress west. I watched Nicky staring at the endless gritty bricks and slates of London's suburbs speeding past our windows, and I wondered if she had finally started to believe me, but her thoughtful silence repelled every question I could think of.

The doors chimed again and she rose to her feet.

"This is us," she murmured, and without looking at me stepped down onto the platform.

"Nicky, wait," I said. "What are you planning to do?"

"I'm going to ask Harry if it's true," she said.

As we approached the smart black railings separating her house from the street I glanced around, trying to see if any of the Turk's people were watching her house from a parked car. One sleek soft-top was parked a little further up, but it was empty. There was no passing traffic—not many churchgoers in this prosperous neck of the woods—so nobody saw us arrive, and I still hadn't decided if that was a good thing or not when we walked up to the front door and Nicky started digging among the flowerpots. I couldn't believe she'd hidden a key there. A house like hers surely needed better security than lazy idiots like me would use, but it didn't feel like the moment to point that out.

Nicky slid the key gently into the lock, turned it silently, pushed the door open and entered, leaving it open for me. I half expected to hear a burglar alarm; what we heard was voices raised in argument—one male, one female.

". . . all the finesse of a randy goat—"

"You still enjoyed it, though. Admit it. That's why you kept going back."

The male voice was Harry's, the female Susie's. Nicky and I looked at each other, and her face reflected mine; we both felt sorry for each other, and sick with betrayal.

"Oh, for the hundredth time, I only slept with him to find out what he knew. You're the one I want, Harry. Please get dressed."

"Stop bloody railroading me—I got enough of that from her."

I felt icy rage boiling up, at Susie and myself. Twice now I'd let a woman drag me along
by my dick. Never again. Nicky shut the front
door so gently behind us the latch clicked
home with barely a noise, and we slowly
edged closer to the library where Harry and
Susie were having their slanging match.

"You said the transfer has to happen today,
before the system upgrade—by the time the
bank finds out we'll be on the other side of the
world—"

"It's not that simple." Harry's voice sounded
grim and business-like, as if he knew something he wasn't going to share with Susan,
however much she pleaded.

"He'll never find us, not with that much
money. We could buy our own island—"

We were right outside the library door now,
and inside I heard the metal scratch of a key
in a lock, and the rattle of wooden shelving—
what was Harry up to?

"For God's sake, Harry, this is the Turk.
You're not going to frighten his people with
an antique bloody shotgun—"

"I know that." His voice wasn't angry now,
just calm and cold.

"There's no going back now. This way we get to be together."

"I don't want us to be together." I heard a heavy click of metal snapping shut.

"What are you talking about? We've been planning this for months—"

"Change of plan," said Harry.

Beyond the door we heard Susie gasp and scream in the same breath. "Harry! Don't—"

The blast was so loud it stabbed right through my ears and deep into my brain. Nicky and I both recoiled from the noise and the shock, and then came a second shotgun blast, and I slammed the library door open and moved fast, right across the room, past Susie writhing on the floor to Harry where he stood by the tall cupboard—the gun cabinet—still wreathed in blue smoke.

He stared at me in astonishment and fear, fumbling with two fresh shells, but I had guessed right—his hunting shotgun had to be broken open to be reloaded, and I was on top of him before he had time to snap it shut. I did that for him, trapping his hand and crushing the lower knuckle of his right thumb. He screamed in pain and cursed until I shut him

321

up by slamming my forehead into his face. He crashed backwards into the gun cabinet and slumped to the floor, stunned and groaning.

He had dropped the gun at my feet somewhere, but I ignored it and ran back to Susie. Her face was white with terror and pain, her blonde hair was glued to her forehead with sweat, and her white blouse was already soaked in blood. She was panting in shallow breaths, clutching the mess of her stomach and staring at me in desperation. There was no recognition in her eyes, no room for anything except agony and fear. I looked around for something to staunch her wound, grabbed a velvet cushion from a nearby chair and pressed it to her belly. She scrabbled and clutched at my hand as if my touch could cure her pain.

Nicky was paying no attention either to me or Susie; she'd picked up Harry's shotgun and was calmly sliding a shell into each barrel.

"Call an ambulance," I said.

Nicky looked at me with the same expression I'd seen a few hours before, when I knelt over Tony's body preparing to massage his heart.

"It's too late" was all she said.

She was right. Susie's grasp was weakening and her frantic breaths becoming more shallow. She blinked a few times, and opened her mouth to speak, but all that came out was a whisper I didn't catch. Then she shuddered and lay still, her eyes half closed.

"Nicky?" Harry stuttered. "Christ, Nicky, I thought—"

He was hauling himself to his feet, leaning on the gun cabinet for support and clutching his nose as if I'd broken it, which I'd hoped to do but missed. He flexed his jaw and shook his head as if trying to rattle his brain back into place.

"Don't, Harry. Move away from the cabinet," said Nicky. Her tone was distant and dazed, like she was trapped in a hallucination. Harry straightened up, holding his palms out in a gesture of innocence as if we hadn't just heard him shooting Susie in cold blood.

"Jesus, Nicky, I know how it looks, but she was going to mess everything up—"

Nicky had the gun pointed at him, but I wasn't sure if she was capable of using it, even with Susie lying there beside us, her life soaking into the rug. I wanted to call an ambulance, even if it was too late; but I held back, because I knew that with the ambulance would come police, and we'd never blag our way out of this mess.

"She wanted to keep the ransom," said Harry. "She wanted to let them kill you." He was slowly closing on her, pleading, and I saw the shotgun shaking in her grip. Did she actually believe him?

"How long had you been sleeping with her?" Nicky's voice was trembling like her hands.

Harry winced, as if the question was in bad taste, and moved closer. "I'm so sorry—it was months ago. I was depressed, I'd had too much to drink, you were at work, one thing led to another. Please, don't point that at me—"

He was close enough now to jump her, I realized. And if I lunged in now to stop him, any one of us might catch a faceful of buckshot.

"You weren't going to pay the ransom, Harry."

"Nicky, come on—"

"It was you who told them I'd gone running

in the park. You gave them my passport. You sold me to them."

Her voice was full of disbelief and heartbreak, and Harry sighed, and smiled. It was a roguish, wicked grin that had worked for him a thousand times before, I knew, because he was good-looking and charming and rich, and guys like him always got away with it, and always would, even this time, because Nicky was smiling back as if she loved him too much to argue. She let the stock of the shotgun drop, and held it out to him. Harry reached out to take it.

"Nicky, don't—" I said.

With one gentle, smooth movement, she pushed the gun against Harry's chest, the muzzle under his chin, and I saw her fingers flick to the trigger. Instinctively I shut my eyes, but I couldn't stop myself hearing another shattering blast, and something splatter on the ornately plastered ceiling, and a moment later the bump of Harry's body falling to the floor. My ears were still ringing as I opened my eyes again and wiped my face, expecting to see brain and bits of bone smeared on my hands.

I saw nothing but sweat. Nicky was standing there, shaking, staring down at what she had done.

"Nicky," I said. I didn't want her going into shock. "It's OK," I said. "It's OK. Just . . . don't touch anything."

I looked down at Harry's body with its ragged mess of a head. His hands were still loosely grasping the gun. If we left now there was a chance this would look like a murder-suicide. Nicky was officially thousands of miles away and the Turk was just a rumour—in fact, if the cops decided to pin this on anyone, it would most likely be me.

"We need to get out of here," I said.

"Wait a second," said Nicky. Stooping over Harry she reached for his right hand.

"Don't," I said. "You can't leave prints—"

"It's my gun," said Nicky. "It already has my prints." Carefully she curled Harry's limp fingers around the trigger. This was the cool, calm Nicky I used to know, the one who thought two steps ahead of everyone else. I was glad to see her again, even if she scared me.

\* \* \*

"A man answering your description was spotted fleeing the scene." McCoy was neither condescending nor sympathetic this time; she was all business. That didn't surprise me. Gutted and headless corpses had been piling up in the suburbs and the police had to find someone to blame, or at least they had to look busy trying, and McCoy had been the first officer on my case, thanks to my idiot impulse to report Nicky's disappearance. McCoy's mute assistant sat at her elbow, staring at me hard as if that alone would make me burst into tears, but I've had harder stares from squirrels.

"He might have answered my description. But so could a lot of guys."

"Your fingerprints were found in Sherwood's office."

"Like I said, I'd been there a few times."

"You'd borrowed money from him?"

"I hadn't. My partner had."

I wasn't sure how long this particular interview had been going on, but I didn't check the clock to find out. I knew I'd be pounced on with those predictable sarcastic questions—"*In a hurry, Mr. Maguire?*"—so I sat there, smiling patiently, helping with enquiries as helpfully as I could. They'd arrested me on suspicion of murder, and that meant they had thirty-six hours to bring charges. Let them do the clock-watching.

"OK, Delroy Llewellyn, your partner in this gym—he'd borrowed money off Sherwood. And Delroy couldn't repay his loan, and you went to see Sherwood."

"That's right."

"And what happened on that occasion?"

"I offered to repay Delroy's loan, and he told me to get lost, so I did."

"That was the second time you met him, or the third?" She already had the answer written down in her notes. Maybe she'd forgotten, or maybe it was a lazy ruse to get me cross.

"The first time, and the second. The third time I met him in the street and told him to stop sending his enforcers round. After that I never saw him again."

"Not even after your friend Delroy's wife was run over and died in hospital?"

"Nope."

"But you were with Winnie Llewellyn when she died. And you left the hospital shortly afterwards."

"Yeah. I went for a run."

"A run." She tried her best to inject weary contempt into the word.

"I was upset. Running helps to clear my head."

"And where did you run to?"

"Nowhere in particular. North for a bit, then west, then south . . ."

"According to our information, from the hospital you went straight to Sherwood's office. You blamed him for Mrs. Llewellyn's death. You confronted him, and things went too far."

"Like I said, this informant of yours is lying."

"Why would he do that?" I saw her stifle a wince at her own mistake—she'd said "he" when she should have said "they."

I wanted her to know I hadn't missed it. "Ask him. He's your informant." And his name's Dean, I thought, and nothing he's told you will ever be admissible in court, and he's never going to testify, and you know that.

"So you're saying you were set up?" said McCoy.

"You're saying I was set up. I'm saying I wasn't even there."

"I think you were. I think if you didn't kill Sherwood, you know who did."

"You arrested my client for murder. Are you saying now you don't think he did it?"

Vora spoke as if he was making conversation with an annoying snot-nosed seven-year-old. He projected confidence and authority, with just a tinge of boredom, as if all this was beneath him. He was expensively dressed too, and there was no sign of the flapping, panicked old man who had passed me Nicky's client files out of desperation.

We hadn't discussed how I was going to pay him, or even *if* I was going to pay him. I suspected he was doing this because he knew I'd rescued Nicky, but I didn't want to ask what he knew about that, and I didn't think he wanted me to ask. He had sat patiently all day in that little stuffy room listening to me re-tell my story with all its holes and evasions, and backed me up whenever he thought McCoy was pushing her luck. Thanks to him the process that was supposed to wear me down seemed to be wearing McCoy down instead.

"I think your client is a material witness," said McCoy.

"And he's told you three times he wasn't there. Can we move on please?"

McCoy shuffled through the folders piled in front of her and picked up a slim one she hadn't opened before. I wondered what she was going to bring up next, and whether we were going to go over Harry and Susie again. McCoy hadn't yet accused me of being involved in their deaths, and by now I was sure she wasn't going to.

Nobody had heard the shotgun blasts, or if they had, nobody had bothered to report them. But then Londoners can live in one street for decades without ever even learning their neighbours' names. It wasn't until the bank officials had noticed Harry's continued absence, checked out his business dealings, crapped their collective panties and called the police that the two bodies were discovered. By then the weekend had passed plus a few days, which probably hadn't helped forensics any. Maybe the Turk's people knew before that point that Harry was dead, as was their plan to steal millions of pounds without so much as pointing a gun. But the Turk's people would have been even less keen to involve the plods than I was.

"Ten days ago you went to see a Mrs. Joan Bisham at her home in Ealing." Her memory refreshed, McCoy leaned forward, her arms folded on the table. The pose was deliberate— relaxed and knowledgeable. My surprise must have been obvious—*Bisham? Where the hell were they going with this?*

"Yeah."

"She says you forced your way into her house and accused her son of burning down your gym."

"I didn't force my way in. But her son did burn down my gym. She believed me, at the time."

"Did you have any evidence for this?"

Only the evidence her son planted and I removed from the scene, I thought.

"Just a hunch," I said.

"You had a hunch a fifteen-year-old boy was a . . . 'psychopath and a murderer,' " she read from the file.

"His eyes were too close together," I said. She didn't laugh. "Talk to him," I told her. "Ask him what he was doing the night my gym burned down, with me in it." And Susie, I suddenly remembered, but I skipped over that detail. If McCoy came across that connection she'd start asking about Susie and me and Harry, and I was having enough trouble keeping my story straight as it was.

"We can't, I'm afraid. Gabriel Bisham died last night as a result of injuries received when he was sleeping rough."

"Sleeping rough?" So his mother hadn't called the cops. I should have known.

"He'd run away from home. Sunday morning he was sleeping in a doorway when someone doused him in petrol and set him alight. He suffered third-degree burns over eighty per cent of his body."

"Jesus . . ." I let myself sound shocked and revolted because I was. The kid had needed locking up, not premature cremation.

"Where were you at one a.m. five nights ago?" asked McCoy. "Sunday the twentieth."

At one in the morning the previous Sunday I'd been on a coach from Victoria to Chelmsford. On my way to strangle Talent Show Tony, as it turned out.

"You've asked me about that already. I was upset about Winnie dying. Went for a run."

"All night?"

"No, like I said, eventually I went back to Delroy's place and crashed there."

Delroy would back me up, if the cops ever asked him, and they probably never would.

Vora waded in. "Excuse me, is this a second murder you're accusing my client of being involved in? On the same evening?"

"We haven't accused him of anything yet."

"You do realize that you've been questioning Mr. Maguire for six hours straight, without a break?"

"I am aware of that, Mr. Vora."

"Because we're getting very close to an abuse of process."

"We're grateful for Mr. Maguire's cooperation," McCoy said through slightly gritted teeth. "We just have a few more questions for him."

"Do you have any witnesses or any evidence that my client was involved in this attack on this young chap Bisham? Do you plan to question my client about every murder that took place in London that night?"

"Only the murders of people he was personally acquainted with."

You're wasting your own time asking me

about Bisham, I thought. You ought to talk to Leslie, the homeless guy with the face like melted wax, whose lover had burned alive before his eyes, who slept on the streets, praying to God for a chance at revenge. Maybe one night in some dark piss-smelling back alley he discovered his prayers had been answered.

I said nothing, of course. McCoy was being paid to find this shit out, and I wasn't about to do her job for her.

"It's fine, Mr. Vora," I said. "I'm happy to help." I smiled at McCoy, but she didn't smile back. She looked like a woman who could smell a whole nest of rats decomposing and she'd pulled up every floorboard in her house and started ripping holes in the ceiling and she still couldn't find it. She glanced at the clock and shuffled her folders.

"Let's go back to your dealings with John Sherwood," she said.

Twelve hours later Vora and I left the police station. The cops hadn't pressed charges, but McCoy had asked where I was living, and if I had any plans for travel. I understood her meaning—don't leave town—but I wasn't bothered, because I wasn't planning to go anywhere. I hadn't killed Sherwood, and they had no hard evidence suggesting I had. Forensics would have told them he was dead before I ever arrived—maybe even before Winnie died.

Vora was less optimistic; he knew prosecutions were brought even when the evidence was flimsy, bent, or non-existent, because it was the job of the police to keep the courts busy. If the judge threw out a case twenty minutes into the trial, the cops could still mark it "job done"—it was no skin off their noses.

But I was past caring whether I was charged or not. I had enough to worry about—like finding a long-term place to live, for a start.

That Sunday morning Nicky and I had left the bodies of Harry and Susan lying in the library and exited the house the same way we had come in. As we walked in silence towards the station I realized Nicky needed to talk about everything she had been through and everything we'd seen and done—all the brutality and betrayal and slaughter. I knew that because I wanted to talk about it, badly, and she was the only one I could ever talk to. But before I could even work out where to begin she said, "Have you got a passport yet?"

I saw then it was never going to happen, because we had no time, and our wounds would have to heal themselves somehow.

"Nope," I said. She grimaced. "You're leaving the country?" I said. "For real this time?"

"We have to. Both of us. Harry was going to make millions for the Turk. You stopped that scam, you killed one of his people, you rescued me."

"The Turk won't even know I was there," I said.

"He'll find out, somehow. And he'll take it out on you. Tony and Kemal used to sit in my cell and tell me about him, about some of the things he's done to people who crossed him. You have no idea what he's capable of."

Actually I do, I thought. I saw Sherwood.

"Where would we go?"

"I have family in Brazil. It's far enough away, we'd be safe there."

"Brazil? I'm not going to Brazil," I said.

"Not even with me?" She took my hand, and for the first time she looked at me with clear affection, and even desire. My heart lurched, because I'd once longed for that. But intense as those feelings were, they had been born out of danger and fear and the violence we'd faced together; how long would they last? Even if we got as far as São Paulo she'd get bored eventually with a big ignorant lug half her age who spoke no Portuguese and whose only skill was hitting people. Then I'd be stranded miles from home with a woman who'd once liked me, and now pitied me, and nothing to look forward to but sunburn.

How Nicky planned to get out of the country was none of my business. She kissed me on the lips, and touched my face, and walked away towards the station, and just for a moment I was ready to shout out her name and run after her. Instead I turned and walked in the other direction, found a phone box and made a call.

Then I headed for Delroy's house.

Seeing my face at his door Delroy shuffled back to let me in without a word. The flame that used to burn in him was dimmed now and flickering. It was like he was going through the motions of living with no clear idea why, but he seemed happy to see me all the same, the way a sick man might be happy to hear a bird sing. He offered me cereal for breakfast, but the milk had gone off so I had toast instead. I had to scrape away the spots of blue mould before I buttered it. I must have smelled as bad as the food in his fridge, because he'd suggested I take a bath before I'd even had a chance to ask.

The water was lukewarm, but it got me clean, and while I soaked Delroy found a T-shirt that I'd left behind months earlier. It had been washed and ironed by Winnie, and kept tucked away in the airing cupboard, and it still smelled of the fabric conditioner she liked to use. I sat in the bathroom with it pressed to my face, breathing in that smell of a time full of hope, until I felt my eyes sting and my throat tighten.

Delroy himself was way past weeping. He set me up in the spare room amid the cardboard boxes of junk he and Winnie had accumulated over decades, and next day I visited a few local charity shops and bought some old new clothes with the last of Tony's wad. The stolen jacket I stuffed into a public recycling bin.

Though Delroy was only speaking in monosyllables I learned of his plan to take Winnie's ashes back to Jamaica after the funeral.

Early one morning I hefted his suitcase downstairs—from the weight I guessed he wasn't planning to come back—called him a taxi, checked he had his passport and his ticket, and walked him up the path to his gate. The taxi driver obligingly heaved the suitcase into the trunk while Delroy and I stood there, realizing it was time to say goodbye, and not sure how.

"You be a good boy now, Finn," growled Delroy at last. "Keep your guard up." He held out a fist, and I bumped mine against his. I wanted to hug him but knew that wasn't his thing—it'd make him uncomfortable—so I let him turn away. Then wished, too late, I had hugged him anyway. The taxi driver held open the door while Delroy heaved himself in and arranged his walking stick between his legs. He didn't turn to look at me or wave as the car drove off; he seemed already to be four thousand miles away, sitting on a porch of a Jamaican shack in the fading light, waiting for Winnie to come and collect him.

\* \* \*

For the time being Delroy's home was mine, and nobody seemed to object. A few letters came that looked official but Delroy had left no forwarding address so I just let them pile up on the sideboard. Then I realized Winnie would have hated to see her house so cluttered, so I tidied them away. I visited my bank to explain how I'd lost my cards and my identity documents in the fire, and because they were a bank they kept asking me for identity documents anyway, and I had to keep explaining why I didn't have any until they gave up and let me have access to the few thousand left in my account. If I was careful it would keep me going long enough to reclaim the money Nicky hadn't stolen from me when she hadn't done a bunk.

I got in touch with the Law Society, and the original spotty lawyer I'd first spoken to told me my case would very shortly be resolved. The police were satisfied Ms. Hale had fled the country, and that was good enough for the compensation fund. And it was true, of course, now that Nicky really *had* fled. I would get my money back—by dubious means admittedly, but seeing as the money came from an insurance pot funded by lawyers that wasn't going to lose me much sleep.

Late one night when I turned off the lights and locked up—Winnie was so present in that house I could hear her sucking her teeth if I even left a mug in the kitchen sink—I remembered Zeto, and wondered if Lovegrove would ever come looking for payback. He'd be a fool if he did. I hadn't sent the footage of him being pleasured by Zeto to anyone else, but I could have it all over the Net in seconds if I wanted, even if the material was a little rich for YouTube. I hadn't attached any threats or instructions; I figured Lovegrove could work out for himself what I expected him to do. I was pretty confident I wouldn't hear of Zeto's case coming up in court any time soon, or any time at all in fact, and that I'd never see Lovegrove again.

So when the back gate squealed at two in the morning, the instant I awoke I knew it wasn't him.

The bedsprings groaned as I rolled off the mattress, dropped to the floor and crouched there, motionless, listening. Whoever had opened the gate was moving up the path towards the back door, and now I could hear them trying the handle. They should have known it would be locked and bolted—it was a friendly estate, but this wasn't the 1930s. I thought they'd try the windows next, looking for one that was ajar, then maybe smash a pane. Instead I heard a grinding, creaking, splintering noise, like someone was wedging a crowbar into a wooden frame and slowly forcing the door.

I rose, pulled on my jeans, wriggled my feet into my shoes, grabbed my hooded sweatshirt and quickly tugged it on. Close by in one of Delroy's cardboard boxes lay a long thick statue of a crocodile carved from some dark hardwood, with seashells for eyes. I had noticed it a few days earlier, and wondered if Winnie had been the one with terrible taste or somebody at her church. Grotesque as the carving was I felt glad of its weight in my hand. I'd been sleeping with my bedroom door open—I always did—and now I pulled it wide and stepped out onto the landing. There I paused again and listened some more.

There was someone out front too—Winnie

and Delroy had planted thick scented bushes all along the garden path and I could hear them rustling. The hairs rose on the back of my neck. This wasn't just some local punk out to fund a fix. For a moment I actually hoped it was a police raid, but then cops usually piled in mob-handed, making all the racket they could, on the basis that if they had to be awake at that time of night so should everyone else. These weren't cops.

The creaking and splintering continued from the back door, and now from the front door I heard a series of clicks, like the lock was being picked. By this point I was at the top of the stairs. The ground floor was a thick pool of darkness; the street lights couldn't penetrate the yellowing nets and heavy green drapes of the front window, and the only light around the back of the house came from the rear windows of homes fifty metres away.

The darkness would give me a moment of advantage, if I timed this right. I lifted my hand to the light switch at the top of the stairs and waited. The clicking from the lock coalesced into one loud, definite clunk, and slowly the front door was eased open. From where I stood I could just see the lower half of the door, which was solid hardwood apart from four glass panes in an arch at the top. I shifted my weight to rest my hand on the switch at the top of the stairs that controlled the hall light. The boards under my feet creaked just a little as a bulky figure stepped into the hall. He raised a hand to the light switch and I screwed up my eyes, so when the hall light flicked on it didn't dazzle me. I heard him take one step into the hall, then I flicked the hall light off again and ran down the stairs into the darkness.

I recognized the silhouette in an instant—Kemal—but he didn't know where to look. He'd half turned to reach back for the light switch when I rammed the rock-hard wooden carving into his right kidney. He yelled and arched his back, and I raised the crocodile and brought it down on his skull so hard it snapped in two, but the son of a bitch was still standing. I dropped the broken carving and planted a straight right under Kemal's ear into the hinge of his jaw. It felt like I'd slammed my fist into a bag of pool balls, but it stunned him and his knees buckled, and when I stamped hard on the nearest one he went down in my direction like a cement mixer going over a cliff. I stepped back, ready to clamber over him and make a break for it through the front door before he recovered, but when I looked up two more heavies in leather jackets were running down the path. I'd never get through the door before they were on top of me. Cursing, I turned back, hoping I'd find better odds in the kitchen.

I did. Dean was standing in the busted doorway, leering at me. He held up his crowbar in his right hand and flipped the fingers of his left at me, inviting me to have a go. I barely had time to wonder if that was the same crowbar that had opened my scalp in the car park before I accepted his invitation with slightly more enthusiasm than he expected. Maybe the silly prick thought I'd be so intimidated I'd stand there and let him jemmy my head open, but by now I knew I was probably going down, and if that happened I was taking Dean with me.

He was gripping the crowbar in both hands ready to drive the hooked end into my face, but as he swung I caught his arm and pushed it upwards. I felt its point part my hair left to right, and saw him spin off balance, and I drove my fist under his ribs so hard I could feel his heart pounding under my knuckles. As he staggered, winded, I swung a left into his face and felt through his cheek two teeth pop out of his jaw. Blood spurted from his mouth and his greasy quiff collapsed over his eyes. He tried to slam his right elbow into my face but there was no force in his blow, probably because his head was still ringing like a bell. I grabbed his arm and wrenched it straight—the crowbar landed with a clang at our feet—and using his arm as a lever drove his face into the doorpost.

All I could think of was Winnie, writhing in fear as she died, and I grabbed the back of Dean's head, ready to keep slamming it into the paintwork until the wood splintered and his face hit brick, but suddenly my head jolted forward, my knees sagged and the room was spinning. Kemal's two pals had caught up with me and were laying into my back and my head with what felt like scaffolding poles. But the worst pain was from inside, knowing I hadn't managed to maim Dean before my turn came.

*   *   *

The bile in my throat woke me up, coughing and puking. Every contraction of my chest shot pain through my body, and I guessed they'd cracked a few of my ribs when they'd rained kicks on my chest and belly. I realized I was still alive, and tried to figure out why, and I didn't like the obvious answer, so I kept my eyes closed a moment longer, until I could at least work out where I was. Something hard was pressed against my forehead, my pulse was thumping in my temples, and my arms were wedged up behind my back and tied together at the wrists. Screw this, I thought, and opened my eyes, as best I could. The left one barely obliged; it was bruised so badly the eyelids only parted a millimetre or two. The right was swimming with tears that were running upwards into my hair. The room seemed upside down.

I realized I'd been placed in a kneeling position on the floor of Winnie's front room with my hands handcuffed behind me, and my body bent forward so my head rested on the floor. I tried to topple over sideways but I was propped up against someone's leg, and I felt another leg pressing into me from the other side. I'd seen old Chinese kung-fu movies where peasants kowtowed to their emperor, with their heads knocking the floor, and that was what I seemed to be doing. As soon as I realized that I tried to straighten up, but it was tricky. Not only were my hands cuffed behind me, but every gram of my flesh felt slashed and battered, and it seemed like I had half a dozen fractures between my toes and the crown of my head.

I could smell blood, and carpet, and the stink of Dean's cheap cigars, but there was another smell in the room that seemed oddly familiar—an expensive aftershave mingled with mint. I couldn't place it. I realized too that nobody was saying anything, as if they were waiting respectfully for someone to speak. Somehow I doubted they were waiting for me.

I snorted with amusement when the answer came to mind: I was in the presence of the Turk himself, prostrate before him. I could already visualize him—a burly guy in his forties with oiled hair, stubble you could strike a match on, and a shiny cheap suit with its buttons straining from holding in his belly. He'd be waiting for me to look up at him and cower.

That realization made me try to straighten up again. The Turk must have noticed my efforts and nodded to the guys flanking me to help, because they each grabbed me by an armpit and hauled me upright. I lifted my head to see the great man properly, and when I did I gaped. I might even have gasped. I was so gobsmacked my left eye nearly opened properly.

I was kneeling in front of Bruno. Bruno, the quiet, would-be boxer I'd thrown out of my gym for beating Nicky senseless in the ring. The room swam and spun, or maybe that was just my head. *Bruno?* Bruno was this Turk everyone was so scared of?

Seeing my confusion Bruno grinned. Not the sunny, gormless grin of Bruno the boxer: this Bruno's smile was hard and sharp as broken glass and his eyes glittered. He wore a white cotton shirt and a beautifully cut linen suit in dark blue, no jewellery, no rings, nothing ostentatious. There was nothing clumsy or gawky about him now. His movements were composed, almost graceful. But when he tilted his head to one side I remembered that look—he'd looked the same way at Nicky before he opened up on her. The look suggested I was a Rubik's Cube he would solve by twisting my limbs around until he found the answer.

"You've cost me a lot of money, Finn. And time and effort." His accent was less London than I remembered, and more educated, but I couldn't place it. I had no idea where he was from, or what his real name was. "Harry Anderson was going make me twenty million pounds in one afternoon."

"No, he wasn't," I said. "He was going to double-cross you, keep the money for himself."

Bruno nodded. "He was going to try, yes." He shrugged as if that was to be expected. "And then there's the matter of my warehouse."

Warehouse? What warehouse? "Oh, right . . ." The mansion where I'd found Nicky. The one they'd used for trafficking girls.

"Right," said Bruno. "That place cost me a small fortune to fit out. And thanks to you we had to walk away."

It'd had taken me half an hour after parting from Nicky, but I'd managed to locate the last public phone box in London and call an anonymous whistle-blower's hotline. The next day I'd caught a radio news report about how five bodies had been found in the grounds of a stately home in Chelmsford that police suspected had been used by a sex trafficking ring. They were trying to trace the mansion's owners, but they'd must have got nowhere, because the item soon slipped out of the news bulletins.

I could guess what had happened: after finding Nicky missing and Tony dead, Kemal and the others had chucked Tony's body into the same pit as the girls who'd fought back, then packed their bags and cleared out. It was gratifying to know I'd damaged their business, even a little.

"And then there was Tony," said Bruno. "He was a good man."

"Good, how, exactly?" I said.

Bruno smiled. "OK, he was a bad man. But good bad men are hard to find. Look what you did to Dean here."

Dean stood in the corner, clutching his face and trying not to whimper. By now blood and slobber from his broken teeth had soaked the front of his shirt under his leather jacket. I could guess how much it would hurt him to chew, and I hoped the pain would last all his life.

"And Kemal!" Bruno—the Turk—laughed. "I don't think I have ever seen Kemal bleed before."

I glanced up to my left. Kemal was staring down at me, his face calm and neutral, but a trickle of blood from his scalp was running down his neck and blotting around his collar.

"What is the English expression?" said the Turk. "You are a bull in a china shop. And all breakages must be paid for."

I saw Kemal's fist rise, and I knew I had no way to go with the punch. It came down like a piledriver on the side of my face and I felt my head try to part from my shoulders. The rings on his fingers had split the skin of my temple and my blood spattered Winnie's good rug.

I knew that was only the beginning, and groped in my foggy brain for some witty last words to say before Kemal broke my jaw. Preferably something so offensive they'd beat me to death that much quicker. Blood filled my mouth, and I hawked and spat. I still felt an absurd twinge of guilt watching it soak into

Winnie's rug. Cold water to clean up blood, she used to say.

The Turk stepped forward, hitched up his linen trousers and stooped down so his mouth was close to my ear.

"Where is Nicky Hale?" he murmured.

"I don't know," I said. I looked at him as straight as I could. His brown eyes stared into mine. I don't know what he saw; I saw a cold, gaping void. My eyes were throbbing and watering, but I knew if I looked away he'd think I was lying, and they'd keep on asking, and I wanted to get this over with.

After an eternity he nodded. "Pity," he said. "No woman has ever hit me like that before. I was hoping to finish our bout. You just can't help interfering, can you?"

That was why his people had been keeping Nicky alive—payback. For all his laid-back airs and lack of bling, the Turk was just another cocky punk, fuelled by ego and insecurity, and guys like that always ended up kissing the canvas. Must remember that, I thought, although the way things were going I wouldn't have to remember it for very long.

Even with my jaw knocked crooked I couldn't help laughing, and I saw Bruno frown.

"You want someone to slap you around?" I said. "Glove up." Out of the corner of my eye I saw the piledriver rise again.

"Kemal," said Bruno. Kemal froze. "I do have many vices," said Bruno softly. "But vanity is not one of them. I don't care about Nicky. I wasn't there to watch her." He straightened up again and waited patiently for me to put it together.

"You were watching me?" I said.

"I wanted to know what sort of man you were. At first I thought the reports must be mistaken. He's big and he's tough, but he's an idiot. He can't read, he has no head for business. All his money will be gone in a year. That's what gave me the idea."

"To clean out Nicky's client account."

"Like your friend Delroy used to say—you want to really know a man, put him under pressure," said the Turk. "And now I've seen what you are capable of, I have to admit, I'm impressed. Now I understand what he sees in you."

"Who?" I asked. But deep down I knew.

"Finn, why do you think you are still alive, and in one piece? I have a job for you."

"I'm not for hire," I said.

"Of course not," said the Turk. Reaching into his pocket he took out a smartphone, unlocked it and started flicking at the screen. "You don't need money, you have nothing to lose, there is no one you care about."

"Nicky's gone," I said.

"And her sister is dead, I know. I was thinking of this one." He held out the phone so I could see the screen.

The footage was smooth; whoever took it had been so close there was no need to zoom in. Close enough to see the stud glinting in Zoe's nose as she laughed at some crack her friend had made. The two women were sitting in some huge cafeteria—a dining room at her college maybe. Now she was emerging from an old house, pushing a bike, wrestling with a bag of books. Every turn of her head and quirk of her mouth burned into my heart, and my aching guts tightened in fear. I couldn't look up at the Turk—I knew I'd see triumph in his eyes.

"What do you want?" I said.

"There is someone I would like to meet. A friend of yours. I need to put a proposition to him."

Something told me this proposition was going to involve a lot of lead and explosives.

"I want you to introduce me to the Guvnor." said the Turk.

*Turn the page for a preview of the companion novel . . .*

# CRUSHER

*an Edgar Award finalist*

"A hard-hitting adventure. . . .
Travels at a gripping pace."
　　　　　*—Publishers Weekly*

"Many twists and turns . . .
leave readers guessing."
　　　　　*—School Library Journal*

The day Finn Maguire discovers his dad bludgeoned to death in a pool of blood, his dreary life is turned upside down. Prime suspect in his father's murder, Finn must race against time to clear his name and find out who hated his dad enough to kill him.

# one

It was a bit early for someone to be banging on the front door. I hurried down the stairs, hair still dripping from the shower, and turned the latch.

"Sorry, son, locked myself out," said Dad, shivering as he stepped in. He'd been out in his slippers, I noticed. I wondered why, until I saw the TV trade mag folded in his hand, and my heart sank.

Dad looked pretty rough. His pale blue eyes were red-rimmed and his fair hair was standing up in spikes that weren't dishevelled or trendy, but made him look like he'd slept in a doorway. I'd heard him come home late last night and stumble around trying not to make a noise, crashing into the furniture and cursing under his breath. But he'd got up the same time he always did, while I was out running, and the breakfast he'd made was still warm on the table: old eggs, thin salty bacon and instant coffee, white. I'd nab a glass of orange juice when I got to work, though the most orange thing about the stuff we sold was its colour.

"Bollocks," said my dad, squinting through his crooked glasses at the magazine's first inside page. That hadn't taken long.

"What's up?"

"Bill Winchester's got a second series of that time-travelling cop show. Jammy sod."

"*Future Perfect*?"

My dad gave a look as if I was being disloyal.

"Never seen it." I shrugged. "I've heard of it, that's all."

"Me and Bill worked together years ago, on *Henby General*."

"Yeah, you said." But he didn't say it very often.

Dad had been big in the early nineties. For a while he was everyone's favourite twinkly-eyed Irish actor— he'd even won an award for *Best Newcomer*. The bronze statuette still stood on the mantelpiece, gathering ironic dust. From then on it had all been downhill. He didn't keep the statuette on display out of nostalgia or vanity— it was there to fuel his envy. Envy keeps you hungry, Dad would say, which I'd never understood, because I was hungry all the time and I'd never got to like it. But all Dad's old acting mates were doing better than him. If it had been true that every time a friend succeeds a little part of you dies, by now my dad would have been a really ripe zombie.

He saw himself as a passionate, committed and challenging performer. Directors soon got to see him as temperamental, pig-headed and impossible to work with. The jobs had already started to dry up when he met my mother, and his last role had been years ago, eating imaginary pizza on a desert island in a commercial, for insurance, I think . . . it might have been for pizzas, or desert islands. He never officially retired, but he grew a beard and stopped going to auditions and quit pestering his agent for work.

He wasn't going to wait for the phone to ring, he said. He was going to make his own luck. He was going to write a TV epic so gripping and authentic that producers would be ripping each other's throats out to make it, and he'd write a really good part for himself, so they'd have to cast him. Not the lead, of course—he had to be realistic, he said. The lead could go to one of his more famous old mates, to help get the show commissioned. He had it all worked out. He'd had it all worked out for years now, and it never seemed to happen.

"Don't sweat it, Dad. You always say success is the best revenge."

"Yeah, but I might be wrong," said Dad. "Maybe the

best revenge is cutting someone's head off with a rusty saw. Maybe I should try that instead."

I carried our empty plates out to the kitchen to wash up.

"So what are you doing today?" I said, more out of politeness than interest.

"Working," he said.

Dad used the term loosely. A lot of his work seemed to consist of staring out the window. He had read every book on writing screenplays the local library could scrape together, and he was always quoting aphorisms and mottos about inspiration and perspiration and pants being applied to the seat of a chair, and he always wrote ten pages a day. The only problem was, next day he'd tear up nine of them. Some days he'd go traipsing round London doing "research," and the notes and jottings and cuttings would pile up on the dining table beside his laptop, and over dinner he'd try to tell me about his latest story idea, but I'd stopped listening long ago.

"You wouldn't believe the stuff I heard last night," said Dad. "London gangland is like the court of Caligula—they're all stabbing each other in the back. That's the real drama, and it's right under our noses, and nobody ever wants to hear about it." Then why the hell are you writing about it? I thought. But I didn't say it. The best thing about Dad was his eternal optimism. Someday, with a lot of effort and a little luck, he'd be rich and famous, and we wouldn't have to scrape by on his shrinking royalty payments and my minimum wage from Max Snax.

"You want me to bring something back for dinner?" I said.

"Nah," said Dad. "I'll probably go down the shops later." He wouldn't go into the shops, I knew, until he'd checked the skips outside for ready meals chucked out after their sell-by date. He'd serve them up with a sermon about the evils of the consumer society and the wastage it produced. I used to think, if wastage keeps us in dinners, I'm all for it.

"You know where the spare keys are?" asked Dad as I laced up my trainers.

"Hanging up," I said. "Rough night?"

"Never mind," said Dad. "Mine will turn up."

"I'll see you later, yeah?" I rose to go, expecting his routine grunted goodbye, but he put the magazine down and looked at me.

"Finn?" he said. "We're all right, aren't we? You and me?"

All right? How were we all right? I was an illiterate dropout with no GCSEs stuck in a dead-end job, and he was an ex-nobody who spent his days writing a script that would never be finished and that no one would ever want to read anyway.

"Yeah, Dad, sure. I have to go."

"See ya," said Dad.

I pulled the door shut behind me, jogged a short distance to warm up, then started to run.

"Yeah, I want the Texas Chicken Special, no salad, no sauce, none of that."

"What, just chicken and bread?"

"Yeah."

He was about five foot tall and five foot round the middle, and I could see why. I always used to wonder how guys like Mr. Spherical kept their trousers up— were their belts stapled to their stomachs? Anyway, without the sauce it wasn't a Texas Chicken Special, it was just fried chicken in pappy white bread, but I wasn't there to quibble with the customers about what the stuff was called, I was there to sell it to them. And smile. And say thank you. "Smiles and thanks—money in the bank!" Andy used to recite that at our weekly pep talks. He was fond of morale-boosting slogans, and thought he had a knack for coining them, but his own were even crappier than the ones on the Max Snax staff training videos.

I punched the order into the programmed till and

handed Mr. Spherical his change. Jerry in the kitchen slid the foil-wrapped package into the chute while I filled a litre beaker with half a litre of ice followed by half a litre of fizzy aerated syrup, wondering for the thousandth time how anyone could consider this chemically reconstituted muck to be food, and how I'd ended up selling it. I pushed the thoughts aside for the thousandth time, but they kept flopping back into my mind, like an annoying greasy fringe you can't cut off getting into your eyes. And it was only bloody Monday.

Hands on automatic, mind anywhere else but here, bish, bosh, sandwich, regulation single paper napkin, drink, tray, deep breath, stab at a smile, recite the fast-food blessing: "Thank you, sir, and enjoy—have a great day." The tubby punter grunted, turned and waddled off to the door, turned round again and bumped out backwards, into the bright April morning that I was pissing away behind this overheated counter in this sweaty polyester shirt.

"Yo, Maguire!" hissed Jerry from the kitchen. "Thanking time is wanking time!" Not quite the approved formula, but he had the Max Snax high-pitched, hysterical delivery down pat. I didn't mind Jerry. He was almost bearable, as long as you didn't try having an actual conversation with him. You couldn't look him in the eye, anyway—either he had curvature of the spine or he spent too much time bent over computer porn, jerking off. Andy wouldn't let him serve the customers, insisting that I gave a better impression of Max Snax. If I did, it was because I ran ten kilometres a day and never ate anything we sold, but I didn't say that to Andy. I flicked Jerry a cheery middle finger. He sniggered and ducked back towards the fryers, while I cursed myself.

How could I have forgotten about the CCTV? Andy had cameras all over the joint, concealed under little black plastic domes, most of them pointed at the staff rather than the punters. I used to wonder why Andy had gone into catering, when he didn't like people. He disliked the punters on a casual basis, but he made a full-time job of despising the staff. That was why he stayed in his office all day, watching us all through CCTV monitors. He wanted to check we weren't stealing the fries or sneaking off to the bogs to smoke a spliff, but he wouldn't join us on the floor to do that. Instead, he would sit poised in front of his six fuzzy monitors, waiting until he spotted an infraction of one of the hundreds of "suggestions" that made up the Max Snax Code of Conduct. Then his office door would silently open, and Andy would emerge like a nervous hermit crab scavenging the ocean floor for whatever it is hermit crabs eat. And now, as I had dreaded, his door was opening. I was about to get a three-minute lecture on proper behaviour for customer-facing operatives, which did not include obscene hand gestures to the kitchen staff.

Andy extruded himself from his office. He was in his mid-thirties, I guessed, and always wore the shirt and tie he considered appropriate to a management position. I was always morbidly fascinated by Andy's hairstyle—he had a decent head of hair, but by carefully calculated use of a comb-over, he managed to make himself look like a balding fifty-year-old. His complexion was blotchy and pale, and he compensated for this with a fake tan—not from an expensive sun bed, but from a bottle. Closer inspection, which I usually tended to avoid, confirmed it. Sun beds generally don't leave pale streaks on your orange forehead or a faint tangerine tinge on the collar of your shirt.

"Finn . . ." Andy bobbed and weaved and avoided my eye. He'd missed my finger to Jerry, I thought. This is something else. Probably a shit job he doesn't have the inclination to do himself—that's what he was paying us the statutory minimum wage for. "We have a clientele turnover issue." I stared at him, doing my best to look mystified. I knew what he was saying, but I wanted to see if he could express it in English. "Over there." He nodded as discreetly as he could towards the table in the corner of the restaurant furthest from the counter.

She'd arrived mid-morning, ordered hot chocolate, and sat there sipping it for the next forty-five minutes. She was about my age, in the brown uniform of Kew School for Girls, although I doubted the stud in her nose was an approved part of the outfit. Her tangled black hair fell across her face and she was wearing too much eyeliner, but it failed to hide the fact that she had clear, pale skin, fine bone structure, and curves even the frumpy uniform couldn't straighten out. Not as curvy as she could have been, for all that: at a guess she was about five kilos under her healthy weight. That was one reason she stood out in here. The other was that she was the only customer. It was too late in the morning even for the student crowd, and too early for the weekday lunch crowd.

"What's the problem?"

"She's blocking our prime seating."

I glanced over. I wasn't aware we had any prime seating. All of them were bright green plastic around bright yellow tables, and all of them had the same thrilling view of our car park, if you didn't allow for the vast window stickers that advertised Max Snax's latest blend of herbs, spices, salt, more salt and chemical gloop that coated our pinky-grey mechanically-recovered-chicken-product.

"But there's no one else here," I pointed out.

"Because she's blocking our prime seating!" hissed Andy. "And her attitude . . . it doesn't fit with our corporate image."

The first few weeks after I started work here I had found Andy's bullshit funny. I used to relay his latest examples of ridiculous corporate gobbledegook to my dad, and we'd both have a go at talking like that— "Could you transfer the sodium condiment across the consumption platform?" Then, after three or four months of it, I'd realized I might be working in Max Snax for years, soaking up the smell of stale fat, rolling myself in Max's special chemical mix until I was permanently coated in it, and the joke was on me, and it wasn't funny any more.

"Tell her she has to order something or re-allocate her custom."

"Re-allocate her . . .?"

"Now, please, Finn."

He darted back towards his office. For a moment his little crab antennae waved, sniffing the greasy air, then he slipped inside and the door clicked shut. I could visualize him settling back into his vinyl leather-look executive armchair, watching the monitor, waiting for me to redeploy unwelcome clientele. Timing me, probably. I sighed and made my way over.

"Hi there."

She had been staring at the traffic turning the corner at the junction outside, as if waiting for a car crash to break up the empty monotony of her morning. She turned to me. Her eyes were bright green, almost too large for her heart-shaped face. I found myself wondering what colour her hair really was under the jet-black dye.

"Can I get you anything?"

"Didn't know they had waiter service here." Her tone was off-hand, a little amused, as if she was flirting, but not really. Her heart wasn't in it.

"We don't."

"Then why are you asking?"

"The manager wants you to buy something."

"I did buy something."

The amusement had evaporated. She knew what I had come over to say, and was going to argue about it. It was pointless, and her morning was spoiled before we'd even started, but a row would do as well as a car crash. I hadn't felt sorry for her till then.

"Let me get you another not-chocolate," I offered. She missed the pun, and I was glad. It sounded ingratiating and pathetic.

"Forget it. It tastes like piss mixed with soap."

"Really? I wouldn't know."

Her nostrils flared angrily. I was angry too, wondering why I'd got myself into a playground spat on

Andy's orders. And wondering whether she'd put stuff on her lips to make them that shape and colour.

"So I have to order something, or you'll throw me out?"

"No, you don't. I'll buy it, and you won't even have to drink it. But that way you can sit here as long as you like."

She sighed, glanced out across the car park again, then flashed me a huge smile. "Actually, Finn, could you do me a Max Snack? One of those big triple-deckers?"

Of course she knew my name. It was printed in big happy Max Snax font on the little badge pinned just over my left tit. Punters always ignored it until they wanted to complain.

"With everything?"

"Yeah, extra barbecue sauce, pickles, the works."

"Sure." I didn't move.

"And a giant cola."

"OK."

"And could you put it all on a tray? With lots of napkins?"

"Sure."

"And then could you shove it up your arse?"

I nodded. "You want fries with that?"

"Oh, just piss off."

She stood up forcefully, as if she expected the chair or

the table to go flying, or both, preferably. But of course they were screwed to the floor and she just winced as she bounced between them. I made sure she noticed me notice.

"Thanks for coming to Max Snax. Have a great day." I heard myself deliver the line with exactly the amount of patronizing insincerity, and a processed-cheese grin of exactly the width that the Max Snax staff training videos specified. She looked at me with even more contempt than I felt for myself at that moment, glanced down at my beige polyester shirt with its fetching perspiration stains under the armpits and down the sternum, and walked out. Even as I watched her go, my skin prickling with embarrassment and humiliation, I wanted to follow her. She had that sort of walk.

And then the place was empty again. An empty plastic cell. Even with me standing there, stinking of sweat and stale fat, the place was empty. Just the little black plastic dome of Andy's CCTV camera watching me. I couldn't even give it the thumbs-up and flash it a mock-triumphant grin; I'd had enough irony for one day.

I went back behind the counter, grabbed a damp cloth and started wiping down the counters, the cash register, the menus, everything in sight. Trying to keep busy so the urge would subside and pass—the urge to rip off this stiff nylon blouse and these shapeless, pocketless trousers and run home in nothing but my tatty briefs. Leaning time is cleaning time. Thanking time is wanking time. Frying time is dying time . . .

Andy was back. He was wearing his blazer, the one with the brass buttons and the shiny elbows. He wore it at the Friday morning Max Snax staff training sessions, or when he announced the month's sales figures, or whenever he gave someone a new pip on their plastic name badge.

He was offering me one now.

"That was exemplary, Finn. Really well-handled."

"It's OK, Andy. Don't bother." He wanted to reward me for getting rid of customers?

"Come on. Three more of these and you're a Max Snax Star. That's a six per cent pay rise."

If I turned it down he'd know I hated Max Snax, and him, and the uniform, and the job, and he'd hire some other school dropout. But I needed the money. I couldn't drive, and I could barely read. What else was I going to do?

"Thanks, Andy."

I took it off him. The first hole on my name badge already had a golden stud—you got that on your first day at work, just for turning up. I snapped the new one into the second little hole, and it didn't hurt much more than punching it into my forehead.

"Keep this up, you'll have a branch of your own someday."

The rest of my shift was a deep-fried blur, and as usual I showered and changed before I left. The workplace shower was another reason I stuck the job. Our shower at home was like being peed on by an old bloke with a prostrate problem, but this one at work fired out scalding hot water that came down like a tropical storm. I was the only one who ever used it, and it felt like the one time and space in the world that I ever had to myself.

I stooped in front of the washroom mirror—it wasn't quite high enough for someone as tall as me—combing my mousy-brown hair with my fingers. I generally kept my hair short, or it would spring up in spikes I could never control. The rest of my reflection I tried not to look at. It wasn't that I minded how I looked; apart from the kink in my nose where a sparring partner had broken it, it wasn't such a bad face, according to my dad—triangular, with a big chin that currently needed a shave and a kind of girly mouth. My teeth were pretty straight and even, and my pale skin was clear (this week anyway). But I could never meet those washed-out blue eyes because they always seemed to ask how they'd got here, and whether they'd spend the next twenty years looking out from behind the counter at Max Snax, and I never had the heart to answer.

I stuffed my uniform into my backpack—planning to wash it at home—laced up my running shoes and headed out across the car park, dodging pedestrians as I built up speed. Pushing my pulse to 140, I pounded along the backstreet pavements, heading home.

The street lights were flickering on as I pulled up, panting, outside the house. I stretched as I got my breath back, glad to see I was still supple enough to touch my knees with my forehead. But as my pulse slowed and my breathing found its resting rhythm I realized something was bugging me. The house was dark, as if Dad had gone out. But he usually worked on his writing till I came in from work—my coming back in was his excuse to knock off for the day.

The curtains were already closed. Had they ever been opened? I fished my keys from my backpack and opened the door. As I reached for the light switch I registered something about the silence.

"Dad?"

It was too deep, as if the house was empty; but it didn't feel empty.

Our house was small—the door opened straight into the living room. The light came on dimly, brightening as it warmed up. Dad disliked the overhead light, and only switched it on when he had one of his fits of tidying-up. Now it flooded the room in the way he disliked, cold and harsh, and fell on him where he sat at the table. Not sat, so much as slumped, the way I'd seen him once or twice when he'd been to the pub and somebody else was buying.

I paused in the doorway, certain something was wrong, trying to figure out what exactly. "Dad?" It was too cold in the room. He couldn't hear me—he still had his earphones in.

I'd found him like that before a few times, early in the morning. He'd be resting his head on his folded arms. Now his arms were pinned underneath him, at an odd angle, and he wasn't breathing. I knew that, even before I consciously worked it out, even before I registered properly that the crown of his head was a sticky mass of blood, and something heavy and bulky lay on the floor by his chair, itself stained with red, with bloody hairs sticking to it.

My dad was dead. He had been sitting at his desk, plugged into his music, and someone had crept up behind him holding his award for *Best Newcomer 1992*, and hit him over the head with it, and kept hitting him until he died. His eyes were open and his glasses had fallen off. There was blood coming from his mouth and clotting in his beard, and pooling on the table, and he was dead. And the house was empty and silent.

# ABOUT THE AUTHOR

NIALL LEONARD is a drama and comedy screenwriter, born in Northern Ireland and currently living in West London with his wife, bestselling author E L James, and their two children. Among his many television credits, he has created episodes of *Wire in the Blood, Silent Witness, Ballykissangel,* and *Hornblower.* He has also led seminars and workshops on screenwriting and script editing for the BBC, the Northern Ireland Film Council, and the Irish Screenwriters' Guild, and has lectured on the creative process at the University of Reading. *Incinerator* is the companion novel to *Crusher,* Niall Leonard's debut young adult novel.